DEVIOUS THINKING

Misadventures in Getting Even

Tom Blomquist

DEVIOUS THINKING
Copyright © 2021 Tom Blomquist

First Edition

Cover Design by Tanya Cummings
www.tanyacummings.com

Cover & Author Photographs by Alex Shi
ShilexPhotography.com

Cover Model
Brittani Lace Phillips

ISBN: 9798592846359

LINDSTROM
LEGACY
PUBLISHING

www.facebook.com/Devious Thinking
www.facebook.com/LindstromLegacyPublishing
LindstromLegacy@gmail.com
www.tomblomquist.com

To Duane Bogie and Cathy Lonergan,
for sharing the adventure with me all those years ago

ACKNOWLEDGEMENTS

I once had the good fortune to serve on the production staff of an American movie in Italy. The film shoot in Rome, Assisi, and the picturesque Umbrian countryside was memorable in innumerable ways, but in the end it was not the fabulous landscape, architecture, or cuisine that made the most lasting impression on me—that turned out to be the Italian people with whom I spent so many hours while living and working on location. The distinctive music of their language and colorful personalities struck a chord in me and, as often happens with writers, that chord led to another and then another, until a whole concerto of characters and plot convolutions was eventually being performed in my head, demanding to be written down.

While DEVIOUS THINKING is a work of fiction, several of its central elements were derived directly from my experiences in Italy. Not only were some of the characters inspired by real people, but certain events unfolded exactly as they appear on these pages. I will happily leave it to you to figure out which ones are which.

I appreciate the individuals who unwittingly served as my research subjects at the time. I am also deeply grateful for the friends, family, and colleagues who in various ways fueled my efforts to get this story told; Roger Badesch, Ann Blomquist, Bobby Bowfinger, Chuck Bowman, Lisa Bowman, Jay Bryant, Andrea Casamitjana, Barbara Dreyfus, Tamara Farsadi, Gaylyn Fraiche, Daniella Serquen Gamarra, Eric Karson, Michael Kennedy, Mike Leary, John Loprieno, Jeff Myrow, Victor Quintero, Scott Richter, Dana Shockley, Lisa Sullivan, Sarah Tatting-Kinzy, and Roger Young.

I owe special thanks and so much more to Steven L. Sears, W. Reed Moran, and Tom Walla for their generous insights, and to the devious team of Bonnie Blackburn (editor), Tanya Cummings (cover design), Alex Shi (photography), Brittani Lace Phillips (cover model), Maryvonne Fent, Oriana Nastrini, Sabrina Nastrini, and Vincent Pastor (foreign language consultants), and the magical Scott Wells (promotional trailer) for their invaluable contributions!

Chapter One
Save Some For Later

The young woman in a dressing room at the posh Rodeo Drive lingerie boutique See Me, Feel Me was hot. No doubt about it.

Smoking hot, to be precise.

If anyone wanted proof, then they should have seen her that afternoon as she shimmied into a shape-hugging red silk chemise with a breathtaking plunging neckline. She was simply stunning. After all, bodies like hers are exactly what garments like this are designed for, where little is left to the imagination and the rest is undiluted fantasy. And make no mistake, thirty-two-year-old Dana Zimmer was well suited for somebody's fantasies. Her physical qualities were further enhanced by her stylish brown pixie haircut, sultry brown eyes, and sensual long stem rose ankle tattoo.

But even with all that going for her, at this moment she was beset by a swarm of misgivings. Having auditioned a succession of alluring poses in the full-length mirror, she unceremoniously jettisoned them all. "Damn it, now I'm totally messed up," she grimaced. "I can't pick. What do you think?"

A fawning sales consultant, who was decades past wearing clothing like this herself, poked her head through an opening in the thick privacy curtain. She had a cherubic face and agreeable disposition that played well with her affluent Southern California clientele. In fact, she reminded Dana of the doting Aunt Bee character in reruns of the old *Andy Griffith* television series. "Oh, that looks soooo cute on you!" she effused with practiced sincerity. It goes without saying that she had offered the same affirmation to countless other women, regardless of what was frequently glaring evidence to the contrary.

"Are you sure?" Dana questioned. "He's expecting something special."

Aunt Bee was incredulous and this time her reaction was completely authentic. Most of her Beverly Hills and Bel Air trophy-wife shoppers would give anything to look like this in such revealing nightwear. God knows many had tried, which made a generation of celebrity plastic surgeons and personal fitness instructors a fortune while assisting them in that often-futile pursuit. "For goodness sake, dear," she gushed as she joined her in the spacious cubicle, "a man would have to be dead to ignore you in this."

She was right, of course. Her trained eye knew the difference between ordinary and special when she saw it. And this young lady was anything but ordinary.

Dana remained skeptical, however. "I dunno. It's gotta be perfect."

Then Aunt Bee had an inspiration that seemed so impish it almost made her giddy. "Why leave it to chance?" she proposed with a conspiratorial wink. "Go out there and give your hubby a little preview right now."

But as she prepared to slide the curtain open with a flourish Dana reached out to stop her. "That's ... not my husband," she confided.

"Oh, I am so sorry," Aunt Bee answered with confusion. Her playfulness awkwardly faded as she muttered, "I could have sworn I saw his wedding band."

"You did," came the straightforward response. Dana held up her left hand. *See? No diamond.*

Aunt Bee's puzzled gape flicked hesitantly from the bare ring finger to the dazzling girl in suggestive sheer fabric as she recalled seeing the couple holding hands and nuzzling earlier. Then her customer's meaning registered: *she was with someone else's husband.* "Oh, my," was all the flustered woman could get out before Dana summoned the confidence to step from the dressing room on her own.

The calming soundscape of the appropriately titled *Longing/Love* track from a vintage George Winston album wafted through the air as Alex Connelly, a rugged and fit Australian who was twenty years older than his mistress, relaxed in the patron's lounge in the center of the store. Smartly dressed in a slim-fitting blue Saint Laurent suit and crisp open collar white shirt, he glanced up from the Nasdaq feed on his iPad and beamed at the sight of Dana heading in his direction.

He was not the only one in the shop smiling, either, because she was not merely walking through the glowing pools of recessed lighting, she was floating above the polished marble floor without touching it. Or so it seemed.

And there were no signs of her previous qualms about her appearance, as this Dana Zimmer seemed to be bursting with self-assured sexuality. A hush fell over the room and heads jerked around to view the marvel of her approach. More than a few of the onlookers no doubt risked whiplash injuries in the process.

"Well, well!" Connelly breathed approvingly.

"That's all you gotta say?" she teased while contentedly waiting for his piercing cobalt blue eyes to finish roaming her body. "Well, well?!"

His amorous gaze finally reached her face. "It's all I *can* say in public," he affirmed as his index finger oh-so-slowly traced the delicate edge of her neckline to the price tag near her left breast. "Twelve hundred dollars," he read aloud. "Worth every penny, I'd say."

Dana grinned and ran her fingers through his salt and pepper hair as she pulled him into a loving embrace that suggested they might go at it right there on the Persian area rug, a prospect not lost on Aunt Bee.

"I guess I'll just put these other things away ...." she mumbled, moving off as inconspicuously as she could.

Neither Dana nor her boyfriend noticed her departure or the people who continued to stare from various areas of the store. The two lovers were blissfully in a world of their own. As a rule, the temperature of their relationship was somewhere north of smoldering, but things here were heating up faster than usual.

A lot faster.

"So, how am I supposed to wait for next weekend after I've had a gander at you in these knickers?" he sighed in her ear.

Dana drilled him with a provocative look that he had enjoyed many times before. But considering what she was almost wearing and the fact that they were in full view of a dozen strangers, it was even more arousing for him than usual. "Who said anything about waiting?" she dared before practically climbing inside his mouth.

Love was in the air on the east coast, too. On a dull overcast September day, New York's magnificent landmark Saint Patrick's Cathedral was the setting for what many people regarded as the society wedding of the year.

A beatific choral rendition of *Ave Maria* that would have made Franz Schubert himself weep ended as the twenty-four members of the wedding party took their places on the steps to the liturgical altar. Arrayed as they were before the 850 attendees, the twelve bridesmaids in their flowing mint tulle dresses and corresponding tuxedo-clad groomsmen resembled a perfectly staged tableau for a magazine cover.

Anchoring the storybook image was the groom, Giancarlo Lombardi, a boyish thirty-eight-year-old Italian with chiseled good looks, lightly tousled dark hair, and fashionable movie star beard stubble. Few among the guests could take their eyes off him, men and women alike.

That was, until the cathedral pipe organ in the triforium thundered the majestic staccato fanfare of *The Wedding March*. As Felix Mendelssohn's regal proclamation of matrimonial splendor filled the mammoth neo-Gothic space and its surrounding 5th Avenue neighborhood, everyone's attention shifted to the luminous bride, Montell Cherie Harrison, and her distinguished father, Grant, as they entered the grand narthex entryway.

Monty was a timeless vision of elegance and beauty in an exquisite Vera Wang gown. She paused in the nave to take in the scene, clutching her father's arm in fierce determination to remember every detail of her special day. She meticulously absorbed as much as she could; from the sculptures of saints lining the sanctuary, colorful stained-glass windows, and ethereal glow of chandeliers hanging from the ribbed ceiling vaults, to the emotion-filled faces of her family, friends, and neighbors framed by rows of imposing cluster columns.

Oh, those wonderful people!

Her eyes leapt from one to another as she concentrated on the love they radiated as they turned to watch her. There was her Uncle Randall, a resolutely stoic man who was uncharacteristically fighting a losing battle with tears of elation. Beside him was her Aunt Caroline, who had the opposite temperament of her husband but was solidly unified with him in her reaction today. Monty next located her adolescent nieces and nephews who were ecstatic to be there, as were her Tau Zeta Epsilon society sisters with whom she had shared so many treasured times at Wellesley College.

Sitting alone at the end of an empty pew several rows behind the TZE contingent was her elder cousin Aaron, whom she loved a great deal, but who was self-isolated from everyone due to a persistent flatulence disorder. After years of humiliating gastric disruptions at family gatherings, everyone appreciated the courtesy of being spared the worst of his condition on an occasion like this.

Monty's view then settled on her mother, Rosemary, and grandparents, who looked absolutely overjoyed in the front row. She forced herself to avert her eyes before her mother's waterworks had time to trigger her own. *It was hard enough to make it down the aisle without becoming a blubbering mess!* She wondered how other brides managed this but resolved to do her best.

Then the affirming squeeze of Grant Harrison's hand signaled that the time had arrived. They started their long walk along the colorful path of rose pedals scattered throughout the aisle and she had to remind herself to breathe. The soothing bouquet of flowers and incense in the air, along with woody traces of her father's Green Irish Tweed cologne, enveloped her.

She focused on the scent of his fragrance, with its comforting masculine quality, and was reassured by having him to lean on. No matter what life event she encountered Monty believed that she could do anything as long as her father was beside her.

Social media bloggers, newspaper society writers, and local radio pundits would rave about the wedding ceremony for days. One columnist went so far as to observe that at age twenty-six Monty was "the most radiant bride in the greatest dress in the history of nuptials". And while such assessments may have been a bit hyperbolic, they did not miss the mark by much. It was obvious even through her veil that this lovely young woman was not merely worthy of her astonishing gown, she surpassed it with her willowy figure, flawless porcelain skin, and lush shoulder-length blonde locks.

No one in the room had ever seen her look more beguiling.

Giancarlo descended the carpeted stairs and Monty's green Bambi eyes filled with tears as he warmly hugged her father before escorting her to the altar. Waiting there for them, resplendent in his formal scarlet red cassock and white lace-trimmed rochet was the Archbishop of New York, His Eminence Cardinal Timothy Dolan. His round Irish face wore a heartfelt ear-to-ear smile. This was the picture-perfect wedding of Monty's dreams.

"Dearly beloved," the seventy-year-old Dolan intoned as his amplified voice reverberated through the cathedral's many domes and alcoves, "what a glorious day this is, as we gather together in this sacred place to celebrate the holy union of Montell Cherie Harrison and Giancarlo Lombardi ...."

Ninety minutes later an ebullient Monty and Giancarlo emerged beneath Saint Patrick's twin Tuckahoe marble spires that reached toward the gloomy folds of low-hanging darkened storm clouds above. The weather had deteriorated during the ceremony, but that did not hamper the deluge of rice, flowers, and cheers greeting the newlyweds as the mighty church organ loudly heralded Beethoven's *Ode to Joy* and nineteen tower bells overhead clanged freely.

There were well-wishers, photographers, and pedestrian passersby everywhere, making the couple's path to their stretch white limousine more of an obstacle course than anyone would have anticipated. After navigating the labyrinth of festive humanity to a lower concrete landing, oversized droplets began falling on them from the sky. Then, when the rain escalated seconds later, the throng reacted en masse by pushing towards the church entrance, thereby blocking the bride and groom's path.

Giancarlo saw the concern on his wife's face, which prompted him to take matters into his own hands. Dramatically swooping her into his arms, he forged a hero's escape route to the sidewalk. And even as people covered themselves from the increasing downpour everyone applauded his gallantry. Especially Monty's parents, who judging from their rapturous expressions felt they had just won the son-in-law jackpot. Although he was not the physician, lawyer, or Wall Street executive they had envisioned for their little girl, the man who captured her heart was a sensitive and talented artist who shared her cultural and spiritual interests. She had found her ideal mate.

Once safely ensconced in their limo, Monty plucked a few errant grains of rice from her husband's damp hair and giggled. "Look at you, such a mess on our wedding day!"

Giancarlo indulged her fussing with amusement before tenderly retrieving the collected granules from her palm. "Montell, since I have you in my life, everything for me is perfect," he proclaimed as he dropped the rice on the floor. Then he kissed her so fervently that he nearly melted her right out of the world's greatest dress.

"For goodness sake, Giancarlo—" she implored with a titter after coming up for air. "Save some for later!"

His Latin eyes sparkled as he spoke in the mellifluous accent that she adored so much, "What you will be learning about *Italiano* husbands, my love, is there is always "some for later"."

While she contemplated the thrilling layers of meaning behind his proclamation, he turned to the elderly uniformed chauffeur and instructed, "Four Seasons Hotel, *per favore.*"

"Yes, sir!" came the lively rejoinder as the driver steered the car into clogged traffic and worsening weather.

Leaning back in the buttery soft leather seat, Monty was Princess Diana beautiful as her face bloomed with delight. "Oh, it was such an enchanting ceremony, wasn't it?" she asked dreamily.

"To make you my bride even a judge at the *ufficio cittadino* would be enough," Giancarlo vouched as he filled two flutes from a bottle of Cristal champagne on ice in the console bar.

"The *ufficio*—what?" she asked.

"Forgive me. The city office."

"You are a dear for saying that, but you know what this day means to me," she remarked. "I just wish that Mother Superior Emanuela and the Sisters *di Sant'Angelo* could have shared it with us."

He handed her a glass and gently reminded her, "Montell, you must understand that I am no longer the child they once cared for. There are now many orphans in Rome who are needing their love."

"I can't help wanting to meet them!" she shared. "They're doing God's work at that orphanage. I know that for a fact, because thanks to them I now have you."

Giancarlo smiled gratefully. "After our honeymoon we will go to *Via delle Muratte* together so that you can meet them. They will love you so much."

"I hope so," she confided. "It's amazing to think of Sisters Adriana, Rosario, Matilde, and Mother Superior as my family now."

"As your family is mine," he returned. "What would I have done without your cousins to protect me at the altar today?"

She responded quizzically. "Sweetheart, why in the world would anyone need to protect you?"

He searched carefully for the right words. "So that you would not change your mind because of the poor life I am from," he acknowledged shyly.

Change her mind?! What?! Monty was overwhelmed by his confession. "Giancarlo, nothing could ever make me change my mind about you," she assured him.

His eyes reddened upon hearing her pronouncement and seeing that warmed Monty inside. She could not have loved the man any more than she did in that instant. Setting their drinks aside she was compelled to draw him into a long and passionate kiss. The taste of champagne on his lips was sweet.

Doing his best to avoid staring at the unfolding sight in his rear-view mirror, the chauffeur discretely closed the tinted window behind him for the remainder of the eight-block trip to the hotel.

Monty and Giancarlo ended up being thirty minutes late to the reception, though the solidifying Manhattan traffic had nothing to do with it. Experience told the chauffeur to drive in circles around Midtown to give the bride and groom additional time alone.

Six hours later, the guests were departing the Harrison-Lombardi celebration in the Four Seasons Hotel ballroom, and the consensus was that it was the finest wedding event that any of them had ever attended. And that was saying something, given the stature of the people on the guest list. As if the ceremony at Saint Patrick's Cathedral were not notable enough, the reception featured spectacular floral decorations throughout the 3,116 square foot hotel ballroom, superb French cuisine that pleased even the most discerning palates, and the sight of the bride dancing to *Moon River* with none other than His Eminence Cardinal Timothy Dolan.

Providing the live entertainment was music superstar Michael Bublé and his orchestra. For his final number Bublé brought everyone to tears when he offered the newlyweds a special rendition of *Three Coins In The Fountain*, the Frank Sinatra hit about lovers sharing their dreams at Rome's *Trevi* Fountain. It was a precious memory that provided an impeccable ending to an ideal day.

Chapter Two
Don't You Ever Get Enough?

Across the continent and embracing the cloudless sky for as far as anyone could see, the lightshow of the setting coastline sun was extraordinary. Massive swatches of brilliant red and orange exploded across the azure blue horizon with a virtuoso painter's touch; a natural visual masterpiece that reflected off an impossibly smooth Pacific Ocean.

Any number of love songs and romance novels have been inspired by a whole lot less.

A flock of crooning seagulls gracefully soared on cliffside currents as invigorating gusts lifted from the water and streamed up the bluff toward the luxurious Ritz-Carlton Laguna Niguel Hotel. After ascending the 150-foot slope, the relaxing draft flowed past patio furniture on a private veranda and through the open French doors of a hotel suite. The cool breeze caused the delicate white curtains in the entryway to dance over the new red silk chemise lying on the carpet beside various hastily discarded items of men's clothing.

Nearby, Alex Connelly and Dana Zimmer were spooning in the king-size bed wearing the whimsical smiles of lovers and nothing else. The warmth of his skin against hers was the ideal conclusion to what had been a most memorable day for Dana; one that started with a long solo morning jog on the beach and culminated with an exceptionally satisfying romantic rendezvous. Dana felt as if she were living an incredible dream from which she never wanted to awaken, because after years of looking for love it had found her at last.

Awe-inspiring, mind-blowing love.

As their relationship flourished during the recent final stages of his divorce, she had begun to long for these Laguna getaways more and more. They were perfect because he was perfect; the way he treated her, the way he did everything. "You know what keeps running through my mind?" she murmured contentedly as the gulls and rolling surf serenaded outside.

He nuzzled the back of her neck, sending chills up and down her spine. "Mmmm ... I can't imagine."

"How the girls in the office are gonna freak when they find out who the boss is dating—now that he's back on the market," she chuckled as she stroked the new diamond necklace that glinted against her tanned skin. "I mean, some of those dopes are totally gonna lose it!"

As she snickered at the concept, Connelly raised himself onto one elbow. His tone turned solemn. "Dana, about that—" he said, hesitating, "I don't want to muck up our weekend, but I'm afraid that things have hit a snag."

Her exhilaration disappeared as she turned to face him. "What do you mean?"

"My lawyers want me to hold off on formalizing the divorce," he began cautiously. His face was etched with regret. "Just for a while."

But when he leaned in to kiss her, she pulled away. "This weekend was to celebrate you finally signing the papers," she reminded him.

"I know, but now Heather is balking at our agreement," he explained. "Suddenly, she wants more assets than she's entitled to— and believe me, if she finds out about us, she'll throw wild accusations of infidelity on the fire."

"Infidelity?!" she repeated as she sat upright. "You lead separate lives."

"We do, but it's more complicated than that," he added, his voice cracking. "... my company and investments, the art collection. She'll take it all if I'm not careful."

The news launched Dana from the bed. "Christ—I shoulda known."

"What are you talking about?!"

"You and me, the shitty marriage you were already done with," she fumed, putting on a robe. "That was all bogus."

"That's not true!"

"You gotta *wife*, Alex. You're still wearing her ring, for Godsakes."

"That's just to placate her until she signs the damn papers," he countered as he took off his ring and tossed it on the bed. "You know that."

"Whatever," she snapped. "This whole deal is way different than you said, and I'm not into being anybody's side glide." She punctuated the declaration by haphazardly stuffing clothes into an overnight bag. She drew the line at being the other woman and would have never allowed herself to become involved with him if she thought that were the case.

"I'd slam the door on her and change the locks in a minute, if it were up to me," he protested as he tried to take her in his arms.

"I thought you did that a long time ago," she disputed.

"You know what I mean," he appealed. "Why does anything have to change between us?"

"Wrong question," she snarled, shoving his hands away. "I am so outta here!"

After hurriedly retrieving items from the walk-in closet, she turned to find him blocking her exit. "Dana, listen to me," he begged, "you don't know what Heather is capable of. That's why I have to be careful. It's not just about the money."

"Of course not," she cynically retorted, pushing past him.

But Connelly was undeterred. "I mean it. There's a lot that you don't know about her," he insisted. "She's emotionally unstable—and she could come after you."

"Because she's *still fucking married!*" she corrected.

"It hasn't been a marriage for a long time," he argued.

"So you told me."

"It's true!" he pleaded. "Why are you acting this way?"

"Gimme a break," she challenged. His news had caught her off-guard and she felt like her whole world was coming apart. As futile as it might have been, it was important to prevent him from discovering her true feelings on her face.

Then, reaching down to pick up the red chemise from the floor, he handed it to her. "Dana, come on. Please. I love you!"

The statement halted her in her tracks. *Did he say what she thought he just said?* "What ...?"

"I just need a little more time," he continued. "Please."

Her heart was pounding fast. "You wanna run that "love" part by me again?"

By now Connelly was gripped by emotion, which had dissolved away his Australian macho swagger. Dana had never seen him so vulnerable. "I'll say it as often as you like," he pledged. "I've been in love with you since the day we met. Head over heels, can't-get-you-out-of-my-mind love."

She did not answer. The room had stopped because she was not expecting to hear those words. "That's the first time you've ever said that to me," she thought, not realizing that her thinking had inexplicably turned into spoken words. *Damn it, what was HAPPENING?!*

"You know how hard it is for me to express my feelings," he admitted. "That's why I need you in my life." He brushed away a wisp of hair that had fallen across her face. "What we have is staggering."

Absorbing his admission took a while. He had never been so open with her, and it made him all the more desirable. "How much time are we talking about?" she finally asked.

"A few months at most."

"Months?!" she blurted as her blood pressure climbed.

"It's not fair, I know," he added quickly. "But please be patient with me—I'll do whatever it takes to make it up to you."

There was another long silence as his proclamation sunk in. This was new territory for her, and she had no clue how to react. Then he touched her with his strong hands and slowly pulled her body to his. The feel of him and the manly smell of his skin were exhilarating, but it was his unforeseen defenselessness that was impossible to resist.

Eventually, the hint of a smile appeared at the edges of her mouth. "Anything?"

"Anything," he vowed as he purposefully opened the front of her robe. "*Any*—thing."

Dana would have preferred to keep her feelings of hurt and indignation alive, but she also knew where things were heading. And, frankly, with Alex Connelly that was a tremendously exciting prospect.

So was the fact that he was still naked. And as usual his toned athletic physique was a significant distraction. "Really," she challenged while pointedly scrutinizing him from head to toe.

He tugged lightly on her robe, causing it to slip from one shoulder. "Oh, yeah."

"Even if it takes all night?" she wondered seductively.

"My God, don't you ever get enough?" he asked with a more playful and assertive pull on her sleeve. The garment dropped to the floor.

"Only one way to find out," she purred.

Chapter Three
Giancarlo, Can You Hear Me?

6,000 miles from Laguna Beach, another young woman was reveling in romantic euphoria. Since arriving on the French Riviera, Montell Harrison Lombardi and her new husband had indulged in connubial pleasures almost continuously, and at this moment they were once more coupled in ecstasy on the silver satin sheets of their Saint-Tropez honeymoon suite.

While they surely must have paused for the occasional meal, to Monty such events were little more than vague impressions— because if Giancarlo's intentions were to demonstrate the supremacy of Italian lovers, then he was succeeding. Guiding her sensations to new heights, he miraculously compounded them one upon another until they could no longer be contained. Monty had no idea how he did it, but she asked no questions as the room spun and she held on for dear life. Her whole body quaked.

Remarkably, as wonderful as their intimacies had been before, the elation consuming her this time outdid everything else.

Twenty minutes later, while Giancarlo watched *I Giallorossi* of his venerated *A.S. Roma* professional *fútbol* club on the bedroom television, Monty was savoring the intersecting sprays of their expansive glass tiled shower. The adrenaline rush of marathon lovemaking with her exceptional husband had left her with a profound sense of well-being.

Monty relished the lifetime of discovery and passion that was ahead of them and she felt genuinely sorry for the rest of the population that had no idea what that was like. Somehow, she had managed to find a kind-hearted man who shared her values. Giancarlo was an artist whose soulful paintings elevated him from the poverty and pain of his broken childhood, and his work nobly explored the traditional Catholic themes of generosity, love, and hope that she revered.

She was the luckiest girl in the world.

Given his obsession with soccer, however, she resolved to learn more about the sport, which she now understood to be a lifestyle staple for Italians and not merely an athletic activity. In fact, she heard Giancarlo speak of *A.S. Roma* players Ciccio Cordova and Fabio Capello with equal admiration as his favorite Twentieth Century Avant-Garde painters Sandro Chia, Enzo Cucchi, and Mimmo Paladino.

Monty smiled as she reflected on how much it would please him if she were to share his reverence for all of those names.

As she rinsed shampoo from her hair, she noticed the morning sunlight pouring through the window. It appeared brighter than usual, but what really captured her attention was the quality of the light itself: instead of soft and welcoming, this time it seemed harsh. Little did she know that the phenomenon would prove to be a harbinger of things to come.

Just then she remembered something and called out, her voice echoing in the large enclosure. "Darling, I want to phone home before it's too late. What time is it in Connecticut?"

But she received no response.

Turning the water off, she cracked the shower door open and tried again. "Giancarlo, can you hear me?"

Again, he did not answer. Nor did the soccer match seem to be on, she realized. That was unusual. Giancarlo would never miss a chance to watch his team play.

Suddenly for reasons she could not explain, a peculiar sense of apprehension spread through her. "Sweetheart ...?"

There continued to be only silence in return.

Monty rushed, dripping wet, into the bedroom to find the suite abnormally still. Unnaturally so. And everything was in a strange state

16

of disarray that she could not identify at first. She took in the sight of toppled furniture and scattered decorative knickknacks with bewilderment, until it came crashing down upon her that the room had been ransacked!

Her eyes darted everywhere, not sure where to look. Her purse was on the floor, but when she retrieved it her throat tightened. *Her wallet and phone were missing!*

Within seconds she saw that the dresser drawers and wall safe were also open. Taking a tentative step forward, she stopped. Giancarlo's and her clothes were a jumbled mess. And everything else of hers was gone ... her jewelry, credit cards, cash, and two suitcases filled with wedding presents. It was like a punch to her stomach.

Yet nothing could prepare her for what came next—the shocking realization that one side of her purse was covered with blood!

As she fell into a chair, disoriented, she noticed one last thing: a long bloodstain on the carpet leading from the purse to the front door. There had been a struggle.

The *Gendarmerie* on *Place Blanqui* is only a half mile from the Byblos Hotel, so it should have taken just a few minutes to travel. However, like everyone else in Saint-Tropez, Monty's taxi driver was in no particular hurry. The end of the summer tourist season had arrived, and the resort town was gratefully easing back to its charming fishing village roots. Nevertheless, completely ignoring the light traffic, the driver was content to slow down or stop for every imaginable reason. It was maddening.

Having arrived at long last, Monty relayed her emotional story to a young police lieutenant and small assemblage of officers in the main room. However, while she had the riveted attention of the men, she did not comprehend that they were far more interested in their attractive guest than any offense that she might be describing. These policemen were, after all, just local boys who reveled in the influx of female vacationers each year, the shiny wedding bands on their hands rarely inconveniencing their extra-curricular activities.

And Monty strongly resembled the captivating celebrities and fashion models who often visited the area, despite her sodden thick hair and lack of make-up.

Lieutenant Jean-Claude Jeunet was notably enthralled. A short and slender thirty-four-year-old sporting a thin mustache, he fancied himself quite the lady-killer, which became evident as he returned her passport with an unctuous grin. "Your photograph is quite nice," he declared.

"My photograph?" she repeated with uncertainty.

Jeunet authoritatively leaned back in his chair. "Please excuse my English. What I meant to say was, it is fortunate that the thieves did not steal your passport."

"Yes, it is," she answered impatiently. "... since everything else is missing, including my husband."

"Of course," he continued while making a notation on a pad. "You have been married, how long?"

"Only a week."

"Ah, honeymooners," he commented as he and his pals exchanged knowing singles bar smirks. "You were having much romance?"

She reacted with confusion, not sure that she heard him correctly. "Romance?"

He leaned forward with an ingratiating half-smile. "*Oui,* lovemaking."

Lovemaking? She could hardly believe her ears. "What business could that possibly be of yours?"

Rising from his seat, Jeunet maneuvered around the desk to strategically position himself on the front edge where he could loom over her. It was always a thrill identifying a worthy destination for his desires, and this one had a mouth that needed to be kissed and a body that could not be ignored. "Forgive me, *Madame,*" he continued with a slightly raised eyebrow, "but a missing husband is many times traced to certain difficulties in the lovemaking."

His insinuation was appalling. "There were no difficulties, I assure you," she proclaimed as she emphatically crossed her legs.

Unfortunately for Monty her flowing skirt was now divulging

a whole lot more thigh than she realized, and the men leered. One more smarmy look passed between them as someone whispered that he would bet her state of marital bliss was true, *"Je parie que c'est vrai."*

Another cop chimed in with a haughty sneer as his eyes indelicately traveled up and down her figure, announcing to the others that he would not mind finding out for himself, *"Ça ne me dérangerait pas de le découvrir par moi-même."*

Guttural laughter permeated the room as Jeunet and the officers chortled, propelling Monty irately to her feet. *"Et ça ne me dérangerait pas de demander à vos femmes pourquoi vous trouvez ma vie sexuelle si fascinante!"* she scolded them in flawless French, asking what their wives would think of their fascination with her sex life.

Startled that their vulgar conduct had been unmasked, the would-be studs scattered like cockroaches when the lights come on in a darkened room.

An indignant Monty was retrieving her belongings when a voice broke in from a nearby office doorway. "Your French is excellent," a middle-aged policeman noted as he approached.

"So are my family's connections with your government," she announced. "I suggest that you don't make me use them."

"There is no need for confrontation," he promised her, extending his hand. "I am *Capitaine* Michel Chouinard. I hope you will not let my childish colleagues color your opinion of the *Gendarmerie*."

Monty did not accept his gesture right away, as she remained unconvinced that his kind face and warm manner were indicators of trustworthiness. Particularly after the tawdry behavior of his subordinates.

He knew what she was thinking and did not take offense. On the contrary, he did not blame her in the least for her revulsion and looked forward to reprimanding his foolish underlings later. They would soon regret their disreputable actions.

He instead graciously beckoned her to the empty guest chair. "I will do my best to help."

She studied him a while longer before finally deciding to accept his offer. *Giancarlo was counting on her.* "Thank you," she said tightly.

As she settled into her seat Chouinard reviewed the notes prepared by Lieutenant Jeunet. "Would you please tell me what happened to your husband?"

"I've already reported that he was abducted in a robbery at our hotel," she snapped. "You have my purse as evidence—which is covered in his blood."

He inspected the bag wrapped in clear plastic on the desk. The menacing stain across its side was a gruesome reminder of Monty's worries, forcing her to turn away. "But the Byblos is such a busy location," he mentioned. "Certainly, someone would have noticed a kidnapping."

His supposition struck a nerve. "God knows what happened to my husband and you wonder why no one witnessed the crime?!" She glanced around the room in the futile hope of finding a higher authority to discuss this with.

Chouinard silently deciphered her comportment as he proceeded. "Security cameras also did not record the incident," he observed, again referring to the notes. "The hotel management has apparently verified that fact."

That did nothing to reassure Monty, who was becoming increasingly exasperated. "And their employees would know precisely how to evade those, wouldn't they," she persisted, motioning to the bloody purse. "Shouldn't you be sending that to a laboratory for analysis?"

"We will scrutinize everything quite thoroughly, I assure you," he conveyed.

"Including the possibility of a theft ring working at the Byblos, I assume."

"Absolutely," he replied. Then, upon seeing that he was proving somewhat successful in reducing her confrontational attitude, Chouinard tried to nudge the interview in a more positive direction. "*Madame*, if I may ask, do you have photographs of *Monsieur* Lombardi that would assist us in our investigation?"

Monty's agitation heightened as she pointed to another item

on the pad. "They took everything except my passport—it's all written down right there!"

"So, I see," he corrected. "Can you explain why the thieves would want these photographs?"

"They were on my phone, *which-was-stolen*," she growled. Her frustration was nearing the boiling point.

"Excuse me," he continued apologetically. "Then perhaps others have been posted on the internet?"

His question had immediate impact and it was as if someone opened a window to let in the fresh air. "Yes, of course!" she chattered excitedly. "There are dozens of Giancarlo's pictures on Facebook." *At last, a good idea!* Monty could not believe that she had failed to remember the photos on her own.

"Excellent," Chouinard stated as he motioned to the desktop computer. "If you would be so kind as to select some for me ...."

"Certainly!" she eagerly agreed as she slid into the other chair and began typing. But before long the computer beeped loudly, forcing her to retry the procedure several times.

Whatever was happening, it was not going well, and she frowned.

Chouinard shifted to her side. "There is a problem?"

"I can't get into my page," she explained, bewildered. "They keep saying the account is closed."

He looked over her shoulder to examine the screen. As a man who had watched his own sister suffer the untimely death of a spouse, he empathized with Monty's situation, but his instincts also said there were too many peculiar details to accept anything at face value, the strange circumstances of the abduction that no one witnessed being one of them. Monty's social media problem was another. "A most unfortunate coincidence," he said with more judgment than he intended to show.

Monty brusquely stood. It was abundantly clear that Chouinard was not taking this seriously. "This is reprehensible!" she contested. "My husband is missing and here you are wasting valuable time on nonsense!"

She was heading for the exit when she spun on her heels to

address him one last time. "My father will be sure to tell his close friend President Macron how unsupportive you have been," she avowed before resuming her departure.

Startled by the threat, Chouinard was wondering if he had just made a fatal career mistake when his telephone rang. *"Allo!"* he barked into the receiver. He listened for a few seconds and then called after Monty, who was now half-way out the door. *"Madame* Lombardi—please stay."

One hour north of Saint-Tropez on the scenic D559 highway, a dozen fire trucks, ambulances, and police vehicles were positioned along the rugged cliffs of the Mediterranean Sea. The outstanding postcard panorama of the coast had been disrupted by vivid black skid marks across the winding two-lane road and a violently shattered guardrail. As *Capitaine* Chouinard and Monty arrived in his Renault *Mégane* police unit, he carefully navigated through a maze of traffic cones and road flares that reduced the busy motorway to a congested single lane.

After being pointed by uniformed traffic officers to a parking place on the narrow gravel shoulder, he turned to her and asked, *"Madame,* are you certain that you want to see this?"

She did not want to, of course, but being obligated to was another matter.

Nodding sluggishly, she extricated herself from the passenger seat, now fully numb from the anxiety that had mutated inside her like a virus.

The brisk ocean air was gusting vigorously as Chouinard escorted her to the guard rail. As emergency personnel respectfully stepped aside, Monty remembered how meaningful it was to take in every detail of her wedding ceremony and she reminded herself to do the same here.

As difficult as that might be, this time it was even more important.

She and Chouinard approached the cliff and her feet felt exceedingly heavy, as if she were trudging through gooey mud several feet deep instead of walking on dry pavement. The first thing that she noticed was the variety of distant pleasure craft braving the choppy grey ocean, entirely disconnected from the calamity she was experiencing. For them this was simply another day of recreation on the water, just as people had enjoyed here for two thousand years.

A group of white *Gendarmerie Maritime* patrol boats, with their distinctive red, white, and blue diagonal racing stripes, came into view after that. They were anchored offshore, and she could see them bobbing in the waves as several small dinghies motored toward land.

Then as she arrived at the broken guardrail, the misshapen wreckage of a blue Mercedes could be seen crushed among large rocks in the foamy surf hundreds of feet below. And while it was clear that no one could have survived such an accident, Monty's mind stubbornly refused to process what she was seeing.

It just did not seem real. The car did not even resemble a passenger vehicle. It looked more like a crumpled beverage can from someone's trash.

"The automobile was traveling very fast," she heard Chouinard explain. "I am so sorry."

She continued to stare at the mangled sedan. "But ... we don't know that it's Giancarlo ...." she mumbled.

He understood her disbelief and crouched to the roadway where he picked up a damaged Mercedes-Benz front grille badge that had been partially obscured by jagged splinters of wood. "A hotel attendant identified your husband leaving in the Mercedes," he recounted as he handed her the emblem. "He was alone at the time."

Monty pulled her open-knit sweater closed against the cold and held the dented metal badge securely. "But that could be a different car—" she protested.

"That was my hope, as well. However, men who have rappelled to the site have checked the registration plate number. It is the vehicle that was rented in your name."

Monty's stomach was in her throat, but she never took her attention from the partially submerged wreck. "He was obviously pursuing the criminals—" she uttered, desperate to find another focus for the conversation. "To get our possessions back."

"That is a possibility," he concurred. But he had his doubts. The absence of witnesses or video evidence supporting that scenario indicated that Giancarlo himself was the thief and that he lost control of the car while making his escape. Chouinard was well-aware of how treacherous this section of highway could be if attempted at a high rate of speed.

Neither of them said anything for several minutes, while the totality of the tragedy worked its way into her awareness. Ultimately, she summoned the strength to ask, "Is … Giancarlo there?"

Chouinard hesitated. He knew this would come up, but it was still a subject that he was not fully prepared to discuss. Especially given her current state of shock. And as difficult as it was for her to ask, it was no less so for him to answer. "No, *Madame*," he answered. "I regret to inform you that he was ejected from the vehicle."

"Ejected—" she mumbled in disbelief.

"*Oui*," he responded. "But to collect all of the facts our work could take many days."

"This can't be happening." Her head was spinning now. All she could think about was what might have been the terrifying end of her husband's life.

It was gut-wrenching for Chouinard to read the pain on Monty's face and know that it was likely to get worse for her before it got better. A lot worse, once her numbness gave way to reality. Then, upon noticing a crew of military divers putting on wetsuits beside a van, he supportively took her arm. "Perhaps we should return to Saint-Tropez," he advised.

When he eased her attention to his car she did not resist.

The next twenty-four hours were a blur for Monty. She had no idea what to do or how to do it. But one thing was certain, she could not bring herself to call her mother and father. At least, not until *Capitaine* Chouinard had information that merited sharing with them. This was the first time that she had ever kept secrets from her parents, but she was in no shape to explain anything, anyway.

It was all she could do to just hang on.

She had never experienced anything like this, after all. Her parents had done their best to shield her from hardships of every sort. Having provided her with an affluent upbringing and unconditional love, they insured that obstacles with which other people grappled were absent from her life. Indeed, the Harrison family was successful, healthy, and happy. The whirlwind nature of Monty's engagement did nothing to diminish her parents from welcoming Giancarlo as their own son. It did not take long for Grant and Rosemary Harrison to revel in his affection for their daughter, and Monty knew that news of his possible death would be difficult for them to accept.

The special unresolved circumstances of it—the robbery and either the kidnapping or fatal chase in pursuit of criminals—might very well kill them.

Meanwhile, she never could have moved forward without *Capitaine* Chouinard, whose compassion exceeded anything that she would have expected after their contentious first meeting. With his assistance she was able to wire funds from her account at Barclay's Bank. And he wisely recommended that she await updates on the investigation with loved ones, which for her meant rising above her anguish to meet the most cherished people in Giancarlo's life: the *Suore di Sant'Angelo* at the orphanage.

Chouinard's help in making flight arrangements to Rome was extremely valuable, but it was his pledge to investigate whatever evidence there might be that her husband was not in the Mercedes that offered her peace of mind. If it was learned that he was killed, she reassured herself, then proof of his heroism chasing the criminals would mean so much to her parents, the nuns, and to her.

She repeated to Chouinard that nothing short of a criminal act would have made Giancarlo miss seeing his favorite soccer club on television. Nothing.

As she packed a bag, Monty felt increasingly grateful for the chance to escape from Saint-Tropez and the painful reminders that were everywhere she looked. She could not help agonizing over how to break the news to Mother Superior Emanuela, however. Giancarlo was utterly devoted to her. He had described her as a caring older woman who played the guitar badly and sang even worse, but who fearlessly persevered in performing popular songs from the radio. The results were often like fingernails being dragged across a blackboard, he said, but he dearly loved her determination to bring culture into his life and those of his fellow orphans.

And then there were Sisters Adriana, Rosario, and Matilde, who Giancarlo had identified as not only his favorite teachers, but the most fun of all the nuns at the orphanage. *Oh, how he loved regaling Monty with stories about Sister Rosario, an amateur magician who delighted the children with card tricks, and Sisters Adriana and Matilde, the eccentric tap-dancing duo whose routines while wearing their habits never failed to be amusing!*

Monty's meeting with them was not going to be easy.

Chapter Four
I Heard She Works Here

Playa Vista is a small Los Angeles community east of Dockweiler State Beach and the Santa Monica Bay that sits in the shadow of Loyola Marymount University, the prestigious Jesuit and Marymount research institution. For nearly fifty years Playa Vista was the location of Howard Hughes' eminent aerospace company and defense contractor, as well as the Hughes Airport, before becoming the Southern California home to such dynamic companies as Google, Verizon, YouTube Space L.A., and Connelly Import/Export Corporation. The area is now popularly known as Silicon Beach.

Alex Connelly's four-story international headquarters was an impressive sight on the industrial campus. As striking as the gleaming modern glass exterior may have been, though, it was the marvelous interior spaces that set it apart from other businesses. Connelly went the extra mile to fill the eyes and soothe the souls of his employees with custom-designed Boca Do Labo furniture and artwork by such noted artists as Kathryn Babcock, Kichung Lizee, and Christy Ann Skuban.

It was no wonder that he worried about what his wife might do to him in a contested divorce. The man had plenty to lose.

Dana left her cubicle in the airy common workspace on the third floor and carried a pair of file folders to the copy room near the elevators. What was a familiar clerical task had been injected with entertainment value thanks to her wireless earbuds and the throbbing guitars of Metallica's heavy metal classic *Seek and Destroy*. As she did for much of each workday, she cheerfully rocked out to her favorite music, which helped to immunize her from the more mundane aspects of her job and the mindless yammering of her co-workers.

While she set up the Canon Image Runner to collate and staple her pages, she was largely unaware of the gossiping clique that had congregated by the coffee machine. At first, only fragments of their conversation bled through the music. A woman with prematurely grey hair was saying, "You're joking ...!"

"That's what I heard," a younger woman verified, her grin baring a mouth full of bejeweled teeth. "He's got a mistress."

A slightly built middle-aged man of Japanese descent chuckled, "Well, I know I wouldn't turn him down. That man is luscious!"

Their blathering was of no interest to Dana, until one name emerged as the song ended and the last of her copies dropped into the tray: *"Connelly ...."*

Her attention now activated, she casually removed her ear buds and pretended to organize her papers. The younger woman continued, "He has someone on the side. Can you believe it?!"

"Alex Connelly?!" one of them screeched.

Dana was amused and it took all the discipline she had not to turn and shout, *"Well believe it, bitches!"* It would be so awesome to drop that bomb on these idiots.

"I heard she works here," the younger woman added.

That prompted the grey-haired woman to squeal, "No way! Do we know who?"

"Are you sure it's a she?" the man added hopefully.

Dana smirked as she was transported in her mind to Laguna Beach, where Connelly's hands glided over her body and set her nerve endings on fire. *If the gossip hounds only knew!*

But her private glee ended when the grey-haired woman asked, "What I want to know is, what will Heather Connelly say now that she and Alex are pregnant?"

"She's pregnant?!" the Japanese man and younger woman exclaimed in unison.

The color drained from Dana's face. *Pregnant ....*

She was unaware of how long she stood there staring at the

copier trying to manage what was happening, but her senses were dissolving into nothingness. And the word pregnant was echoing in her mind with such intensity she feared her co-workers could hear it.

How could this be?! Alex said their marriage was dead and buried! Oh, God.

Then she thought again. *But wait, what if the pregnancy news was just sick speculation? The rumor mongers didn't know anything!*

Dana's singular thought was to see Alex. But when she tried to leave, her feet stubbornly refused to move. She also realized that she had been clutching the copier tightly like a life preserver. She was incapacitated. Eventually she regained control of her body. After taking a few measured inhalations, she persuaded her legs to lift her leaden feet.

As soon as she could escape from the room without being noticed, Dana was moving fast along a glass-walled corridor of executive offices on the fourth floor. Memories of intimate moments with Connelly and the things he said pummeled her: like during their conversation at a company party when he confided in her and said, *"Heather and I are finally calling it quits ...."* And when he told her during a late-night phone call that he and his wife, *"... no longer even speak to each other ...."* And what he said while making love to her in Laguna-Niguel, *"You're the one I've been waiting for, Dana ...."* And the text message that was waiting for her when she woke up this morning: *I'm not happy unless I'm waking up beside you.*

Blood pounded ferociously in her head. *What she heard in the copy room had to be a mistake! Had to.*

When she arrived at the large corner suite, she stopped upon encountering Connelly's executive assistant seated beneath oversized stainless-steel lettering that identified his eponymous business. Though still in her forties, the woman gave the distinct impression of being past retirement age. And if it is true that a smile can light up a room, then her frown, which was accentuated by her sharply jutting chin, could suck the oxygen out of one many times the size. She had a disagreeable snooty quality, as if she thought she was the Queen of England or something. This part of the Connelly empire was her domain and she fiercely protected the boss. Everyone in the organization feared her.

Dana paused in Connelly's open office doorway and peered inside. The Queen of England queried, "May I help you, Miss Zimmer?"

"I hafta see Alex right away," she answered, hoping that her face did not reveal what she was really feeling.

"Mister Connelly isn't in."

But there was no stopping Dana. She continued into the office and was immediately confronted by the sight of a framed 8x10 glossy color photo on the credenza—a professionally shot portrait featuring a radiantly pregnant Heather Connelly with her loving husband.

Dana came up short upon seeing the picture, which was a new addition to the decor. The sparkle in the couple's eyes was unmistakable. Heather Connelly was pretty, in her late thirties, and gleamed with happiness. *Connelly was not in the throes of a long-awaited divorce. This was a couple still very much in love.*

It was all she could do to not throw up.

As Dana fidgeted with the diamond necklace that Connelly gave her, the Queen of England appeared behind her. "I was about to say that Mister Connelly is away on business."

"Oh, yeah … I guess I forgot …." was all Dana could get out in an attempt to cover her actions. But it was not very convincing. She was pale and trembling and strangely unable to control either.

Whether the Queen of England knew of Connelly's affair with her or not, and she probably did, she rather liked this spirited young woman. The heartache that Dana was experiencing was palpable.

"He's at the Raphael Hotel in Rome," she informed her. "If you want to contact him there."

Chapter Five
My Husband Grew Up There

Monty's trip from Saint-Tropez to Rome took nearly four hours, including the ninety-minute drive to the airport in Nice. *Capitaine* Chouinard had thoughtfully supplied an official car to take her, which was driven by a capable associate and not one of the lascivious miscreants from the *Gendarmerie*. That relieved her of having to think about anything, and she managed to sleep during most of the ride. It was the first rest that she was able to get since Giancarlo's disappearance.

The Alitalia Airlines flight took about the same amount of time as the journey to Nice, but it felt longer thanks to the colicky infant that cried incessantly in the seat behind her. She was trapped by the sounds of an inconsolable child and the troubling feelings that filled her heart and mind. The annoying tinny classical music discharging from her cheap airline headphones did nothing to help.

Gazing out the window of the Embraer 190, patches of the blue Mediterranean peeked through a carpet of fluffy white clouds whenever they could. She held the dented Mercedes grille badge in her hands and tried to think cheerful thoughts; like the way Giancarlo swept her off her feet on the first day of her vacation, their mutual fondness for culture, and the romantic hours they shared before their wondrous wedding at Saint Patrick's Cathedral. And, of course, the impassioned days and nights of their honeymoon.

They were all events that she should have been treasuring, but knowing she might never again be held in his arms made them feel unbearable. And then there were the images of the crash site that she unsuccessfully tried to block out, as she fought to maintain at least a shred of hope that her husband was still alive.

Unfortunately, there were serious questions that could not be sidestepped. *What would she do if Giancarlo were really dead? Did he have funeral or memorial preferences? If so, what were they? Who besides the nuns should be notified?* She had never discussed any of those things with him. Their relationship was too new and, she wrongly assumed, they were too young for such morbid considerations.

When Tomaso Albinoni's despairing *Adagio in G Minor* came on the jet's music channel she removed her headphones. Given her sullen mood even a screaming child was better than being forced to listen to that, she thought as she concentrated on her hope that Giancarlo might have survived.

But what if her implorations were granted and Capitaine Chouinard called with miraculous good news? With the possibility came so many more uneasy questions that she did not feel at all qualified to answer. *What if Giancarlo were to need extensive medical or psychological care? Physical injuries can be healed, but the emotional trauma of a violent incident could take years to resolve.*

Monty knew nothing about her husband's medical history, either. *Why had she never discussed those things with him?!* Hopefully, Mother Superior Emanuela and the Sisters *di Sant'Angelo* would have the critical information that she lacked.

Monty's anxieties did not dissipate during the forty-minute taxi ride from Leonardo da Vinci International Airport. They only continued to darken. As the flat green coastal Italian countryside along the *Autostrada Roma-Fiumicino* airport highway gradually gave way to the seven hills of the Eternal City and the Aurelian Walls that once protected them, her concerns became disjointed and severe, like shards of glass piercing her heart. A mental image of Giancarlo making love to her would suddenly mutate into one of him being savagely beaten by thieves during the robbery. Another of him holding her hand on a romantic date at *Spiaggia di Focene* would morph into one of the Mercedes crashing into the sea in agonizing slow-motion, before exploding on impact like a nuclear bomb.

She tried everything to purge the disturbances, but that only seemed to inflame them. Monty saw Giancarlo's face wherever she looked—one second, he would be walking down the street as her taxi drove by, and the next he would be watching her from a passing car. She even had the harrowing surprise of seeing him pull alongside the cab on a motor scooter and derisively sneer at her. It was as if she were trapped in a horror movie playing repeatedly, without end and without a hero to save the day.

But Giancarlo was supposed to be her hero!

When the sinister apparitions finally disappeared, however, all that remained were Monty's increasing apprehensions about how to inform the nuns that their dear Giancarlo might be dead. She had to stay strong.

As her taxi crossed the Tiber River, for once she did not care about the places she passed. The person who previously would have noted neighborhoods and legendary structures to explore later was no longer interested. Her destination was nearing, and it was as if the gargantuan city of Rome were swallowing her whole. Trepidation grabbed her hard and a heavy weight had been placed on her chest.

Monty stepped from the taxi not far from the fabled Trevi Fountain. Michael Bublé's clever customized song dedication at her wedding reception recounted the evening that she and Giancarlo tossed coins over their shoulders to guarantee her return visit, but she resisted the memory. Instead, she was struck by the boisterous hum of the city and exhaust fumes mingling with kitchen odors in the air. She had always enjoyed the sensory experience of Rome, but this time all she could think about was the terrible task looming at the orphanage.

The harsh metallic booming of nearby cathedral bells reverberating through the neighborhood intruded on her consciousness. It felt like the gloomy moment before an execution. Consulting a slip of paper on which she had written the orphanage address, Monty would have given anything to avoid meeting the nuns under such circumstances. Her angst was further heightened when the address on *Via delle Muratte* that Giancarlo had given her turned out to be that of an inconsequential souvenir shop, not a venerable Catholic home for orphaned children.

She was lost.

Monty lugged her suitcase the entire length of the street from *Via Santa Maria In Via* at one end to the *Piazza Di Trevi* at the other. As she examined the entrances of dozens of 18th and 19th century buildings, her search was to no avail. While she did find several cafes and boutique hotels behind variegated brick, stone, and plaster exteriors that seemed to have been patched over the years rather than maintained, and even a McDonald's Restaurant that seemed woefully out of place in these historic surroundings, she was unable to locate Giancarlo's orphanage.

She was growing more depressed by the minute. With nowhere else to go she doubled back to the souvenir shop.

The sugary aroma of scented candles and incense was strong as Monty passed jumbled rows of *Italia* t-shirts and refrigerator magnets, plastic religious curios, and colorful framed likenesses of Jesus, Pope Francis, and Mother Teresa that were crammed into the miniscule store. An overweight shopkeeper with thick grey eyebrows and an unpersuasive charcoal black toupee greeted her. *"Buon giorno. Posso aiutarvi?"* he opened in a friendly voice.

"I'm sorry, I don't speak Italian," she replied. *"Parlez-vous Français?"*

The shopkeeper smiled. "My English is better. How may I be of service?" He proudly gestured to a display case filled with inexpensive costume jewelry. "I have an excellent selection of treats for a young lady such as yourself."

"Thank you, but I'm not shopping today," she explained as she handed him the folded paper. "I'm looking for an orphanage that should be at this address. I would appreciate any information that you might have."

He briefly squinted at the note before returning it. "The number is the same, but as you see there is no orphanage."

"It's operated by the *Suore di Sant'Angelo*," Monty continued.

"My husband grew up there."

The shopkeeper could only shake his head. "We have the *Sant'Angelo* Bridge and the castle, but I do not know about any nuns." He plucked two postcards from a rack and handed them to her.

Monty was crestfallen as she took in the photos of an ancient bridge and castle, which prompted him to offer another suggestion. "Why don't you ask at the church down the street?" he said pointing to the left of the Trevi Fountain. "The priest there might have information. His name is Father Vitale."

The Church of *Santa Maria a Trevi* is a Baroque Roman Catholic basilica with an incongruously plain exterior, given its proximity to the opulent Trevi Fountain around the corner. Conversely, the inside is an architectural gem that is distinguished by a single nave with four arched niches on each side, sumptuous gold decorations, and a masterful Antonio Gherardi ceiling fresco depicting scenes from the life of the Blessed Virgin Mary.

The tiny sanctuary was the opposite of Saint Patrick's Cathedral, which was a blessing. Monty did not need additional mementos of her wedding day.

Contributing to the sacred feeling around her as she sat alone in one of the well-worn dark oak pews was the evocative bouquet of frankincense and myrrh. Ordinarily, she would have savored the room's inspirational ambiance for hours, letting the transcendent values of the artwork and Christian symbols wash over her. But of course, there was nothing ordinary about her being there. She silently prayed to Saint Maria, who was herself a murder victim, to send a sign that Giancarlo might somehow be spared. If anyone should understand the injustice of his possible death, she hoped, it would be Maria Teresa Goretti.

Eventually an aging priest with narrow sloping shoulders, high forehead, and large hook nose took a seat beside her, wincing from the arthritis in his knees. "Mrs. Lombardi," Father Demetrio Vitale began, "I have made inquiries at the convent next door and they are not familiar with an order called the *Suore di Sant'Angelo*."

Monty shifted her weight apprehensively. "Then I must have the wrong name. Mother Superior Emanuela and the sisters are the only family that my husband has in the world."

Vitale peered at a father and young daughter lighting votive candles on a nearby tiered metal stand and paused to clean the lenses of his glasses with a sleeve on his cassock. But if truth be known, he was just buying time. There was something that he was not looking forward to talking about.

"Yes, from when he was a boy at the orphanage," he reprised.

"Surely you can understand how important this is, Father," Monty implored. "They deserve to know what has happened."

The priest hesitated again. Understanding how invested she was in the information that she had presented, he wanted to be as compassionate as possible. "*Signora ...* I do not know how to say this except to be direct," he said returning his glasses to his nose. "The church orphanages in the city were closed many years ago."

"But that's impossible—" she argued. "I made a donation to them just last month."

He cocked his head. "May I ask the amount of this donation?"

"Ten thousand dollars," she answered, hoping the substantial amount would prove meaningful. "My husband handled the delivery to Mother Superior Emanuela himself. Whoever gave you your information is mistaken!"

Father Vitale clasped her hands, consoling. "Then may our Lord Jesus Christ provide you with the answers you seek."

Monty stood and thanked him as she reached for her suitcase, only to be overcome by a wave of dizziness. When she gazed up at the altar it became distorted and blurry. Sensing her distress, the priest eased her back into the pew where he sat with her in silence and prayed for God to relieve her suffering.

Chapter Six
You Got What You Wanted

Although Dana's reason for flying to Rome was similar to Monty's, in that they were both motivated by broken hearts, the comparisons ended there. Monty had seen the city many times and enjoyed all that it had to offer, including falling in love with her future husband, but Dana had never been to Italy. Or to Europe, for that matter. Other than a memorable date years ago with one of the Scaramucci twins, an up-and-coming rock duo on the Hollywood club circuit, the closest she ever came to experiencing Italian culture was *Angelini Osteria*, the Beverly Boulevard restaurant that was a favorite Alex Connelly date spot.

Connelly. There was that name again! She wondered if there would ever come a time when everything did not remind her of him.

Dana entered the cozy bougainvillea and Virginia creeper-enshrouded courtyard of the five-star deluxe Raphael Hotel and strode past the intricately carved front desk. The Raphael was old and elegant, with renovations that resembled something from a Hollywood movie set, which was appropriate since many movie stars had stayed there. Renowned actors Richard Burton and Elizabeth Taylor helped make it famous in the 1970's when they named it their favorite Roman hideaway.

While Dana would not have ordinarily appreciated the collection of Picasso ceramics, Mayan artwork, or museum-quality paintings on display throughout the ground floor, at least she would have noticed them. Not today, however. Today she was oblivious to it all as she waited for the elevator to arrive. Still, her lack of attentiveness had nothing to do with jetlag from spending the past fourteen hours in the last row of coach seats. For her, time-itself had been suspended. Connelly's betrayal of her trust—and his manipulation of her emotions—were a one-two punch that sent her reeling into a state of disbelief that compressed everything around her into a dull, generic backdrop.

Dana had been used and there was no escaping that fact. The image of Connelly's unsuspecting pregnant wife burned into her brain was a haunting reminder.

In his spacious corner suite upstairs, Connelly and one of his young executives, Greg Lange, sat in the living room and referred to notes in their matching Connelly Import/Export leather folios.

Connelly checked his watch impatiently. "It's been an hour, Greg. You don't think they're having second thoughts, do you?"

"It's the mafia, Alex. I'm not sure anybody can read their minds," Lange surmised.

A former college intern at the company, Lange was a newly minted Loyola Marymount MBA graduate and there was little question that his career ambitions exceeded his professional expertise. But his ego and ruthless nature made up for it, which were the traits that caught Connelly's attention in the first place. His protégé reminded him of himself at that age, though without his athletic build and arresting good looks. On that score Lange did not compare very favorably—his forehead was excessively large, and his lips were so thin they were barely visible. Topping off his appearance, literally, was a gnarled clump of curly red hair that had to be kept short to avoid looking like a comical Halloween wig.

"On the other hand, I think they want this agreement as much as we do," Lange surmised. "And they sure have cash to launder."

"I don't like being kept waiting. Cash or not."

"It's their turf," Lange added while checking a text message on his phone.

Connelly stood to stretch his legs. "You're right," he acknowledged. This deal was worth millions of dollars and he knew that he would need to rein in his anxiety.

"I'm glad you agree," Lange said as he held up his phone screen, "because they want to reschedule."

"For when?"

"They'll let us know."

Connelly shot him a look. "The bastards are testing me—"

"Sounds like something the mob might do."

"Smart move, seeing what I'm made of," Connelly mused as he paced. "But this just gives us more time to polish our pitch. Where do we stand on the players?"

"Well, I only met Citrano that one time in New York and he does a lot of talking," Lange described, "but DeLuca has the real clout now that the families are joint venturing."

Connelly was intrigued by the reference, given the customary competition for drug trafficking, loan sharking, and prostitution in Italy. "So, DeLuca worked things out with the 'Ndrangheta and Camorra, after all?" he asked, referring to the ruthless mafia organizations in Calabria and Naples.

"Rome's where the action is," Lange verified. "And a few weeks ago, he became the man to reckon with."

"Nice work, mate," Connelly observed as he sipped the last of his Americano-style coffee, which had gone cold. "I want to know more about how the families made their truce, so I don't walk into the middle of something."

"I'll have that for you in the morning," Lange answered, making a note of the request.

Just then there was a firm knock in the entryway. "That must be room service," Connelly said, setting his cup aside. "Good timing."

But when Lange opened the door, the men were startled to discover Dana standing there. She was unsmiling as she zeroed in on her lover. "Lemme guess, you're surprised to see me."

Surprised, indeed. But Connelly did what he could to mask it with forced pleasantries. "Dana—what are you doing here?" Moving to greet her as she advanced into the room, he could tell there was something different about her.

Little did he know how empowering the information that she

had about him was. "Let's just say I couldn't wait to hear the latest update on your divorce," she derisively revealed. "When'll that be? Before the baby or after?"

Her eyes were sharp and unblinking. Energized.

Turning to Lange he said, "Give us a minute, will you Greg?"

"Wow, a whole minute?" she noted acidly as the executive stepped into the next room.

"Darling, I can't tell you how sorry I am you found out—" Connelly swore.

"I'll bet," she interrupted.

"—before we could talk it over," he finished in earnest. "This's been a nightmare for me. I don't know what happened!"

Dana glared at him, incensed. "Gimme a fucking break!"

"You know what I mean," he continued, hoping to turn this around.

But she was having none of it. "Do I?"

"It was Heather! She did this to me deliberately."

"Amazing, considering you're not even on speaking terms with her," she caustically pointed out.

"It's more complicated than that," he said in what he hoped sounded like an apology. "I've been tricked by a devious woman."

"She didn't look so devious in that new photo of you at work."

"I had nothing to do with that," he maintained.

"It's in your office."

"That's just to mollify her until she signs the damn divorce papers," he professed.

"... Like your wedding ring," Dana remembered.

"Exactly!"

"The baby bump in the picture was a nice touch," she added. "She looked extra mollified to me."

Connelly let the remark pass. "Nothing has to change between you and me."

But for once she had clarity. Searing clarity. "You never meant any of it, did you."

"Of course, I did ... and I still do."

"Jesus, be honest!" she cut in. "I'm nothing more to you than a great lay."

"That's enough!" he demanded sharply. There was a finality to his demeanor, an unspoken threat that did not go unnoticed.

"Why?" Dana said defiantly as she stepped closer. "I'm the girl who never gets enough, remember?"

His eyes turned to ice and there was an ominous dark edge to him. "Greg ..." he summoned. "Get her a car to the airport."

"You got it," Lange confirmed as he reached for her arm.

But when he grabbed her, Dana spun her body to break free and twisted his hand behind his back. It was a self-defense move that had served her well with a parade of jerks over the years. "Try that again and you won't pee standing up for a month," she warned.

Lange whimpered from the pain and nodded hastily. She released him with an emphatic shove before turning to Connelly. "So, does the little woman know what a two-timing piece of shit you are? Or have you got her snowed, too."

Connelly glowered at her. "Why is that any business of a root rat like you?" he challenged, using Australian slang for a woman who cannot get enough sex.

"Because you used me, that's why."

"You got what you wanted," he commented while grimly looking at her diamond necklace. The one he bought her in Laguna Beach. "Now, piss off," he added, pointing to the door that Lange was holding open.

It was all Dana could do not to slug him, but he was too big and strong for that. Besides, she said what she came to say, even if the outcome was less than ideal.

Without a further word, she turned and left.

After a lifetime of becoming a self-proclaimed expert on men, Dana was entirely undone. Her assumptions about love, romance, and the male gender had been proven wrong. And nothing had prepared her for Alex Connelly—certainly not her experiences with a long line of would-be studs who thought they were God's gift to women. She thought she had seen it all, but now saw that she could not have been more wrong. She felt like an idiot.

As she wandered the streets of the city, she could not help thinking about her time with Connelly and what might have made her so susceptible to his ploy. He was rakishly handsome, absolutely, but there had been other great-looking men in her life. He was also a wonderful lover, but she had known a few of those, too.

Then she thought about how much older he was than her previous boyfriends. Given her intensely negative feelings about her drunken loser of a father, who was out of her life before she was a teenager, Dana could not help wondering if Connelly's appeal had something to do with her dad's absence as she was growing up.

A freaking daddy issue?! How twisted would that be!

Still, she had to consider it. No matter how nauseating it might be. She could not deny the appeal of having a stable older man in her life, and while her past loves were younger than Connelly, every one of them was older than her. *Was it possible that the attention Connelly showed her filled some sort of dark need inside her?*

What was left of her spirits was crushed by the possibility.

She decided there was only one thing for her to do: show this city what a pissed-off woman on the rebound looked like.

Chapter Seven
There Must Be Another Explanation

Upon checking into the quaint Inn At The Spanish Steps, Monty arranged an emergency appointment with the United States Embassy. Despite the stubborn Roman traffic and a chatty Middle Eastern driver who spoke no English, but who seemed intent on making her acquaintance, she arrived at the American complex on *Via Veneto* minutes before the entrance was scheduled to be locked.

She was escorted to an upstairs interview room, where she meticulously recounted the details of the robbery, kidnapping, and car crash to an assistant. She was then ushered into an austere office, where she sat across from a diplomat senior enough to be her mother, but who lacked any discernable maternal qualities. Meredith Jacobsen also had misaligned wide-set eyes that pointed in opposite directions, making it impossible for Monty to tell whether the woman was looking at her or something behind her.

Framed photographs of celebrities who had visited the Embassy were displayed on a bookshelf, including one featuring Jacobsen with Monty's father and Bill Gates. Conspicuously, there were no family pictures anywhere. Nothing of a personal nature.

"How well did you know your husband before you were married?" the officer asked in a diminished New England accent.

Monty was discouraged by the diplomat's lack of empathy, especially given the details of misery contained in her report. "What difference does that make?!"

"I'm only trying to sort out a complicated problem," Jacobsen asserted while reviewing the papers. But her words had a hollow feel.

"Giancarlo is missing," she reiterated. "Is that complicated enough for you?"

Jacobsen cast her unnerving, skewed eyes at Monty, or whatever might be behind her. "I'm sure your father would agree that having a complete background would be helpful."

Monty forced herself to calm down. The diplomat only agreed to see her after Monty invoked her well-connected father, but her cynicism was unmistakable. And while Monty's urge to look over her shoulder to see what Jacobsen might be looking at was troublesome, she was too upset to worry about that now. "We met eight months ago."

"I see," came the reply with a hint of condescension.

"My own grandparents had a brief courtship during the Vietnam War," Monty added defensively. "Giancarlo is the most caring man I've ever known."

"I'm sure he was."

"Furthermore, I prefer that my husband be discussed in the present tense," she admonished. "No one has convinced me that he's dead."

"It isn't very convincing that he's alive, either," Jacobsen said flatly as she checked her watch for the time.

That was it. Monty was done with this halfwit. It might have been the end of a long day, but that was no excuse for this abusive treatment. "I can't believe that someone from my own government would say something so insensitive!" she erupted.

But the diplomat was unruffled. "What I meant was, we have checked with the Italian authorities and there is no record of Giancarlo Lombardi having ever been born."

The revelation nearly knocked Monty over. "No record—"

"None."

Monty deflated and even the dispassionate woman could not avoid feeling sorry for her. "Would you like me to place a call to your father? I'm sure he would appreciate an update."

"No ... thank you," Monty quickly responded. "This is something that I should tell him myself."

Inside the Municipal Police station on *Via della Greca* in the center of the city, Monty was in urgent need of assistance. Where the Roman Catholic Church and her own embassy had failed to help, surely Italian law enforcement officials could do more, she thought. As luck would have it, the cluttered desk of Sergeant Cesare Fazio was the one she happened upon. Unlike the gruff American diplomat, he actually cared about his job—not to mention the plight of this young woman, who was by now looking quite haggard.

Fazio's appearance was a bit rumpled, too. A somewhat unkempt desk jockey who recently turned forty, he had gained a few pounds and was having a little trouble fitting into his blue *Polizia* uniform jacket. When she entered his office, he tried to suck in his stomach without much luck. *He really needed to start hitting the gym!*

Disappointingly, after having her wait in the lobby while he investigated the details of her case online and by telephone, he did not have good news to share. "The information that your embassy gave you appears to be correct, *Signora*," he disclosed as she took a seat. "I can find no record of birth for your husband. I am sorry."

"That can't be—" she answered.

"I wish that could be true," he replied. "However, there is also no evidence of a driver's license in his name."

"But he has a passport," she reasoned.

He reacted with increasing sadness. "Again, our government has no record of that."

"Then, someone has made a terrible mistake."

"Regrettably, that is not the only issue." He handed her a page from his file. "As you can see, I have also established that what the priest has said is true. There is no documentation of the *Suore di Sant'Angelo* in Rome."

Monty's face flushed with indignation. "Well, that is absolutely ludicrous! My husband knows perfectly well who raised him."

"I have seen the database," he explained. "It is not a mistake."

Monty reeled. She was emotionally depleted. "Then this is some sort of cover-up," she countered.

The accusation caught Fazio off guard. "Cover-up?"

Yes, a cover-up! Of course! A surge of adrenaline jolted her awake as the possible explanation swirled in her mind. She excitedly asked, "Has it occurred to you that your government may be conspiring with the church?!"

"Why would they do such a thing?"

"I don't know," she retorted, folding her arms defensively. "When was the last time anyone around here investigated the Vatican?!"

Fazio's thick mustache hovered above the cup of cappuccino that looked comically small in his beefy fingers. "The Vatican," he repeated.

"Of course!" she confirmed as the plausibility of her idea became increasingly clear. "Giancarlo's records mysteriously disappear and all traces of the Catholic orphanage where he was a child vanish into thin air?! One hardly needs to be an investigative journalist to see a connection."

Astounded by the assertion, Fazio set his cappuccino down and fingered the unlit cigarette he was never without. "But I do not think—"

"You don't think," she interrupted. "How reassuring."

He gathered himself carefully. The interview was spiraling out of control and if nothing else, he prided himself on his ability to communicate with the public. "In spite of what you may believe, I am not your adversary," he expressed.

Monty stopped. The man was trying to help her, after all. He had done nothing to warrant her rebuke. "Forgive me, Sergeant. I didn't intend to take this out on you," she apologized. "You can't imagine what this ordeal has been like for me."

"I imagine more than you realize," Fazio offered as he set his cigarette aside and leaned forward. "A wealthy American woman meets an intriguing man in Rome, and to her few places are as much for romance as the Eternal City."

Her left eye twitched as the synopsis hit close to home.

"Because she is in love," he went on, "there is a brief courtship. She asks no questions, knowing only what her exciting lover has told

46

her. Then he disappears with her valuables."

Monty's face paled as she gawked back. He had just recapped her entire relationship with Giancarlo! She wanted to be outraged but no longer had the vigor for that. "Please, Sergeant, is there anything you can do to learn what happened to him?" she implored. "I have to live with memories of the accident scene in Saint-Tropez. I can't handle more bad news."

Fazio shifted in his chair. "Yes, the accident. I am afraid to say that I have difficult information about that, as well. I have spoken to *Capitaine* Chouinard. He has determined that the floor pedal of your car, the accelerator, was immobilized before the crash."

Her stomach sank. "What ...?"

"Divers have not recovered a body from the ocean. The French believe that these details can mean one thing only: the incident was a deception."

"Deception," she restated as her heart seemed to stop.

And even though Fazio's heart was beating, he felt as if it were also breaking. "Yes," he added with difficulty.

"But there must be another explanation!" she insisted. "What about the blood on my purse?"

"The laboratory has found that it was not human blood. They suspect that it came from a package of meat."

Monty's body weakened. "Meat."

"*Capitaine* Chouinard and I agree that the facts are these," he submitted, "... whoever your husband is, his name is not Giancarlo Lombardi ... the orphanage does not exist ... he was not abducted in a robbery ... and he was not in the Mercedes when it crashed."

"I think I'm going to be ill," she mumbled.

Sergeant Fazio rushed to catch her when she fainted.

Upon learning the dreadful truth about her husband, Monty walked aimlessly for miles. Sergeant Fazio assured her that he would try to determine Giancarlo's real identity, though that did nothing to ease her pain.

Nor did the splendid autumn day. For Monty, the sunny crisp

weather brought only emptiness, not the renewal for which she had hoped. Her unconscious mind guided her to the 400-year-old Borghese Gardens with the glorious city views, trees, walkways, and illustrious museum that had bestowed on her so much pleasure in the past. But today they failed to penetrate her desolation.

She was removed from it all as she roiled with misery and confusion.

Swarms of people around her were enjoying the day and each other, happily holding hands and taking pictures. *How could they be so jubilant?! Did they not see that she was suffering? Did they not care?!* Inevitably, the answer was that she was invisible to them. She had never felt so alone and despondent.

Despondent ... what a terrible word that was! Perversely, she wondered if there might be a more fitting depiction of her state of mind. *Dejected and downcast* were strong candidates, she thought, and just as bleak. But they did not fully capture the profundities of her despair. And *unhappy* did not even come close.

That triggered another word in her mind: *hopeless.* Yes, that seemed more accurate. How pitiful to be defined by such an adjective, she considered. And that realization brought an amended revelation: *pitiful* was another depressing word that portrayed her perfectly.

Hopeless and pitiful! Hardly the emotional status that she expected on what was supposed to be her honeymoon.

Monty recognized that her mental word game was sending her further into the abyss, so she did what she could to shift her attention back to her superb garden surroundings. The late afternoon shadows were cast long by the setting sun, making the branches of trees in the park look like giant arms waving on the ground. She contemplated continuing to the *Galleria Borghese* and the works of Bernini, Caravaggio, Canova, and Raffaello in the 17th century home of Cardinal Scipione Borghese, but the pain of having visited the Villa with Giancarlo early in their relationship was too much. There would be no relief there; only things to make her feel even more hopeless and pitiful.

Then the disquieting occurrence from her airport drive replicated itself—as Giancarlo's face appeared on every man she saw.

What had been sociable smiles morphed into sadistic images of her husband rejoicing over her dire circumstances; mocking her for allowing him to exploit her inexperience so easily.

It was truly frightening, and Monty knew she was losing her equilibrium. The little girl who once believed in love story happy endings was now a miserable lost soul who was no longer sure what she believed in.

Chapter Eight
This Was All Your Fault

That evening across the Tiber River from Sergeant Fazio's office, a middle-aged gentleman in a white dinner jacket was playing pleasant piano interludes at *La Cucina di Isabella*. It was a sophisticated place with thick white tablecloths, soft ambient lighting, and authentic *Emilia-Romagna* cuisine prepared by the owner's wife, a talented chef.

On this night, however, the antics of a boisterous drunken American female were spoiling the atmosphere for everyone: Dana Zimmer, who was drowning her sorrows as a trio of middle-aged men competed for her attention. "Hey, did you guys hear about the Italian chef who died?" she yelled. "He pasta away! Get it? Pasta away ... sounds like *passed away*?!"

They cracked up on cue, though they did not understand most of what she said. But being red-blooded Italian males, their interest in the sexy tourist in a miniskirt and revealing lowcut top was the only motivation necessary. The language barrier was irrelevant.

"Okay, that one was over your heads," she recognized. "But stay with me, boys. This one you'll like! In La-La Land we call this a depth-charge." She drunkenly plopped a shot glass of tequila in her beer and chugged the foaming concoction. The men howled uproariously and obediently followed suit.

It was a rowdy scene for a subdued room like this and twenty-five feet away Monty took it all in with revulsion. Perched on her bar stool she was every bit as drunk as Dana, but in her state of mind she was in no mood to listen to an obnoxious loudmouth. She did not know why Americans often seemed louder than people from other countries, but in her travel experience they were.

This one certainly was.

Monty turned to the mild mannered fifty-seven-year-old proprietor Alfredo Barone, who was attentively serving her from behind the bar. "It is a depressing study in contrasts, isn't it?" she lamented. "A talented artisan rendering Chopin, while a beer guzzling strumpet makes an absolute spectacle of herself."

She downed her glass and continued, "Another *Chianti Classico*, please."

Alfredo nodded respectfully at her request. But while he might have saved for years to open this establishment, he never overcharged anyone. "*Signora*, would it not be cheaper to purchase a bottle?"

Monty sloughed off the idea. "Oh Alfredo, I could never drink an entire bottle."

"But you have already finished one," he informed her.

She looked stupefied before grinning a loopy grin. "Well, isn't that something?"

Just then a raucous cheer erupted from Dana's table, where she was having a beer chugging contest with the Italian men.

Wiping her mouth, Dana noticed the glaring diners around her. "Ya know what's wrong with this joint? Elevator music!" She turned to the pianist. "Yo, Yanni, what's your jam, man? Hip it up a little. Know any Mariah Carey?"

The man did not react.

"No Mariah? Okay, how about some old school JIM Carrey?" She did a bleating Jim Carrey laugh but got only blank stares in return. She could not believe it. "Come on, *Ace Ventura Pet Detective* ... it's a classic!"

Eventually Monty could not take it any longer and called out, "Excuse me, but would you please keep it down?"

Dana glowered at her. "You gotta problem, honey bun?"

"As a matter of fact, I do," Monty sniffed.

"Don't tell me you like that garbage he's playing."

"I'm talking about the vulgar inebriate who seems intent on ruining everyone's evening."

Dana had to think about that a moment. "That means me, right?"

"If the profanity fits," came Monty's curt answer.

That got Dana on her feet and staggering in her direction. "You got some kinda mouth, lady."

"At least what emanates from it isn't detritus."

Dana gaped. "I don't even know what that means," she said, slurring her words badly.

"Next time bring a dictionary," Monty sneered.

Unsure what Monty was saying, Dana paused vacantly.

"Effluence," Monty specified as she stood and smoothed her skirt, "... sewage ... waste ...."

"Bite me, bitch!" snarled Dana.

Monty tossed a glass of wine in her face in return, which prompted Dana to drive her head into Monty's stomach and shove her hard, a tackling maneuver that she had learned from years of watching WWE television wrestling with her older brothers while their mother held down two full-time jobs. This particular move was known to her fellow diehard wrestling fans as "The Spear".

Restaurant customers scattered as the women crashed into a table. Alfredo tried to intervene, only to get punched in the nose. Terrified, he scrambled behind the bar and dialed the police as his wife and her back-of-house workers wisely barricaded themselves behind the kitchen doors.

Dana was a ball of unchecked fury. And given her highly intoxicated state, what was most effective for her was her proficiency at fighting dirty. However, while Monty was someone who had rarely raised her voice in anger, let alone physically assaulted anyone, she was surprisingly impressive with a frenzy of slapping hands and hair-pulling countermoves.

And that made for a most colorful catfight, indeed.

Unluckily, since Dana had a short haircut, she had the upper hand when it came to hair-pulling, and she managed to get more than one handful of Monty's luxurious long and thick tresses. She yanked Monty right off her feet several times and slammed her to the floor.

But Monty held her own. It was a flamboyant match-up worthy of a pay-per-view cable TV event.

The fight progressed that way as the screaming duo rolled from one end of the restaurant to another, scattering chairs, tables, and people. In the process, Dana attempted other theatrical wrestling moves that she learned from television: in addition to "The Spear", she also tried such outrageous WWE classics as "The Boston Crab", "The Sharpshooter", and something called "The Shining Wizard Combo".

Yet in her severely drunken state, none of those really worked. Dana wound up falling on her face as much as she did hurting Monty.

At one-point Dana struggled to her unsteady feet to grab a bottle for a weapon. Monty threw a water pitcher at her and missed, crashing it instead into the elaborate glass shelving behind the bar. Alfredo screamed as his entire inventory of liquor and glassware collapsed with a deafening explosion.

Until then, the bar held the only unbroken glass in the establishment.

The brawl came to an unceremonious end when Dana attempted another TV wrestling maneuver by jumping from the bar onto Monty's shoulders, missing her target and falling into a pool of red and white wine just as a squad of policemen burst into the restaurant.

Startled by the bizarre scene that greeted them, none of the officers who took Monty and Dana into custody had ever been confronted by anyone quite like them. Nor had they tackled anything close to the pandemonium the women had created—notwithstanding their work in a city of three million citizens and over ten million tourists each year.

The women's concrete holding cell area in the Municipal Police station was chilly and damp. The three large lockups were teeming with a peculiar assortment of female prisoners that evening. Monty and Dana were still intoxicated as they occupied the first and third cells with grubby street people, hostile drunks, and one inmate with wild eyes who Monty feared might be an escaped mental patient.

Even now, with their torn wine-soaked clothing and two hours spent on uninviting jail cots, they still looked better than the other inmates; the scruffy fifty-year-old hooker passed out on Monty's shoulder, in particular.

When the prostitute burped loudly in her sleep Dana shot Monty a look through the bars. "I hope you're happy," she slurred.

"Don't speak to me," Monty mumbled. "I have nothing to say to you."

"Why not?" Dana sniped. "This was all your fault!"

Monty glared back. "Are you deaf? I just said, I have nothing to say to you!"

"You are such a bitch, ya know that?"

"Duly noted, thank you."

Just then, in the center cell a braless butch-looking woman wearing a stained and wrinkled man's sleeveless undershirt stepped into their line of sight. "You are both Americans, yes?"

"You know it," Dana answered.

"As disconcerting as that seems at the moment," Monty pointedly added.

"Well, let me tell you, American girls ..." the butch woman continued in a booming voice, "SHUT THE HELL UP!"

Which they did. Immediately.

So did everyone else in the cell block. The only remaining sound was the dripping faucet in Dana's cell and the faint buzzing of an unseen ventilation fan. The butch woman flopped onto her cot and rejoiced in her newly achieved peace and quiet.

Chapter Nine
He Is A Good Hunting Dog, Yes?

The same evening that Monty and Dana were being arrested, Giancarlo entered the Chapter Hotel's industrial-chic lobby bar on *Via di Santa Maria de Calderari* and signaled to the bartender, Leandro Rossetti. As he had done many times before, the chubby thirty-year-old had called to describe a good-looking female hotel guest who was drinking alone. Having successfully accomplished his financial objectives with Monty, Giancarlo was already on the prowl for his next victim.

Because his conquests were as much about the thrill of the hunt as the money he managed to extract from them, Giancarlo savored the feeling of being a free agent once again. And in addition to his tendency to over-pour Giancarlo's drinks, Leandro had proven to have an excellent eye for tourists worthy of his consideration.

It was late when Giancarlo arrived, and the number of patrons in the bar had dwindled. Leandro pointedly placed a bright red cocktail napkin on the bar near one particular woman, who was desirable, indeed. Giancarlo discretely slid him a gratuity across the counter before approaching the stool beside her.

The young woman was even more appealing up close, he discovered. She was in her early twenties, and had shining dark hair, creamy smooth skin, and a voluptuous figure. Her clothing and jewelry also suggested that she had wealth. *Leandro certainly came through with this one!*

"Do you mind if I sit?" he asked her on arrival.

"Not at all," she responded while motioning for him to join her. "I would hate to think the bartender went to all this trouble for nothing."

Giancarlo was surprised. "I do not understand."

"Telephoning to inform you that I was here alone," she said directly. "He is a good hunting dog, yes?"

He reacted bashfully. Like a kid being caught with his hand in the cookie jar. "Was it that noticeable?"

"I saw him watching me when he phoned you," she explained. "And then replacing my white napkin with a red one when you walked in as a signal … it was not the most subtle move I've ever seen."

He submitted his hand. "My name is Giancarlo."

Her eyes connected with his as she warmly accepted his handshake. "Olivia Zironi."

The bartender arrived with a glass of wine for Giancarlo and a fresh gin and tonic for her. "Leandro, my good and loyal friend," Giancarlo amiably informed him, "I am afraid that our little game of romantic deception has been discovered. *Signora* Zironi was not fooled by your attempt to introduce me to her."

Leandro was embarrassed. "My apologies to you both," he submitted as his face turned bright red. "Please forgive me, *Signora*."

"Not being deceived is different than not being pleased," Olivia told them.

"Then I have your permission to stay?" Giancarlo asked hopefully.

"How could I not want to know more about the man who went to so much trouble to meet me?" she answered, sizing him up.

"It was worth the effort," Giancarlo said as he lifted his glass. "Has anyone told you that you bear a strong resemblance to Sophia Loren?"

"Who?"

The question hung in the air as he tried to imagine a world where the glamorous Italian actress was not revered by everyone. "Sophia Loren," he recounted. "*Two Women … Yesterday, Today and Tomorrow …?*"

She could only stare impassively. "Nope, sorry."

"The movie star and sex symbol," he added.

"She still doesn't sound familiar."

"Really?" he asked incredulously. "That is not possible!"

The befuddled look on his face was finally too much for Olivia, who broke into a boisterous laugh. "Just kidding! Of course, I know who she is!"

Giancarlo laughed with her. "You really had me going there!" he admitted while still holding his drink in the air for a toast. "To Sophia Loren."

"To Sophia Loren," she returned.

An hour after the lobby bar closed, Giancarlo was still deep in conversation with Olivia in the darkened room. A bottle of wine and row of gin and tonics had been left by the bartender before he left for the night. Giancarlo was attentive to her every word as she talked about her art history professor at the University of Florence and her lack of any real feel for what he was teaching.

"He assumes everyone loves classical art," she moaned.

A perplexed look came over Giancarlo's face. "But how could they not?"

"No way," she yapped, cringing at the thought. "How boring!"

"I cannot imagine such studies ever becoming boring," he declared as she downed the rest of her drink. "What is it that interests you more?"

"Owning a successful business someday, like my father," she told him as she picked up another drink. "By the way, it was thoughtful of the bartender to leave us well supplied."

"Leandro is a good man, even if his attempt to introduce us was not very clever," he answered before returning to the subject at hand. "If you do not mind my asking ..." he broached, "would your research assignment not be easier at home? There is much wonderful art in Florence."

"I suppose," she agreed. "But this trip gave me an excuse to get away. And I heard a rumor that Rome has art someplace."

He nodded with mock earnestness. "I have heard that rumor, also," he quipped. "And as it happens, I am an artist."

"Are you making fun of me?" she asked with an inebriated flirtatious smile.

"No!" he ensured her. "I hope that you will one day see my work in a gallery of my own."

"Wow, your own gallery?" she exclaimed. "I'm impressed!"

"It is still just a dream," he depicted, pausing for effect. "A very expensive one for a simple artist like me."

She held his look, contemplating. "Well, in the meantime maybe knowing a real painter will make me like art a little more."

"Then your first lesson is to never refer to an artist as a painter," he instructed with a patient smile. "Painters decorate buildings. Artists interpret the world around them."

"Really?" she replied. "I'm so sorry!"

"It is not a problem. How could you know?" he pointed out.

Olivia took a sip from a new drink. "You said that was my first lesson," she remembered. "What's the second?"

"Come with me tomorrow and let me share with you my favorite art in all of Rome."

Chapter Ten
Where Does Deluca Figure Into It?

The next morning Connelly and Lange were having breakfast at the Raphael Hotel's rooftop *Mater Terrae* Restaurant. Ignoring the 360-degree city view that attracts as many regulars as does the food, Connelly was thinking about one thing only: his pending relationship with the Italian mafia.

"So, what'd you find out about the crime families?" he asked.

"It's a little more complicated than I thought," Lange reported as he consulted his notes. "There are forty-five organized gangs here, plus the four main mob families—the *'Ndrangheta, Camorra, Cosa Nostra,* and *Sacra Corona Unita*. But instead of letting competition take them to war, they decided to collaborate on this deal instead."

"Collaborate? Interesting!" Connelly effused. "Where does DeLuca figure into it?"

"He made it happen. The deal is, they all get to keep control of their neighborhoods and regions around the country as long as they work together in Rome."

"That's mighty sophisticated footwork," Connelly commented. "I wonder how he pulled that off."

"Money talks, I guess. There's plenty to go around in global distribution."

"This's amazing stuff, Greg," Connelly raved. "Keep going."

Lange closed his notebook. "That's all I have for now, but as long as we have extra prep time I wanted to ask about the planes."

"What about them?"

"DeLuca might want to know why you have Airbus 300's in the proposal instead of Boeing 737's or 757's."

"That's easy," Connelly explained. "Airbus gives more bang for our buck. The Boeing jets only hold 24,000 and 36,000 kilos. That's less than we need."

"He'll like the sound of that," Lange observed.

"He should," Connelly came back. "He'll make a bloody fortune."

Lange nodded. "Do you want me to follow up on rescheduling the meeting?"

"Either he calls, or he doesn't," answered Connelly. "But if he keeps me hanging too long, then he can find another partner."

Chapter Eleven
Hey, American Girls …

Sitting at his messy desk in the police station, Sergeant Fazio gazed at the booking photos of the bedraggled Monty and Dana. Even after the chaos of their drunken fracas the previous night, they were still the most beautiful women he had ever seen. Mussed hair, smeared make-up, and all.

No, he corrected himself, what these Americans possessed was more than beauty. They were fundamentally flawless, like the airbrushed models featured in magazines. And he did not make that assessment lightly, since he worked in Rome, where he routinely encountered appealing female visitors and local residents.

Other than his interview with Monty the day before, however, Fazio had never actually had an extended conversation with such a woman. *Rock stars and fútbol players had all the luck,* he thought. Certainly not underpaid civil servants like him, which was much to the consternation of his mother, whose relentless campaign to find him "a nice girl" had grown tiresome long ago. While he had tried, he had not met anyone with whom to settle down. Sadly, there was no explaining that to Magda Fazio, who harkened from an era when Italian mothers were evidently right about everything.

Particularly in matters of the heart.

Complicating things was the fact that his dear mother's namesake was the esteemed operatic soprano Magda Olivero, which was a distinction akin to sainthood. As such, she would never approve of his fascination with Monty and Dana. Not only were the women out of his league, but they were not even Italian!

It was time for a return to reality, however disappointing it may be.

Fazio would soon be discharging the two Americans from jail and then he would never see either of them again. He let out a slight sigh and dug through piles of papers to find their release forms. Losing them would mean having to revisit his superiors for their signatures. As his mother was fond of saying, while he had many fine qualities, he did not inherit his lack of organizational skills from her.

Locating the documents at long last, he sat back in silent victory and fingered his unlit Marlboro cigarette before waving it under his nose for a long appreciative inhalation. The sweet aroma of dry tobacco was calming, though he was getting better at not indulging in the mesmerizing scent. Smelling a cigarette was meant to be a step away from lighting one but resisting the urge to smoke continued to be a struggle.

However, today his mind was exclusively on the Americans. The temporary solution that he devised for their release would work only if they agreed to terms. But as much as Monty and Dana's good looks set them apart from other people, they also could not have been more different from each other. While his dealings with Monty were difficult, as he was forced to watch negative information about her missing husband crush her spirit, he was not acquainted with Dana Zimmer beyond the time spent booking her. It was apparent that she was every bit as stubborn as she was lovely, however. Based on the tumultuous events of the preceding night he had no reason to believe that either woman could agree with the other on anything.

Fazio entered the holding cell area. It was evident through the dusty shafts of sunlight streaming through dirt-encrusted casement windows that his prisoners were miserable. *The Americans' hangovers must be awfully painful,* he concluded.

Monty saw him first, and in her excitement slammed her body against the jail bars. "Oh, Sergeant Fazio, thank God you're here," she blurted. "Please release me from this detestable place!"

"Disorderly conduct and assault are serious offenses, *Signora,*" he answered upon arriving at her cell. "As is resisting arrest."

"But to be imprisoned here seems disproportionately severe," she countered. "The mortification that I feel is punishment enough, don't you think?"

One of the women in her cell translated the exchange into Italian and those who had regained consciousness by that point listened with amusement. *Was she kidding?! This lady was hilarious. It was almost worth spending a night in jail to hear!*

Dana thought it was funny, too. While she did not remember much about the night before, she knew that she and Monty both contributed handily to what turned out to be a real cluster.

"What I think is not important," Fazio explained to Monty. "It is what the owner of the business you destroyed thinks that matters. And he is very angry."

Monty saw an opening and went for it. "Of course, he is. If you could have seen how that raving amazon behaved—"

"You better not be talking about me, princess," Dana warned.

"I most certainly am!" Monty quarreled.

Fazio interrupted the exchange. "I believe you were the one who hit him, *Signora*," he informed Monty.

"That is outrageous," she disputed.

"So the witnesses have indicated," he answered. "We have their written testimonies."

She opened her mouth to disagree further, but Fazio raised a cautionary hand and Monty reconsidered. As her memory slowly sharpened through the haze of her hangover and fatigue, she knew he was right.

Fazio continued, "I have spoken to the proprietor of *La Cucina di Isabella* and he will decline to press charges if you agree to make restitution."

"Excellent! I can have the funds transferred by the end of the day," Monty confirmed. "For my share only, of course."

She gave him her best doe-eyed look and he could not resist. "Very well," he said.

Monty brightened. "Sergeant, you are an angel!"

Fazio met her look. "I must warn you that the destruction may be more severe than you realize, considering the amount of alcohol in your blood when you were taken into custody."

"Really," Monty said as she cocked her head with uncertainty. "How bad could the damage have been?"

"Napoleon caused less devastation in his 1809 invasion."

"Oh," she replied, duly chastened.

He unlocked her cell door and Monty stepped through with less energy than she would have, had he not made the point about Napoleon's army. As she awaited his instructions, Fazio hastily stepped back from the cloud of stale wine that accompanied her. "*Signora*, if you will allow me? You must accept your loss. Your husband is gone."

Dana and the other women reacted to the exchange as she absorbed the statement.

"My colleague in Saint-Tropez, *Capitaine* Chouinard, agrees," he continued. "We are both worried about you."

All eyes were on Monty as her resistance faded, and she reluctantly nodded her agreement.

"*Signora* Zimmer, you will also pay for damages?" he asked, moving to Dana's cell.

"I don't have that kinda bank," she divulged.

"If that means money, perhaps you could make other arrangements with the proprietor."

Dana shook her head. "I can't compete with Miss America over there," she said, referring to Monty. "No way."

"How will you know unless you try?" he asked as he opened her cell door. "Alfredo Barone is a reasonable man."

Dana emerged from confinement, and as the women met face-to-face for the first time since the fight, the stench of wine that greeted Fazio intensified. He took another judicious step back. But while Monty and Dana might not have recalled a lot about their altercation, it was clear to Fazio that they vividly remembered not liking each other.

Then, ignoring the alcohol cloud engulfing them, he forced himself to step forward again. "You will both remain in Rome until the magistrate reviews your case. Until then, I am required to keep your passports," he commanded. "Is that understood?"

"Yes," Monty and Dana answered.

"Very well," he concluded. "Now, if you will both accompany me, the clerk will administer your release."

As they headed for the door, the large butch-looking prisoner leaned into the bars. "Hey, American girls—" she bellowed. "Get my phone number from the Sergeant and give me a call. I'll show you the best time of your lives!"

Monty turned to answer, only to be silenced by the sight of the woman forcefully clutching her own oversized breasts, as if to show them off, while unleashing a full-throated grating cackle that echoed off the walls and ceiling. The other inmates soon joined in and it was the most unsettling sound that Monty ever heard.

Monty completed her discharge paperwork faster than Dana and took the opportunity to flee from the building and, she hoped, further dealings with her obnoxious adversary. As she exited the graffiti-marred door that seemed better suited to a back-alley drug den than the city of Rome's Municipal Police headquarters, she headed for the corner. She was hungover and dispirited, both of which were foreign sensations for her. So was being duped by a heartless con man. She could not believe she had been so stupid.

How could she have trusted a man she had known for less than a year? How could she have convinced herself, and her parents, that he was the life partner she had been looking for?!

Until yesterday she had steadfastly believed in the fundamental goodness of people and the power of love. Monty now understood just how sheltered she had been all these years and it was embarrassing. Her romantic ideals were nothing more than wisps of smoke amounting to nothing.

As she limped from the police station on a broken shoe, she was little more than a shattered remnant of her former self. The bravado that she expressed to Sergeant Fazio in the jail was for Dana's benefit only. She did not want her, of all people, to perceive how overcome by anxiety and fear she really was. Monty had been a naïve chump and she knew her father would tell her it was time to take responsibility for her actions. And that is exactly what she planned to do; she would apologize to the owner of the restaurant and then retreat to her hotel until the legal case against her was resolved.

Pausing to let a scrawny dog pass at the corner, someone suddenly rushed up behind her. It was Dana.

"Hey, wait up!" she barked.

Monty recoiled. "Oh, it's you—" was all she could say as she picked up her pace. In her zeal to ignore Dana, she was oblivious to the park across the street and what was once the location of the largest chariot racing track in the Roman Empire, the famed *Circus Maximus* where the real-life plot of her father's favorite movie, *Ben-Hur* starring Charlton Heston, unfolded 2,000 years ago.

Dana scrambled to stay at her side, though they were hardly together. Monty grimaced at the arrival of her new companion and could not get away fast enough.

"Well, the Ramada Inn it ain't back there—" Dana proclaimed.

"I'm sure you've seen far better jails in your travels," Monty curtly answered.

"Look, I'm not fishing for another hassle with you," Dana began. "The fact is, I came on a little strong last night."

Monty could not help but scoff. "A little strong?!"

"Okay, a lot strong. I was looking to get bent and you were an easy target," Dana conceded. "No offense."

"Do you always get so ... bent?" Monty asked as she continued her pace.

Dana shrugged. "Nah, this was a special occasion," she disclosed. "I'm sorry I was your buzz-kill."

Then without warning, someone materialized from a recessed doorway and yanked Monty's new Fendi handbag off her arm before bolting away! "STOP—THIEF!" she screamed at the top of her lungs.

Dana shook her head. "Like he's gonna listen to you."

"Well, what would you have me do instead?!" Monty cried.

"Gimme a break," Dana grumbled as she kicked off her shoes.

Then, tracking the culprit's bright yellow t-shirt among the sidewalk pedestrians, she took off after him. Being barefoot and running in a tight miniskirt did not slow her down, either. Little did the criminal, who she now identified as a teenager with an ostentatious man-bun know, Dana stayed in shape by running five miles every morning.

There was no doubt the lady could move.

The foot chase traversed the busy *Via dei Cerchi* and then turned left, continuing for a third of a mile to the *Ponte Palatino* Bridge. When the teenager peeked over his shoulder, he was distressed to find the woman gaining on him! He shifted into high gear as he finished crossing the 509-foot span over the Tiber River and headed for what he hoped would be refuge in the Piazza *Castellani* 350-feet ahead.

But Dana picked up her pace. As the gap continued to close, dozens of wild green parrots screeched loudly, as if mocking the thief from the trees along the riverbank where a mythical she-wolf rescued Romulus and Remus before the Roman Empire was founded.

There would be no she-wolf rescuing anyone on this day, however. Now in a full-on panic, but more determined than ever to keep the expensive designer purse, the teen veered into the maze of narrow alleys and streets behind the *piazza*.

By the time he reached the narrow *Via dei Salomo*, it dawned on the young thief that he was never going to out-run her. Though he was almost sixteen he looked like a boy of eleven or twelve, and his legs were losing strength. He was exhausted and sweaty and more than a little freaked out by the unexpected pursuit. After all, he had been snatching purses from unsuspecting tourists for years. *Where the hell did this woman come from?!*

He was quickly running out of places where she could not catch him. Then seeing a tall stone wall lining the street, he scrambled to the top.

As he paused to catch his breath, he locked eyes with Dana when she arrived at the corner and gave her his best cocky and impudent sneer. Taunting her. He towered over her by at least twenty feet. *No way could she get him now!*

Wind whistled through the canyon of buildings as Dana casually approached the wall. It was a spectacle worthy of a classic western showdown. Much to the thief's amusement, she methodically took aim with one of her stiletto heels, which she was still carrying. Then his grin disappeared as she unleashed a bullet pass that would impress any National Football League quarterback. She improbably even got the shoe to spiral!

It was astounding.

Whack! She nailed the poor jerk right between the eyes, which sent him tumbling to the other side of the wall, dropping the purse to the street as he fell.

A minute later Monty hobbled up gasping for air and looking even more frazzled than before, which was saying something. Dana calmly handed her the bag.

"How … did … you … manage …?" Monty wheezed.

"He fumbled at the goal line," Dana shrugged as she headed down the street. "What a tool."

Monty had almost caught her breath by the time they reached the corner. But she remained amazed by Dana's prowess. "I still can't believe you did that!" she squealed. "Wow!"

"No problem," Dana answered. "It saved me from having to work out later."

Monty brushed dirt from the bag. "Well, I just want to say that I appreciate your recovering my purse," she told her.

Dana was nonchalant, like she chases thieves in foreign cities every day. "So, what's your name, anyway?" she asked.

"Monty."

"Dana," she came back, extending her hand. "Nice to meet ya sober."

Monty smiled gratefully, but before she could accept the welcoming gesture, she abruptly shrieked, "Oh, my God!"

Dana jumped back; a reflex derived from years of dodging lunatic drivers on Los Angeles streets. "Now what?"

"Look at my hair!" she complained.

Her hair? Dana was flummoxed. She could not believe this chick was upset about a reflection in a storefront window.

"Someone should have told me I looked like this," Monty protested as she attempted to run her fingers through her gnarled mane. But her effort was pointless. Whatever design her cut once had was long gone. "Do you have a brush?" she asked.

"Lost it when the cops rushed me."

"What?"

"Last night," Dana clarified. "Shitstorm at the restaurant."

Monty nodded. As they continued along the haphazardly repaired sidewalk that resembled a timeworn concrete quilt. Dana took the opportunity to bring up what motivated her to come to Monty's aid in the first place. "Monty, listen, I heard what the cop said about losing your husband. I just wanna say I'm real sorry."

Monty tightened at the reference. Her pain and embarrassment were still too fresh to discuss with a total stranger. Particularly this one. "Thank you for your interest," she politely said. "However, that is a personal matter I'd rather not discuss."

"Come on, lady," Dana challenged. "I just ran a marathon for you and it's pretty clear that you got kicked in the gut."

Monty sized her up and grudgingly concluded that she needed to unload her burden more than she needed to be pedantic about Dana's qualifications as a confidant. Her solitary day of walking the city was a powerful reminder of that. "We might want to sit down," she told her. "It's a long story."

Designed in 1723, The Spanish Steps are vast marble stairs that ascend a steep slope between the *Piazza di Spagna* and *Piazza Trinità dei Monti*, dominated by the *Santissima Trinità dei Monti* church at the top. As Monty and Dana sat in the middle of the irregular butterfly design, hundreds of tourists crisscrossed the 138 steps around them.

Monty gazed absently at Pietro Bernini's *La Barcaccia* fountain of an old fishing boat at the bottom of the stairs while Dana dug hungrily into a cup of raspberry gelato. The depiction of a sinking ship was a fitting image for her situation, Monty thought as she finished telling Dana the story of her distressing odyssey.

"No way—he faked his death?!" Dana gasped as the totality of the scam consuming Monty hit her.

"He falsified his birth, too," Monty added. "There is no record of him anywhere."

"What a douche!" Dana growled.

Monty looked at her gloomily. "Now you know why I was loath to tell you about it," she explained. "I hope you don't think less of me for being evasive."

Until a few moments ago it would have been impossible for Dana to think less of Monty. She hated her at the start of all this, but now things were different. Now the annoying rich woman was struggling with the pain of rejection, just like her. "If you don't mind my asking," Dana asked, "how much did he rip you off for?"

Monty stared at her feet. It was difficult to say it out loud. "Over thirty thousand, plus the filigree ring that I designed."

Dana practically choked on her gelato. "Holy crap!"

"That's one way of putting it."

"What about that cop, Fazio? He seemed like an okay guy. Can't he bust him?"

"There's no trace of Giancarlo anywhere," Monty lamented. "Sergeant Fazio looked into it thoroughly."

Dana paused. It felt strangely satisfying to meet somebody with a worse problem than hers, and to have that to think about instead of Alex Connelly. "But the guy's gotta be around here someplace," she proposed.

"Not according to the Italian authorities, Catholic Church, and American Embassy," Monty recapped. "I don't know where else I could possibly go for information."

Dana was fully engaged now, as she absorbed Monty's troubling facts as a problem-solving challenge. "You're right. Damn ... okay ..." Dana continued, thinking aloud. "What about his best man at the wedding? Can't he help track him down?"

"That would be too easy," Monty answered unhappily. "The best man and all eleven groomsmen were my family. Giancarlo was supposedly an orphan, remember. And his closest friend passed away last year."

"Sure, he did."

"It seemed so sad when he spoke about it."

Then Dana stopped. "Wait a minute, if he had eleven guys with him, then you had twenty-four people in your wedding party?"

"My parents went all out."

"No shit, Sherlock!" Dana exclaimed before realizing she was steering the conversation off course. "Okay, so he covered his bases by not having anybody at the wedding," she said, summarizing the situation. "What a miserable piece of dog crap."

Monty's eyes filled with tears. "This will kill my parents when they find out."

Dana was surprised. "They don't know?"

"I was too distraught to even tell them he's missing."

"Roger that," Dana accepted. But despite her signal of support, Monty's admission came as yet another surprise to her. Monty seemed to be full of them. "I thought they're sending you dough to fix the restaurant," Dana remarked.

"They think I'm investing in art pieces," confessed Monty. "I hate myself for lying to them, but I didn't know what else to do. Daddy was fairly skeptical about Giancarlo at first, but I eventually persuaded him to trust my judgment."

"Ouch."

"Precisely," Monty confirmed.

"But he went with what you wanted at the time," added Dana. "You two must be close."

"We are," Monty shared before putting the rest of her answer into words. "Now I understand what he was trying to tell me—that fantasies should never be mistaken for reality."

Dana shook her head. "You must be reading my mail."

"What do you mean?"

"That fantasies and reality thing," Dana repeated. "Been there."

Monty absorbed the observation, and the similarity of their situations was becoming increasingly clear. "It's not like me to be so impulsive, but it didn't seem that way at the time," she continued. "If I wanted to be with Giancarlo then I only had two options: marry him or live with him. And we agreed that our mutual faith required marriage."

Dana could only shake her head in disdain. "Mutual faith— right."

"I honestly thought we were soulmates," bemoaned Monty.

"Again ... been there," Dana sadly concurred.

Monty nodded in commiseration. "And now I've even lied to my bridesmaids that I can't get back on email or social media until Giancarlo lets me out of bed," she went on. "But they won't believe that for long. Soon everyone will know my husband is nothing but a charlatan ... a common parvenu ...."

Monty dissolved into uncontrollable sobs and Dana did not have a clue about what to do. She awkwardly put her arm around her before Monty added in a subdued voice, "I keep thinking about our family dog, Matisse. He is the sweetest boy ever, but he did not take to Giancarlo at all."

Dana was not much of a dog person, so people's stories about their furry pets rarely made it to her radar screen of interest. "Really," was all she could offer.

"He did not like it one bit whenever Giancarlo came near me," Monty explained, unaware of Dana's fading attention. "I thought he was just being territorial."

"Sounds like he was trying to tell you something," Dana finally said.

"I should have listened."

They sat there in silent reflection for several minutes, until the words of a poem began to flow from Monty's lips. It was more of an involuntary whisper than a recitation.

"Can death be sleep, when life is but a dream,
And scenes of bliss pass as a phantom by?
The transient pleasures as a vision seem,
And yet we think the greatest pain's to die."

Dana was immediately drawn in by the words. "That's nice. Did you write that?"

"Oh, that I could be so clever," Monty responded. "It's by John Keats. I've always adored his work," she continued as she pointed to a building at the base of the steps. "He died in that house in the early 1800s. He was only twenty-five."

"No kidding," said Dana. "Well, thanks for trying to cheer me up."

Just then a cheerless female Municipal Police Officer approached them. *"Non é permesso sedersi qui."*

"I'm sorry, what?" Monty asked.

"We don't speak Italian," added Dana.

"You are not permitted to sit here," the woman reiterated in English.

"What are you talking about?" Dana dissented. "This is a public place."

"It is the new rule," the officer retorted. "You must move."

Dana was about to give the cop a piece of her mind when Monty stopped her with a hand on her arm. "It's alright, officer. Really." She emphasized her point by standing and practically lifting Dana with her. "We didn't mean to cause any trouble."

Dana concurred, if unenthusiastically. "This sucks—bigtime," she notified the cop. "You know that, right?"

Before the woman could say anything more, Monty was leading Dana down the steps. "It's time to leave."

"Yeah, yeah," Dana groused.

"We hardly need another international incident," said Monty as they descended the stairs. "Besides, now it's your turn. Why were you on a rampage last night?"

Dana looked away, as if to dodge the subject. "You don't wanna hear all that—"

"As you know, I have nothing but time until they return our passports," Monty reminded her. "Would you please tell me what happened to you?"

Dana calculated how little information she might get away with divulging. This was painful terrain, and she hated the idea of acknowledging her delusions that her relationship with Connelly was more than it was. That she thought their feelings for each other were the result of true love. "Well," she explained slowly, "I was doing the dirty deed with my boss, who's married—which was supposed to be history, but wasn't. When I found out his wife's having a kid, I followed him here and got in his face."

"My God, what happened?!"

"He kicked me to the curb."

"Dana, that's terrible!" Monty said in what felt like the understatement of the year.

"I've had better weeks."

Monty put a consoling arm around her as they reached Bernini's fountain in the *piazza*. "It hardly feels like the idyllic city they depicted in *Roman Holiday*, does it?"

"If you ask me, it's more like *Gladiator* and they just fed us to the freakin' lions," Dana agreed as they headed towards Monty's hotel entrance in the middle of the block.

"Do you think it's too early for a glass of wine?" Monty asked.

"I think we could get wasted just smelling our clothes," answered Dana.

Monty met her look. "Would you care to join me, anyway?"

"Just try and stop me," Dana replied. But the simple truth was that as good as a drink sounded, she liked the idea of not being alone even more.

Monty and Dana shared a bottle of Chianti at the Inn At The Spanish Steps rooftop bar. "Ya know, I'm not normally a wine person, but this stuff isn't half bad," Dana noted.

"The Antinori family has been making wine for over 600 years."

"That's kinda random—how'd you know that?"

"My parents have a very nice wine cellar," Monty explained. "You don't grow up in the Harrison home without developing a certain appreciation."

Dana studied the ornate label depicting a vineyard. "In my house it was beer and tequila after my old man split. There wasn't much of that around when he was still there, because he drank it all."

"I take it he had a problem with alcohol."

"He had a lotta problems," Dana rejoined before changing the subject. "So, where's this house with the sick wine cellar, anyway?"

"Darien, Connecticut."

"That's kinda upscale, I take it."

"It was a charming place to grow up," Monty told her. "And you?"

"We bounced around ... Culver City, Hollywood, Van Nuys, Burbank ..." she described. "We pretty much did the whole L.A. circuit."

Monty thought about that, still not fully grasping the disparities in their upbringing. "I've been to Laguna Beach," she submitted. "I love the galleries there."

Dana was grim. "That's where Alex and I used to go. Laguna."

"I'm sorry," said Monty. "I didn't mean to bring up a sore subject."

"No sweat," Dana assured her. "But since we're dredging up painful stuff, what am I gonna say to the owner of the restaurant we trashed? I wasn't kidding when I told Fazio that I don't have money."

"I've been thinking about that, too." Monty refilled her glass and smiled. "What if I take care of the repairs and you pay me back?"

Dana was shocked by the offer, and more than a little dismayed. "That's nice of you to say, but that'd take forever."

"I can wait," answered Monty.

Dana could not believe what she was hearing. She had never met anyone this generous. "Really?"

"How could I knowingly send you back into the arms of that awful woman in the jail?" Monty asked, before imitating the butch inmate's departing comment to them, "Hey, American Girls!"

Dana nearly spit good Chianti all over the tablecloth as they laughed at the absurd memory. "Wow, thank you so much!"

"It's my pleasure, believe me."

Dana dabbed wine from her chin. "Okay, then I gotta ask, where'd a classy chick like you meet an asswipe like Giancarlo, anyway?"

"It was a dance club on *Via Veneto*," Monty recalled.

The reference made Dana brighten, as an idea came. "Well, I say let's finish the bottle and then go hit it."

But Monty was slow to grasp her meaning. "Hit what?"

"The club," answered Dana. "Let's go find your scumbag husband."

Monty blanched at the notion. "Oh, I don't know—"

"Sure, ya do," she said as she tapped Monty's arm reassuringly. "I'll be back in an hour, if I can get the wino stink off me. You might wanna do the same."

Chapter Twelve
Art Is Everything To Me

The *Galleria Borghese,* where Giancarlo brought Monty on one of their first dates, was a favorite destination for his romantic forays. Not only did the display of artworks by such artists as Tiziano, Raphael, Rubens, and Botticelli usually have the desired effect on his companions, it provided him with the opportunity to share artistic insights that he plagiarized from a pamphlet years ago.

Especially about Michelangelo Merisi da Caravaggio, for whom he pretended to have the most passion.

Giancarlo's amorous history was celebrated among the museum staff, who always enjoyed watching the parade of magnificent women that he brought to the facility. The *Galleria* workers were not his only admirers, however. There were countless concierges and taxi drivers in the city who also wished they could be more like him. The bartender at the Chapter Hotel was merely one of his devoted fans.

One waiter even hired him to mentor him in the art of seduction, but no one could match Giancarlo's success in that area. How he managed to snare one woman after another was a mystery— though the rumor was that he was a freak of nature, physical endowment-wise. *Why else would women keep coming back for more?*

In another era, the lore surrounding him would have been the stuff of folk songs commemorating his sexual exploits. In fact, after a long night of partying, two alcohol-fueled *Galleria* staff members tried to write just such a song, but the results fell far short of capturing what they regarded to be the majesty of his prowess. Had they known about his defrauding operation, they would have no doubt felt less reverence for him.

On this particular day, the gallery staffers eagerly anticipated the results of their betting pool that endeavored to guess the age, hair color, and nationality of Giancarlo's latest starry-eyed contender. As he entered the Villa, his date was Olivia Zironi from the Chapter Hotel. Security guard Renzo Giambalvo stole a peek at the entrancing creature as the couple moved past his station and grinned. His hunch that Giancarlo was overdue for an Italian conquest meant that he would be taking home the one hundred-euro winnings this time. *Victory at last!*

The exquisite young woman in a breezy sundress would not only be putting money in Renzo's pocket, she possessed all the qualities that Giancarlo wanted, too: she was the daughter of a wealthy family, she was young and impressionable, and she seemed to be quite smitten with him. An easy mark, to be sure.

"An art museum is a different idea for a date, Giancarlo," she said with a wily smile. "The men I meet in Florence usually try to impress me with an expensive dinner or good seats at a concert."

"This is more than a museum, my dear. The collection of art is like no other," he explained. "The *Galleria Borghese* has the most Caravaggio pieces in the world."

"Caravaggio? I think my professor talked about him once."

"I would be astounded if he did not," he answered as he guided her to a prominent artwork in one of the main floor rooms. "Caravaggio was a genius at using light colors on dark backgrounds," he effused while never taking his eyes off the painting. "This is one of his final works, *Saint John The Baptist*. Do you see how the contrast and light effect make him seem young and alive?"

Olivia was captivated, though less by the painting than his words. She could not help being drawn to this sensitive man and his respect for the portrait. "I wish I had your enthusiasm for art."

"Art is everything to me," he replied simply.

She slid into his view with a seductive edge. "Everything ...?"

Giancarlo smiled. "Well, perhaps not everything."

Chapter Thirteen
This Little Spinner Right Here Is Mine

Alex Connelly was drenched in sweat as he ran on a treadmill in the Raphael Hotel fitness center when Greg Lange entered.

"I hope you've got good news," Connelly opened.

"Sorry, Alex," Lange answered. "Still no word from DeLuca."

Connelly slowed the treadmill. "That's okay. There are worse cities to be stranded in."

Lange held up two color photos of Airbus cargo jets. "In the meantime, what do you think of putting your logo on these and adding them to the presentation?"

Connelly stepped off the machine and wiped his face with a towel. "Very nice!" he pronounced. "Those will spice things up."

"Thanks, I thought so," Lange affirmed, as he proceeded to hand him several other photos. But instead of jets this time they were of scantily clad women. "And speaking of spice, a buddy of mine recommends this escort service, if you feel like a night on the town."

"Now you're talking, mate!" Connelly said with a wide grin, admiring the array of exotic-looking Asian and Middle Eastern women. "I can use a new resource in this part of Europe. And this is top shelf merchandise."

"You could say he's something of a connoisseur," added Lange. "His uncle runs a strip club in Vegas."

"Well, send him my thanks and get us a couple for tonight!" Connelly directed before pointing to one of the photos in particular. "This little spinner right here is mine."

Chapter Fourteen
Ya Wanna Find This Hairball Or Not?

Swarms of motor scooters populated the *Via Veneto* as if they were swirling gnats mocking cars that dared to share the road with them. Being one of the most famous and expensive streets in Rome, the wide sidewalk was filled with pedestrians and the flavors of many languages blended themselves into a lively musical sound that filled the air. It was classic Rome.

Federico Fellini immortalized the avenue in his acclaimed 1960 film *La Dolce Vita* which explored, ironically, the fruitless search for love and happiness. During the *Via Veneto's* golden age as a cultural landmark, it would not be unusual to find Frank Sinatra at the piano in Harry's Bar and such jet-setting stars as Audrey Hepburn, Tennessee Williams, and Coco Chanel socializing with princes and other members of international high society.

One block down the hill from Harry's Bar and the Borghese Gardens, groups of young people on the sidewalk heralded the proximity of the hottest dance club in the city, *Dolce Disco*. As Monty and Dana approached, they were the two hottest women, too, though the contrasts between them were never more conspicuous than how they looked now: Monty was elegant in her stylish Prada ensemble, while Dana's eye-catching leather mini, fishnets, and Jimmy Choo knock-off stilettos would stop traffic at the Indy 500.

Monty's negative emotions surged upon seeing the entrance to the club. "Dana, I don't have a good feeling about this," she admitted with hesitation.

"What are you talking about? You said it was a good idea," Dana pointed out.

"I know, but something tells me we're wasting our time," said Monty. "Why don't we forget it and have dinner instead? My treat."

Dana stopped. "Ya wanna find this hairball or not?"

"Of course, I do," she insisted somewhat feebly. She was still aching inside and her worries that running into Giancarlo would make things worse were daunting. "But even if he is in Rome, the odds of him being here tonight are slim," she added.

"I know," Dana agreed.

The answer confused Monty. "Then why did we come?"

"Because you don't know where he lives and this's where you met him," Dana reasoned.

"That doesn't mean he'll be here now," Monty stressed.

Dana knew she was stalling but tried to be as encouraging as possible. "Look, guys stick with what works, okay?" She pointed at a group of college-age girls entering ahead of them. "And this's where Giancarlo finds his strange at least some of the time."

"His what?" asked Monty.

"You know, his next whirl," Dana explained.

But when Monty still did not follow the concept, Dana broke it down for her. "Meets chicks he's gonna nail."

"You don't know the meaning of the word *nuance*, do you," groused Monty.

"I call 'em like I see 'em, kid."

Monty nodded halfheartedly. "Fine. But if we don't find him, then can we please have dinner?"

Dana shrugged. "If you're buying, you bet."

Inside the disco, Monty and Dana encountered an ultra-hip meat market with a dynamic futuristic industrial vibe, jammed with what must have been every sexually active adult in Rome. Thumping techno music and spinning colored lights animated a sea of eye-catching men and women heaving to the hypnotic beat. It was energized, sensuous, and otherworldly.

They were also confronted by odors ranging from colognes and perfumes to the rank stench of perspiration. It was a powerful array of scents, to say the least.

Dana walked through a gauntlet of undressing eyes like a woman with nothing to prove. She was in her element. "Whoa, look at the guns on that guy ... sah-weet!" she announced to Monty over the blaring music.

"Someone has a weapon in here?" she asked with alarm.

"You could say that," Dana advised as she took in the spectacle of slender men in tight trousers and shirts ogling the parade of women. "So, what was uptown talent like you doin' at a humpfest like this in the first place?" she asked.

"The concierge recommended it."

Dana threw her a look. "And you were here long enough to hook up with somebody?"

"I hadn't planned to stay," Monty clarified. "I had just ordered a drink when a man offered to pay for it. I turned and found myself gazing into the most penetrating eyes I'd ever seen."

"What'd he do, kidnap you?" Dana joked.

"As a matter of fact, Giancarlo was a perfect gentleman," Monty corrected, as if the incident needed defending. "When he realized how uncomfortable I felt here he suggested that we go somewhere else."

"Yeah, his bed!" snorted Dana.

"It was an all-night cafe, thank you very much," Monty countered. She paused uneasily before completing the story. "... it was several more hours before I saw his bed."

"Got it."

"Please don't judge me," added Monty. "I feel foolish enough as it is."

Dana shrugged. "Monty look, guys are guys, remember that. L.A., Rome, Cleveland, it's always the same game."

"Your insights about men are impressive."

"I gotta coupla years on you, that's all," explained Dana.

"You're not that much older."

"And I grew up with six brothers," Dana disclosed, completing the thought. "Don't get me wrong, I love 'em like sisters, but they're the same as all men—peckers with feet."

Monty reacted quizzically. "Your vocabulary is astonishing."

"What can I say? I spent my whole life watching them in action."

"Yet, you were still hurt by one."

Dana nodded. "Rookie mistake, I was playin' outta my league. But Giancarlo I know, trust me. And this place's chock full of Giancarlos."

Monty followed her gaze across the room, where dozens of dead ringers for Giancarlo could be seen. All with cashmere sweaters tied around their shoulders and gold chains. And all putting the make on available young women.

Monty took in the totality of the scene for the first time, startled by Dana's discovery. "My God, you're right!"

"You also aren't the only notch on his *pistola*," added Dana. "And panty melters like him usually run in packs. So, if he's in town, one of these maggots is gonna know about it."

"But how will we find that out? I don't even know his real name."

Dana thought about that. Then it hit her. "He's a painter, right? How's he sign his stuff?"

"With his first name—Giancarlo," Monty remembered.

"There ya go," Dana calculated. "It's his last name that changes with each score."

Monty was getting into the deduction flow now. "So, that's why there is no record of his birth!"

Dana put her hand on her shoulder. "That's what I'm trying to tell you. Fifty bucks says somebody here knows who he really is."

As Dana moved into the crowd Monty watched her go with admiration.

"Extraordinary," she said to herself before following her. *Somehow this woman knew more about her husband than she did!*

Chapter Fifteen
I Try To Be Good At Everything

Thirty minutes after the girls exited the disco and hailed a cab, another taxi arrived to deliver Giancarlo and Olivia. They entered the club, arm in arm.

The couple danced and wordlessly flirted with each other for an hour while she demonstrated an arsenal of moves that checked all the boxes on his scam victim wish-list. Then, when she was not expecting it, he slid in close and kissed her, taking her breath away.

"You are a very good kisser!" Olivia whispered as the music pounded around them.

"I try to be good at everything I do," Giancarlo returned with a sly smile.

Before he knew what hit him, she was shoving him into a nearby alcove and kissing him hard. Giancarlo could not believe his good fortune—it was almost as if she were trying to seduce him, rather than the other way around. He mulled over the hotel bartender's perceptive intuition about this girl: she was young, cute, and she had money.

Olivia also seemed to be very playful, which he suspected would be a major bonus.

Chapter Sixteen
All It Takes Is Money

Connelly and Lange sat drunkenly in the living room of Connelly's hotel suite as loud music played and two enticing Vietnamese call-girls danced on the large marble coffee table.

"Suddenly waiting for DeLuca to call doesn't seem so bad," Lange enthused.

Connelly never took his eyes off his date's diminutive body as she expertly cavorted above him. "He can take all the time he wants!"

The women removed their brassieres in unison and slowly lowered them onto the men's grinning faces. "You'll get no argument from me," Lange stated as he put a bra around his head like a headband.

Connelly's date stepped from the coffee table to sit in his lap. "Mmmmm," he announced as she took a drink of his scotch. "This reminds me of the good old days in Queensland!"

Lange tittered, "Are you kidding me? If life was like this for you, why would you ever leave?!"

"Because the Gold Coast isn't the only place with talent like this," Connelly smirked as the call-girl kissed his neck and chest. "All it takes is money."

Just then Connelly's phone rang. He glanced at the screen and tossed the phone aside, dismissively. "The wife."

"Aren't you going to answer it?" Lange asked.

"No can do," Connelly smirked as he took his alluring playmate by the hand and headed for his bedroom. "I'm in an important meeting."

Chapter Seventeen
What Are You, Royalty Or Something?

Monty and Dana entered the *Piazza Navona* from the south end the next day, where they encountered one of Rome's most meaningful attractions. The massive 35,000 square yard plaza occupies the footprint of what was once the Stadium of Domitian, a huge sports arena. Today four- and five-story structures containing restaurants, bars, shops, apartments, a church, and hotel encircle the illustrious statuary fountains by Borromini, Della Porta, and Bernini that would be in a museum if they were in any other city.

Dana's jaw dropped at the sight of hundreds of artists hawking their work throughout the area. "Dude, this's epic!" she roared. "Look at the size of this place!"

"It boggles the mind, doesn't it?"

"It's freakin' awesome!" Dana replied. "There's painters everywhere!"

"That's why our information makes sense. If a struggling artist is showing his work, he shows it here."

"Yeah, but if their stuff's any good, how come they're selling it on the sidewalk?" Dana wanted to know.

Monty lovingly scanned a lengthy row of still lifes. "Because the *Piazza Navona* is where many emerging artists develop their reputations."

"There's a shitload of 'em, that's for sure."

"Ironically, this tradition had very different beginnings," Monty explained as they walked together. "In ancient times prostitutes would exhibit paintings here that illustrated their specialties to potential clients."

"How is it you're so dialed in on art, anyway?" Dana asked.

"I studied for one college semester at the Louvre," Monty answered as a dozen pigeons scrambled out of their path. But upon noticing Dana's expressionless look she felt compelled to clarify, "A museum in Paris."

"You went to school at a museum? What are you, royalty or something?"

"I was only there for sixteen weeks, but it was a wonderful education. There's nothing like learning technique from the legends of the art world, let me tell you," Monty expressed. "For example, here's a most promising talent—just look at the broadly brushed influence of Abstract Expressionism. Delightful!"

"It looks like crap to me," Dana said.

Monty labored to be patient. "The French painter Edgar Degas said, "Art is not what you see, but what you make others see"."

"And this one still looks like a bowl of steaming crap to me," Dana finished as a handsome strolling singer with a guitar caught her eye. He was the kind of guy that she would normally go for, so she was duly distracted when he winked at her.

"I understand," Monty continued as she reveled in the paintings they passed. "Abstract art isn't for everyone. You might be more attuned to Realism, where you almost feel that you could step into a painting and join the people there. Sometimes I wish I could do exactly that."

Just then Monty rounded the *Fontana del Moro* and gulped, "Oh my God, Dana! We've found him!"

It took a few seconds for Dana to pull her mind from the enjoyable flirtation with the musician. "What?"

"That painting!" Monty yelped as she pointed at something among a cluster of large canvases. It consisted of bursts of colorful lines and paint smears resembling an explosion of laser light. "Giancarlo gave something just like this to my father."

But when Dana took a closer look, she pointed out, "His name's not on it. This guy's somebody called Parisi."

"I'd recognize that distinctive stroke anywhere," Monty avowed. "Giancarlo is an expert with a palette knife, and this is his work!"

"Are you sure about that?"

"If there is anything I know, it's art."

The young artist, who had been watching the women and trying to listen to their exchange, thought he had a live one in Monty. Dressed in torn jeans and a paint-tinged denim work-shirt, the local artist was barely out of his teens. "You admire *Chiaro e Scuro, Signora*," he opened in a thick Italian accent. "*Light and Dark,* it is the favorite of all my work."

"Your work?! Don't be absurd," Monty jeered.

Dana checked the signature on the canvas again. "So, straight up—where'd you get this."

"From here," he said, tapping his heart melodramatically. "That is why the price must be one hundred euro. I am sorry."

Monty could hardly contain her anger. "How dare you represent stolen art as your own creation!"

"Stolen? No ...!" he protested. "This is mine. It is signed right there, do you see? *Parisi.*"

Monty turned to Dana with conviction. "I swear that I'm right about this. He must have added his signature over Giancarlo's."

Having overheard only part of Monty and Dana's exchange, the artist reinforced what he assumed was the start of a negotiation. "It is nice to meet someone who has such appreciation for fine art," he imparted with a proud smile. "For you, I sell my work for only seventy-five euro."

Monty's face tightened as her emotions rocketed to unbridled rage, causing Dana to nudge her aside and take charge. "Look ace," she warned the artist, "all she wants is the four-one-one on the meat puppet who really did paint this. Giancarlo."

The artist tried one more time, though meekly, "... fifty euro?"

"I'm only gonna ask one more time, *capisce?*" Dana added as she cocked her fist. "Where'd you get this thing?"

The young man froze in abject fear and his Italian accent disappeared to unmask a chunky Brooklyn dialect. "Hey, come on, lady!" he cried. "Gimme a break, will ya? I'm just tryin' to make a living here!"

Monty and Dana exchanged incredulous looks before bursting into simultaneous laughter.

"Are you kidding me?!" Dana boomed.

"What happened to your accent?" Monty followed.

"Is she gonna hurt me?" he asked fearfully, flicking his eyes at Dana.

Dana tightened her fist. "The jury's still out on that."

"I'm from Brooklyn, okay?" he nervously divulged. "That's what happened to my accent. I'm not even an artist. I buy this stuff in bulk from a factory across town."

Monty was stunned. "Then, this is all a lie?!"

"Try and keep up," Dana scolded as she unclenched her fist and turned to him. "I gotta ask, is your name even really Parisi?"

"Ralph Lutz," he told her sheepishly. "Parisi had a better ring to it."

Dana howled in amusement. "Man, you got some kinda balls!"

The young man was greatly relieved to see that Dana was not going to hurt him. "I'm really sorry," he added, "... how 'bout I cut you a killer deal on the painting?"

Monty and Dana spent the next hour talking to vendors around the *Piazza Navona* confirming what the phony artist had told them. Monty was appalled to learn that almost everyone was aware of the bulk art factory near Rome's main railway station, *Stazione Termini*.

It was nothing less than notorious within the art community.

Monty and Dana entered the dark and dank tunnel entrance to the basement of a seedy-looking structure on *Via Gioberti*. Inside they discovered an assembly line of people applying paint to canvases, but it was less the art factory described to them than a subterranean crypt. Harsh industrial fluorescent lights hanging from the water-stained ceiling illuminated dozens of people at easels, where one man sprayed a canvas with paint while the next slapped on various background details. Women further down the row brushed on part of a scene or applied smeared bursts of color with palette knives, and so on. At the end of the procedure an older couple dried the works with heat guns.

Stacks of completed paintings stood in the corner and all that remained to be added were the signatures of the fake artists who would purchase them. Many of them were identical to what Giancarlo had represented as his original work.

The scene took Monty's breath away, as did the paint vapors in the dense motionless air. "This is a ... a cultural outrage!" she sputtered. "I can hardly believe my eyes!"

"What are you so steamed about? Dana asked. "It's not like they're killing baby seals or anything."

But Monty's indignation ran deep. "Dana, this is even more horrific than I imagined," she complained. "Surely you have to see that mass production violates every precept of artistic expression."

"Except raking in the bucks. It don't violate that," Dana countered flippantly.

"I can't believe I was so easily deceived. I thought I was educated." Monty was still shuddering. "There should be a law against this."

"Look, even if they don't know squat about art, Giancarlo and that knuckle dragger from Brooklyn got the money part down," Dana decreed. "Ya gotta give 'em that."

"That doesn't make what's taking place here any less nauseating," Monty said as she panned her inspection around the room one more time. "To think that daddy has something so offensive displayed above his Louis Majorelle rosewood desk ...."

"And he was duped, too, right?"

"Utterly!" Monty answered. "I don't know how that happened, either."

"Maybe this garbage is better than you thought," Dana speculated. "Even if it does come from an assembly line."

Monty flinched. "I feel like I need a shower after being here," she told her while rubbing her arms. "Do you have any hand sanitizer?"

"You're kidding, right?" But even as she asked, she saw that Monty was completely serious. Just then Dana noticed a man eying them from his office window. "Okay, it's time to suit up. I'll see if I can dig up a name and address for lover boy."

"How will you do that?"

"Call in the heavy artillery," Dana said with a wink as she adjusted her top to accentuate her cleavage. "Why don't you find me a nice Elvis on black velvet?"

"What?" Monty asked.

Dana shook her head. "Just cool your jets for a few minutes," she replied as the man continued to ogle her. "This won't take long."

Rome may be the twelfth most visited city in the world, but some neighborhoods are more popular with locals than tourists. With walls and previously neglected buildings that are covered with unconventional street art, the *Ostiense* district is one of the most edgy places to live. As such, it has become a hip artist's haven.

Monty and Dana were two silhouettes in glowing sunlight by the window of a cramped café. Their table faced a tree-lined median and bright yellow apartment building adorned with a large colorful mural.

"So, that's where he lives ...." Monty observed as if in a trance.

"It still don't look familiar?" asked Dana.

"I was only here once, remember? That first night."

"And you were hammered," Dana reminded her.

Monty broke out of her stupor to regain her defensiveness. "It was raining, and the visibility was poor," she told her. "Are you absolutely sure that's the correct address?"

"I checked the mailbox out front," Dana corroborated. "Giancarlo Nunziato, the same name he uses when he scores his paintings." She slid an invoice across the table. "That's the most recent invoice."

But Monty pushed it back without reading it. "I'll take your word for it."

"You might wanna look at it," Dana advised.

"And drive the dagger further into my heart? No thank you."

Dana returned the invoice and firmly held it in position. "Giancarlo's real name's right there, clear as day: *Nunziato*."

"They just gave this to you?" Monty asked as she indignantly clutched the document. "I guess they don't care about privacy laws in this country, do they."

It was then that Dana noticed Monty's trembling hands. "Are you cool?" she asked her. "I mean, you're not gonna hurl, are you?"

Shaking her head sadly, Monty looked away from the invoice. "It's overwhelming that's all, sitting here ... and ... and ...."

But that was as much as she could get out. Monty pointed a quivering finger at what she saw across the street: Giancarlo and Olivia Zironi getting out of his Peugeot. Olivia looked lovely in the sunlight and, judging from the fiery kiss that she gave him, she was not his little sister.

Dana eased Monty's extended arm downward and closed her gaping mouth, smiling self-consciously at the café customers who were gawking at them. "Subtle, Monty," she dryly observed. "You ever think about going into surveillance work?"

Monty did not respond. The sight of her husband kissing the beautiful young woman was more than she could endure.

Twenty minutes of histrionics later, Dana talked Monty into accompanying her into the apartment building. It was clear that Monty had been secretly holding out hope, however unlikely it may have been, that there might be a logical explanation for everything that had transpired with Giancarlo. That by the end of their investigation he would not prove to be a heartless cheat and rat.

Dana could see the difficulty Monty was having processing her pain and she became more determined than ever to be there for her new friend. After all, she could relate to what Monty was going through better than anyone.

The interior of the building needed cosmetic attention thirty years ago, but at the very least a gallon of paint and updated lighting would have accomplished wonders. As they arrived on the second floor Monty was as white as a sheet. Moving across the creaking and scuffed wooden floor planks she became more petrified with each step. "I can't do this—" she mumbled.

"Sure, you can," Dana insisted, guiding her towards the end unit.

But Monty only became more rigid. "No, I can't."

"Let's go, Monty. Wheels up." Dana took her arm and nudged her forward, but Monty was becoming an immovable object. "Look at you. You are totally stalling."

"I am not," Monty argued. "I thought I could confront him, but now—oh Lord, I should have used the restroom!"

"See?"

"What?"

"You're a hot mess," Dana declared. "You know it, I know it, and by now all the damn neighbors know it."

Monty looked at her in horror. "Then maybe we should leave."

"You're kidding."

She was not. In fact, Monty was looking for any way she could find to avoid doing this. "We know his identity," she querulously pressed. "So, now Sergeant Fazio can arrest him."

"Okay," came Dana's answer as she released her arm.

Monty had not been expecting the move, to say the least. "Really?"

"Sure. But ya gotta give me a minute with him first."

Monty stepped back. "You're planning to do something vile, aren't you."

Dana's eyes were unflinching. "Just let me handle it and that Gucci skin flute'll be sorry he ever messed with you."

"Gucci skin flute?" Monty asked.

"Figure of speech."

Monty was still considering Dana's offer when the sounds of wild lovemaking could be heard on the other side of the apartment door, where a young woman was clearly enjoying herself. Really, *really* enjoying herself.

Monty responded with a spontaneous yelp, "Oh, my God!" And then she dropped like a stone to the floor, out cold.

Dana crouched beside her to make sure she was still alive. "Freakin' amazing."

A few seconds later Olivia Zironi cut loose with a cry of unrestrained sexual ecstasy. Dana paused to nod respectfully at what was unmistakably Giancarlo's phenomenal carnal performance. *Wow!*

Chapter Eighteen
A Very Dedicated Student

Giancarlo's apartment consisted of a single 25x30 foot room with a hotplate, refrigerator, and minuscule attached bathroom that also served as the shower. With no stall or curtain to contain the water, the design was such that the spray completely saturated the toilet, sink, walls, ceiling, and floor. And with almost no ventilation to provide relief, the entire dwelling had the fragrance profile of a malodorous locker room.

In every other respect, however, it was a bachelor artist's haven—from the paintings displayed on the walls and an easel holding a newly finished work, to the piles of canvases, supplies, and art books everywhere. Dominating it all was a cringeworthy round bed that seemed to have been taken from an R. Kelly playbook.

The lack of amenities did not matter to Olivia, who after making love to Giancarlo was a very contented woman. His physical gifts and technique were nothing less than a revelation. "Giancarlo, I was thinking ...." she related as she ran her fingers through his hair. "Maybe I should think about delaying my trip back to Florence."

"Why would you do that?" he teased, already knowing the answer.

"You have convinced me that there is more research to do in Rome."

He kissed her hand. "You must be a very dedicated student."

"I guess you could say I'm eager to learn," she chuckled as she snuggled against his chest. "As it turns out your talents aren't limited to works of art."

"Perhaps you bring out the best in me, Olivia," he replied. "You are a miracle that has visited my life when I needed one most."

"A miracle?" she asked.

He rose to one elbow and gazed woefully into her eyes before launching into one of his perfected heartbreaking stories. "Yes, my heart has been heavy lately," he began. "You see, one of the nuns at the orphanage where I was raised is extremely ill. I owe everything to Sister Rosario because she encouraged me when no one else would. Even the dream of having a gallery of my own came from her. This wonderful time with you has been so healing for me."

His sensitivity caused her to melt in his arms. "How will I ever repay that bartender for bringing you to me?" she asked.

That evening Giancarlo entered the Chapter Hotel lobby bar and caught the Leandro's eye. "Giancarlo," the bartender called out as he was drying glasses. "Where is your adorable companion?"

"Upstairs getting ready for our date," he reported as he took up a seat on a barstool.

"You are really something else," Leandro added with a chuckle. "I think I finally figured out what you've been doing with all those incredible women of yours."

Giancarlo shrugged. "Can I help it if they have romantic needs?"

"That's not what I mean," Leandro corrected as he lowered his voice. "I'm talking about how you always seem to ignore the poor ones and never keep the rich ones for very long."

Giancarlo feigned innocence. "Perhaps poor women are not interested in someone with less money than them."

"And the rich?"

"... always seem to be quite generous with me," Giancarlo finished with a wry smile. "I should probably be paying you commissions on what I get each time."

"No, no, just watching you in action is enough for me," Leandro came back. "You are a ray of sunshine in my dull life, believe me. You are amazing!"

"I could not do it without your help, old friend."

Then Leandro leaned forward on the bar, like he was waiting to hear a naughty secret. "I only want to know one thing, if you don't mind ...."

"For you, anything!"

"How is Olivia in bed?"

Giancarlo grinned. "Energetic and highly creative."

"My God! You are my hero!" came the exuberant reply.

At that moment Olivia entered the room and she was beaming ear to ear. "Giancarlo, I have great news! I told my father about your wonderful paintings and he has agreed to be your investor in the gallery!"

Leandro winked at Giancarlo and moved off.

Giancarlo clasped her hands as she sat beside him. "Darling, are you sure?"

"Your timing is perfect. He said he's been looking for another business venture."

"But he knows nothing about me," he reminded her.

"I told him all about Sister Rosario and the orphanage and how she inspired you. And he was very impressed by your loyalty," she crowed. "Besides, I get to handle everything! He said it's time to get serious about my business career."

Emotion filled Giancarlo's eyes, though her perceptions of his gratitude were not at all what he was feeling. For him, his limited time investment on this so far was setting up to be one of his best scams ever! "He sounds like a wonderful father," he remarked.

"The important thing is he loves his little girl," she responded. "And soon you will, too, I hope."

Giancarlo kissed her again. It would only be a matter of time before he would tap this revenue source in a big way.

Chapter Nineteen
A Delicious Fantasy

Leaning against the embellished wrought iron railing of her private terrace overlooking the Spanish Steps and *Piazza di Spagna*, the city lights magically sparkling through the prisms of a light autumn rainfall were no consolation to Monty. She was very much alone and feeling it.

Dana appeared in the open doorway with a tray of food and the most upbeat bearing she could muster under the circumstances. "Yo, room service."

"No thank you," Monty replied before drifting back into the fragrant fresh scent of the drizzle as it washed away the usual smells of the city. She could only wish for it to do the same for her mood.

Dana took a few seconds before trying again. "Can't say I blame ya," she acknowledged. "This joint might be better than the fleabag where I'm staying but check out what these clowns do to a sandwich. They cut the crust off! That's sick."

There was still no progress in engaging Monty, however.

"What I wouldn't give for a juicy In-N-Out burger right now," Dana added. But this comment fell flat, as well. "It's a kickin' L.A. burger place," she explained, even though Monty could hardly care less. Having failed to connect with her, Dana picked up a carafe of red wine. "Never mind," she continued as she poured two glasses. "At least they know how to stomp grapes. Know what I mean?"

Monty shook her head. "None for me, thanks."

"Yeah, I get that," she told her as she considered her next move. Dana could vividly feel Monty's devastation over witnessing the truth about Giancarlo. It was rough, just as it had been for her to be confronted by Connelly's duplicity. Her own misery was more intense than she could describe, so she suspected it must be even worse for a fragile girl like Monty.

She decided to keep pressing. "Personally, I wish I had something stronger," Dana said of the wine. "Like AsomBroso tequila … now that's good stuff. But it's also two hundred fifty bucks a bottle and my ex ain't here to pay for it."

Still there was no response.

"No offense, Monty," she continued, "but you look like you could use some of this." She held out a glass.

Monty accepted the wine but did not drink. For someone who had always subscribed to the adage *We are each the authors of our own lives*, the idea that she might have created this catastrophe was disturbing. Her problem, she was beginning to realize, was that she had always led with her heart. Yet the heart is not cognitive, and her critical thinking strangely abandoned her the day she met Giancarlo.

He was handsome, he was an artist, and he loved her. Or so she thought.

She was mortified that she accepted his stories and lifestyle portrayals simply because she desperately wanted them to be true.

But she could not begin to explain all that to Dana. Instead she shared an abstract thought that seemed oddly relevant. "Did you know that Romans used to hang phallic symbols as wind chimes over their doors for good luck?" she said, once again gazing at the city lights. "I guess Giancarlo has no need for any such assistance."

Progress at last! Dana thought. *Monty was finally talking, and she was talking about Giancarlo!*

"I'll drink to that," Dana affirmed as she drank from her glass. But Monty still had not had any of hers. That prompted Dana to state the obvious. "You do know we're getting soaked out here, right?"

"I don't mind," Monty told her. "I've always loved the rain … it's always so special at night. Back home in Darien I would spend hours listening to the sound of the droplets softly hitting the leaves of trees. There is something so soothing about it. It's like everything in the world stops, even bad things," she described.

"If you say so," Dana responded.

"At first, it's one uniform experience, you know?" Monty continued. "Then it gradually discloses many individual sounds as the raindrops hit roof tiles, metal downspouts, concrete, wood objects, and the leaves of trees and shrubbery. Rain is a symphony if you only listen."

"Sorry, but I don't hear any of that," replied Dana. "It's just rain to me."

"Admittedly, it's a unique sensation here. I don't know why," Monty added. "Maybe when it rains in Rome the spirits of thirsty souls drink the droplets before they hit the ground."

"Spirits?" Dana shivered a bit more than necessary in an attempt to engage Monty even further. "I gotta be honest, that's a little Stephen King even for me."

"The city has been here for 2,500 years," Monty pondered. "There must be spirits everywhere."

"I don't know if I believe that stuff."

"I do," Monty answered. "And most religions believe it, too."

"Have you actually seen a ghost?" Dana asked. She still did not believe in spirits but asked anyway as a tactic to keep Monty talking.

"I once visited the Museum of the Souls of Purgatory at a local parish," Monty explained. "That was enough."

Dana was surprised that the subject was inadvertently turning out to be interesting. "They gotta museum for that?" she asked.

"It's the most chilling thing I've ever seen," Monty portrayed. "They have documents, objects, and clothing with graphic handprints and fingerprints burned into them by deceased souls." She shuddered at the memory.

"Sounds like a tourist trap to me."

"The church is meticulous about verifying such things, believe me."

Dana motioned to Monty's full glass. "Well, since the ghosts in this place are drinking the rainwater, what do ya say to some *vino*?" she asked. "I still say it's a good idea."

Monty shook her head. "Drinking won't solve anything. We learned that the hard way, remember?"

"Maybe—" said Dana. "But it'll kill some time 'til somebody sends that sausage peddler off a cliff for real."

Monty locked eyes with her and relented. "Perhaps just one."

"Cool," Dana chirped as she held up her glass. "Here's to a real toad stool, Giancarlo, King of the Beef Whistles."

The remark forced Monty to smile, in spite of her low mood. "It is shocking how much of the language they failed to teach us at Wellesley," she observed.

After they both downed their glasses Monty turned to face her. "Dana, I want to say something—" she began. "I don't know what I would have done without you. Never in a million years would I have imagined becoming a member of the *Hashtag MeToo* movement."

"It sucks, I know," Dana conceded. "By the way, you don't have to actually say hashtag."

"Really?"

Dana nodded and Monty sunk even lower. "Well, aren't I pathetic? I'm so inept it turns out I'm not even qualified to correctly state my own victim status."

"Hey, give yourself some credit," Dana advised as she refilled their glasses. "There's a wild woman inside you. I met her once, remember? She was really shredding it in the restaurant."

"And it only took a whole bottle of Chianti to unleash her," Monty confessed.

The remark was not lost on Dana, but she let it pass.

"That's the wonderful thing about you," Monty continued. "You confronted Alex under your own power. I'd give anything to know that satisfaction."

"Yeah, well don't lose any sleep," Dana told her, glancing away. "It didn't exactly scratch the itch."

"I don't understand."

"You ever hear the saying, *Find a man who ruins your lipstick, but not your mascara*?" Dana asked.

"That's a new one for me," she answered.

"Well, let's just say he did a number on my mascara," Dana exposed. "But it was my fault. I fell for a married sack of shit player and I crashed and burned." She downed half of her wine before making the rest of her confession. "The truth is, telling him to shove it didn't come close to evening the score."

They stood wordlessly in the rain, side by side, and soaked to the skin as they drifted into their respective thoughts.

"Evening the score ..." Monty echoed. "What a delicious fantasy."

Dana finished her wine and turned to her. "These sandwiches are a soggy mess and I'm so hungry I could eat my own arm. You got any dry threads?"

When Monty and Dana stepped into the hotel elevator twenty minutes later, they were dry and wearing some of Monty's casual clothes. As the doors closed, a woman who was at least twenty years older than her thirtysomething male companion joined them.

The hefty scent of the young man's cologne arrived in the car before he did, and Dana guessed it would probably linger long after his departure. It made her nose wrinkle. The woman, on the other hand, appeared unable to wrinkle her nose even if she wanted to, since her face had been stretched into a perpetual open-eyed look of surprise from what Dana identified as shoddy cosmetic surgery.

The young man gave Monty and Dana a fast approving look before resuming an ongoing argument with the woman. And he dared not allow his attention to drift from that. *"Tu me rends fou!"* he complained to her in French.

"Et tu es désespérément insensible!" the woman replied. Her voice had a piercing nasal quality, as if she had an untreated adenoid problem.

Dana turned to Monty and whispered, "Okay, you went to school in Paris ... she's pissed about something. Clue me in."

Monty leaned closer to Dana. "He said she drives him crazy, but she thinks he's insensitive."

"An insensitive guy?" Dana smirked. "No way."

Meanwhile, the young man persisted, *"Et ces vacances? Je n'avais pas à t'amenerà Rome."*

"He didn't have to bring her on this vacation," mouthed Monty.

"Faut pas te plaindre. Il y a douze femmes par homme, ici!" the woman snapped.

"He doesn't mind the odds, a dozen women for every man," Monty explained.

"A cougar—nice!" Dana approved under her breath.

The woman glared at her young companion before scowling at Monty and Dana. *"Et ces filles là. Tu les regardes. Je t'ai vu!"*

"His eyes are on other women," Monty continued.

"There's a shocker," Dana cracked. "A guy checks out the action, film at eleven."

But now there was a profound shift in the young man's mood. His face took on a pout and his voice softened considerably. *"Peut-être aimerais-tu savoir ce que je pensais quand j'ai vu ces filles?"*

Monty leaned in slightly to hear better. "He's going to tell her what he thought when he saw those women."

"He didn't really say that," Dana griped.

Monty nodded that he did.

"What a groin pull!" Dana pronounced. "Twenty bucks says he feels lucky to be with her."

"Je pensais que j'avais de la chance d'être avec toi, mon amour," the young man professed.

And Monty was astounded. "My God, you're right!"

Dana could only shake her head. "He's baggin' this broad."

Monty and Dana emerged from the hotel and opened their umbrellas as drivers whizzed past treating auto safety as if they were competing in a crazed video game.

The traffic was the furthest thing from Monty's mind, however, as she continued to dwell on the hotel elevator exchange. "What was wrong with that woman?!" she groaned.

"Yeah," replied Dana. "Wearing that dress with regular underwear ...."

"How could she fall for such a glaringly transparent ruse?" Monty resumed, paying no attention to what Dana just said.

"You mean like we did?" asked Dana.

Monty glanced at her as the comment sunk in. "Are all women this feeble?"

"When our bullshit detectors don't work, sure," Dana confirmed. "Anyway, you owe me twenty bucks."

"What? Why?"

"The elevator," Dana proclaimed. "A bet's a bet."

"I'll deduct it from what you owe me for the restaurant repairs," Monty retorted.

Dana was going to dispute that idea when they stepped off the curb and a maniacal driver in a white Fiat adorned with scratches and dents appeared out of nowhere. It was like Pamplona for the running of the bulls, and had Dana not yanked Monty onto the sidewalk, they would have been roadkill.

Monty shrieked in terror and Dana gave the Fiat a defiant *up yours* fist gesture. The car stopped at the curb and the men inside whistled loudly at them, as if the near hit-and-run was their clever version of romantic foreplay. A translation of their ensuing flurry of Italian declarations was not necessary. What they wanted from the girls was clear.

"Wow, that was close!" Monty glowered, her heart racing.

"Yeah, but I say we give it a shot."

Monty was aghast. "I'm not going with those men!" she said, momentarily casting angry eyes at the lingering occupants of the Fiat.

Catching her look, the men became encouraged and increased the speed and volume of their indecipherable Italian taunts.

Dana ignored the men and gaped at Monty as if she were crazy. "I'm talking about evening the score, like you said upstairs," she said. But by now the men were growing impatient. They were like ravenous animals staring at fresh meat and Dana addressed them with two raised middle fingers. "Take a hike!"

The men whined in exaggerated pain at the gesture. It was only when Dana raised her hands higher to emphasize her fingers that they ultimately gave up.

As the Fiat drove off, Monty shot her a look, "That was quite a non sequitur."

Dana threw her a blank look. "What."

"What you just said about evening the score."

"What's wrong with it?" Dana wondered.

"You just resumed a conversation that ended ten minutes ago!" Monty explained in amazement.

Dana looked at her and shrugged. "Hey, is it my fault you can't keep up?"

In the *Piazza di San Lorenzo in Lucina* the girls were making their way through a carafe of red wine and bowls of pasta as they sat under a large market umbrella at an open-air *trattoria*. The city's usual aggressive sounds had been subdued by the rain that continued around them. Cool gusts of wind made the umbrella fabric flutter as an eclectic mix of American and British pop music hits, rather than Italian classics, could be heard from outdoor speakers concealed in large planters serving as traffic barriers.

"Why don't you just call his wife?" Monty was asking.

"And what would I say that didn't make me look like a total whore?" Dana came back.

"For one thing, he deceived you," Monty reminded her. "You didn't know the truth about his marriage."

"I knew he was still married," Dana objected.

"No, he told you that it was over," corrected Monty. "That hardly makes you a whore."

"She'd still hate me—and she'd be right."

"Then what do you propose?"

"I want to see that asshole suffer, that's what." Dana punctuated the remark by cutting a meatball with her fork and stuffing a chunk in her mouth. "And I sure as hell don't want him doing this to anybody else," she added. "Same goes for Giancarlo. He's already found his next victim. Don't you want to help her?""

"I thought you agreed that calling Sergeant Fazio was a good idea," Monty reiterated her before taking a sip of her wine.

"Man, that won't even come close to giving him what he deserves," Dana snarled. "I wanna hurt that guy bad—just as much as Alex."

"As do I," Monty consented, "but the concept of retribution goes against everything I stand for."

"I'm not talking about having them killed," groused Dana.

"What then?"

"I dunno," Dana answered, her mind scrambling for an idea. "What if we could give 'em a taste of their own medicine?"

Monty thought about that and, regardless of her moral standards, had to concede that what Dana was describing was compelling. "Alright," she replied, "but as appealing as that might sound, we would need an elaborate scheme of some sort. And we don't know anything about schemes."

Dana could only laugh. "We're women, aren't we?"

Then Monty made the mistake of showing a negative reaction. "Don't give me that look," Dana chided. "We've been pulling shit on men forever."

"That isn't true," rejoined Monty.

"As if," Dana jeered. "Ever let some dip stick feel smarter than you just because he was smokin' hot?"

"Never," Monty claimed. But the pronouncement was not very convincing.

"Baloney," Dana noted. "There isn't a chick alive who hasn't pulled that. Strike one. Ever wear a push-up bra to kick your boobage up a notch or two?"

"Absolutely not," Monty stated crossly.

Dana burst into a grin. "You mean to tell me you never weaponized your knockers to reel a guy in?" she hoisted her own breasts to punctuate her point. "No way, Jose."

Monty blushed. "Well, it's not like I had surgery," she answered meekly.

"Strike two," Dana mocked. "Now my fastball: ever fake an orgasm?"

"Dana!" Monty objected. She could not believe she was having this conversation.

"Give it up, Barbie," Dana hooted. "Have you or have you not done the "Oh, baby, you're the best" act for some love slug who didn't get the job done right?"

Monty poured herself more wine. "I don't care for this game very much."

"Oh, darling, you are sooooo good!" Dana mimicked with extra vigor.

Monty downed her whole glass, hoping for a way to thwart Dana's question but finding no place to hide. "Okay, okay," she succumbed. "I almost hate to admit it."

Dana cheered as she poured herself more wine, "YEEESSSSS!!! She swings and whiffs! Strike three."

"That doesn't solve anything," Monty corrected in the hope of regaining control of the discussion. "Giancarlo would see me coming a mile away."

"Sure," Dana agreed with a slightly tipsy lilt, "but he voted you off the island, remember? Alex did the same to me. We're off the grid, which means Giancarlo wouldn't see me coming any more than Alex would see you."

"I'm sorry, but you've lost me," Monty divulged.

"Think about it," Dana asked as she leaned forward conspiratorially. We know more about those jokers than anybody. We know the secret handshake."

Monty was still clueless. "What?"

"Try and keep up," Dana chided. "We know stuff only lovers know."

Monty processed that and then reacted with revulsion. "You want to trade men?!"

"Why not? They're low-hanging fruit."

Monty was flabbergasted. "But exchanging lovers is so ... unseemly."

"Hey," Dana replied, "ya don't hafta play Hide the Salami with him."

Monty just stared. "I'm not even going to ask what that is, let alone play it."

Just then a waiter arrived with a dessert plate. "For you, *Signora*," he said addressing Monty.

"We didn't ask for this," she explained.

"It is a gift from the chef," he replied, pointing to the *trattoria* window where the man in question and what seemed to be his entire kitchen staff were watching and beaming like schoolboys. "It is his dessert specialty."

Monty gazed at the plate admiringly. "Umbrian apple-walnut roll-ups ... I love these!" she stated. "Please thank him for us, would you?"

The waiter handed her a slip of paper with a knowing smile. "He would like you to have his telephone number, if you prefer to thank him yourself."

As the waiter moved off Dana snickered before cutting into one of the roll-ups. "Yeah, you never worked a guy over with your looks—right."

Chapter Twenty
My First Business Deal

Olivia Zironi was jubilant as Giancarlo approached on the street corner outside her hotel the next afternoon. "I thought you would never get here!" she greeted him with an accompanying hug.

"I'm sorry, am I late?"

"No, silly! I'm just excited, that's all," she explained. "I can barely stand it!"

"So, what is the big surprise that you have for me?" he wondered.

"Come with me," she commanded, taking his arm in hers and guiding him north on *Via Aranula*.

"Aren't you going to give me a hint?" he asked.

"Only that sometimes dreams really do come true," she revealed with a youthful giggle.

Before he could ask any more questions, she stopped on the sidewalk across from the *Piazza Benedetto Cairoli* park. "Look what I found—the perfect space for your art gallery!" she added with a sweeping gesture to an empty storefront.

He was dumbfounded. "What?"

"I saw the sign in the window yesterday," she chattered. "The landlord showed me inside. Wouldn't this make a fantastic showplace?!"

Still caught off guard, Giancarlo peered into the empty space. "It ... looks wonderful, Olivia."

"You must be in shock," she gushed. "But this location would be so good, with all the tourists who come here. I already sent my father pictures from my phone and he's all for it!"

Giancarlo could not believe it. *This girl was actually hustling her wealthy father for him!*

"He is?"

"It's my first business deal ever!" she enthused. "But other people want the space, too, so we shouldn't wait too long."

"Of course," he answered as his brain came back online. "What are the terms for the lease?"

"Oh, right—sorry. I'm so nervous that I forgot to show you." She took a contract from her bag and handed it to him. "The lease is 3,350 euro a month. Other people have looked at it, but it's ours if we wire him six months' rent by the end of the day. We can sign the contract at his office tomorrow."

Giancarlo's mind raced with the possibilities. Until now, he had planned on simply stealing her credit cards, *but now there was a chance of landing her father's cash!* He quickly calculated ways to get his hands on the deposit before vacating his apartment and vanishing from Olivia's life. "And your father has agreed to this?"

"Absolutely!" she chattered. "But he has two stipulations."

"What are those?" he asked cautiously.

"Well, because he's not accustomed to partnerships with strangers, he wants you to make the deposit as a show of good faith. Then after the lease is signed, he'll reimburse you."

"I don't know," he wavered. "That is a great deal of money." And it was, of course, but he also knew that when the reimbursement arrived, he could close his bank account, which he had done many times before, and get a refund of his deposit. "He is a wise man," he finally suggested. "And the other stipulation?"

"This is the really tough one—you must let my mother decorate the gallery," she added with a frown. "I'm terribly sorry, but she does have good taste. I promise to control her if I can."

Giancarlo smiled. "That will not be a problem."

"Really?" she wondered hopefully.

He held her close. "Do you think she will mind if we put a bed in the back office?" he asked. "For whenever the mood strikes us?"

Three miles from the storefront that afternoon, Olivia was with Giancarlo at the Bank of Italy as he happily filled out paperwork for a transfer of 20,100 euro to the landlord's account. "This is an exciting day, Olivia ... so very exciting," he declared as he signed the form. "And it's all because of you."

"My professor is going to die when he finds out I'm running a real art gallery!" she replied.

"Perhaps we can invite him to give a special lecture to our customers."

Olivia cringed. "I thought you wanted to be successful."

He laughed and set the pen down as the bank manager stated, "Ladies and gentlemen, the bank will be closing in five minutes!"

Giancarlo smiled. The accommodating young woman had kept him so busy in bed that afternoon, he nearly missed the bank's business hours. Fortunately, they were able to arrive just in time. He handed her the lease and asked, "Would you help me double check the landlord's account number?"

She eagerly complied, "Of course! IT60-X054-2811-01546."

"Perfect!" he verified as he studied the transfer order. Then, putting his arm around her, they moved to the teller's window and he slid the form across the counter with his identification. "I would like to transfer these funds, please."

The teller nodded and turned to a computer screen.

Olivia pulled Giancarlo's arm closer, wrapping herself in his embrace. "What are you thinking?"

"That I want to get you back to your hotel and celebrate," he answered with a wink.

"So, I wasn't enough for you this afternoon?" she asked.

"I could never get enough of you, Olivia."

She grinned mischievously. "Then let's stop at a pharmacy on the way," she replied. "I have something special in mind."

Fifteen minutes later Giancarlo was with Olivia outside a small drug store near the bank. They were about to enter when she kissed him on the cheek. "I want you to wait here ... and no peeking."

He smiled at her playful move. "I cannot imagine what you might be planning."

"That's the whole idea, silly!"

He lit a cigarette as she entered the pharmacy, and his smile did not fade. It did not really matter what kind of sexual adventure she had in store, he thought as he inhaled the smoke. This would be their last time in bed together before he disappeared, so she might as well enjoy it!

Taking another inhalation, he tried to sneak a look through the window to see what she might be purchasing, but the glare on the glass obscured his view. He turned away and focused on all that he would do with her father's investment money—like pay off his gambling debts and move into a larger apartment.

After a few minutes of indulging those fantasies, however, there was still no sign of Olivia. He entered the store and became uneasy when he could not find her. Approaching the female druggist, who was glowering at him from behind the counter, he asked, "Excuse me, what happened to the young woman who came in here a few minutes ago?"

The druggist could scarcely hide her contempt for him. "I know what you were up to, *Signor*. You should be ashamed!"

"What are you talking about?" he asked with confusion.

"A man your age, stalking a sweet young lady!"

"What? No—she is my girlfriend!"

"That is not what she told me," the woman snapped. "But good for her. Now she is free of you, once and for all!"

"Free of me?! I don't understand."

"You should leave before I telephone the police," the woman added as she picked up her phone.

"Please, there has been a terrible mistake," he muttered. "Where is Olivia?"

"You will never catch her," came the curt judgment. "She left through the back and my son gave her a ride!"

Giancarlo was stunned. Disoriented, a sense of panic welled up inside him as he exited the pharmacy and punched her number into his phone. But all he heard was her outgoing message: "This's Olivia.

Giancarlo, I'll see you at the hotel."

He hailed a taxi and instructed the driver to get to the Chapter Hotel as fast as possible. Then he phoned his bank to call off the money transfer, only to remember that they were closed for the day. *There would be no stopping the transaction until morning!*

Giancarlo repeatedly tried to call Olivia throughout the twenty-five minutes that it took to arrive at the hotel. He practically leapt from the taxi and ran into the lobby, where a pleasant middle-aged woman was on duty behind the desk.

"Welcome to the Chapter Hotel!" she cheerfully greeted him.

"I must reach one of your guests right away, Olivia Zironi," he blurted. "It's an emergency—she's not answering her cell or room phone."

The desk clerk shook her head. "Oh, her. She's long gone."

"Gone?!"

"Skipped on her bill. She used a stolen credit card the whole time she was here," the woman recounted.

His heart sank as he repeated her words. "Stolen card."

"Everything was charged. Her room, food, even the gift shop," the desk clerk added. "Her name is not Olivia Zironi, by the way."

"It isn't?" he asked weakly. The answer was already clear, of course. His head was spinning. *He had fallen for one of the oldest scams there is. She was posing as someone else, and she manipulated him into transferring money to her account!*

"The real *Signora* Zironi reported her cards missing days ago," she added. "They have all been frozen."

"But how could this happen?" he asked, almost in tears. "Didn't anyone confirm her credit when she checked in?"

"Her fiancé handled that when no one was watching," the woman replied. "I never would have thought him capable of such a thing!"

"Fiancé—" he gulped as his world continued to cave in on him.

"Our bartender Leandro," she disclosed. "They were in on it together, but now he is gone, too. Such a popular employee. I guess you never really know people."

Giancarlo gasped in horror. *Leandro!*

The only thing that Giancarlo could think to do was run to the empty storefront around the corner. The landlord's phone number was not on the lease, but he remembered seeing it posted on a sign in the window.

When he arrived, a group of construction workers were finishing up for the day and an official-looking man stood ready to lock the door behind them.

"Can I help you?" the man asked.

"I need to speak with someone about a lease," Giancarlo mumbled as he unfolded the contract with trembling hands. "The landlord, *Signor* Vetere."

"That would be me, but I'm afraid the space has been taken," the man told him.

Giancarlo handed him the lease. "I need to ask about a deposit … it was transferred to this account," he explained, pointing to the routing number printed at the top.

"This is one of my contracts, but that is not my account," Vetere told him.

Giancarlo sank. His worst fears had been realized. He had been conned, but he felt compelled to ask anyway. "It isn't?"

"No way," the landlord answered. "Somebody added that. You see? They typed over where my phone number is. Only an imbecile would put his bank information out there for the whole world to see."

"Of course," was all he could think to say.

"What's this all about?" Vetere wanted to know. "Why would you send me money?"

But before he could respond, a ping on Giancarlo's cell disclosed a new text message. Opening his phone app with his quivering hand, he found a selfie of Olivia and Leandro holding glasses of champagne and laughing. The sight of the image forced Giancarlo to sit on the pile of lumber behind him as the strength went out of his legs.

Then he read the accompanying text message:

Leandro was right when he said I'd have fun with you! Wow!

Anyway, I'm finished with this phone, so don't try to reach me. Thanks for everything. Ciao!

He slumped in defeat. He had been played by a woman and someone he thought was a friend, and now he was broke! *Totally, miserably, embarrassingly broke.*

"*Signor*, are you feeling poorly?" the landlord asked.

"That is a good word for it," Giancarlo feebly replied. "I am very poor."

Chapter Twenty-One
Even God's Got An Hourly Rate

In Alex Connelly's suite at the Raphael Hotel, he and Greg Lange sat with two men who reeked of influence and danger: Tazio Citrano and Augusto DeLuca. Citrano was younger than the taciturn DeLuca by fifteen years, and powerfully built. The senior DeLuca had oily jet-black hair and monitored the room from behind tortoise shell sunglasses.

Not sitting with the others, but watching closely from the door, was Beppe Caruso, a brawny goon with dead eyes and a face like a callus on someone's foot.

Citrano leaned back in the comfortable cushions of the living room chair. "We have reviewed your proposal, Connelly. Why have you come to us for financing?"

Connelly had been expecting the question and answered with unwavering board-room confidence. "Because no bank needs our services like you do."

"How interesting that you know so much about our needs," Citrano replied derisively.

Connelly poured the men cups of coffee from a shiny silver pot. "We do our homework, *Signor* Citrano."

"You have cash requiring circumspect handling," Lange added. "At the same time, your expanding operations are hampered by law enforcement actions that restrict your ability to move product."

Connelly grinned as he handed them their cups. "How are we doing so far?"

"Please continue," Citrano responded noncommittally.

Lange initiated the core of the pitch. "Connelly Import/Export represents the ideal investment. We're experts at specialized deliveries."

DeLuca calmly added a spoonful of sugar to his coffee, his Rolex watch sparkling at the edge of the sleeve on his Boglioli suit. "We are aware of your work for the Colombians last year," he affirmed. When he saw the surprise register on Connelly's face, he remained scrupulously poised. "You see, we also do our homework."

Connelly nodded. He liked negotiating with professionals and these men were certainly that. "Then you can appreciate the return that fifty million dollars would bring your organization—namely through a fleet of Airbus A300s leased in my name."

"Discreetly transporting 39,000 kilograms of your cargo on every plane to cities all over the world," said Lange. "Like FedEx."

"And the A300 does not require a main deck high-loader like some other planes, which gives us flexibility of airports for deliveries," Connelly added.

Citrano scrutinized the proposal top sheet and Airbus photos one more time. "And we need you for this … why?" he asked.

Connelly smiled. "Because if you were to do this on your own, you'd draw attention to yourselves that you don't want," he explained. "As for me, I already ship tons of goods for companies all over the world, day in and day out, all year long."

The Italians showed no reaction at first. Finally, Citrano remarked, "*Signor* DeLuca places great importance on trust. How can we know that you are trustworthy?"

Connelly looked directly at DeLuca, though he could not read his eyes behind his tinted sunglass lenses. "Because I know what happens to people who are not."

DeLuca sipped his coffee before purposely spitting it on the floor. "I hope the quality of your work is better than your coffee."

Connelly was unfazed by what he knew was a gesture intended to shock him. "It is," he stated simply.

Meanwhile, having bribed a priest to let them into a cramped storage room on the top floor of the *Santa Maria della Pace* church, Dana slouched on a crate near the antique leaded glass window while

Monty monitored the Raphael Hotel next door with binoculars. The room's thick beveled windows refracted sunlight into a spectrum of colors on the wide timbers of the timeworn floor.

As Monty scanned the rear of the hotel in search of Alex's room, Dana's sinuses grew stuffy from the musty draperies and pungent scent of beeswax, turpentine, and linseed oil in the air. She moved around peeking in various containers, more out of boredom than curiosity.

Eventually, she asked the question that had been brewing in her mind. "So, what's your deal, Monty? You said before that you didn't have much experience with men, but how could somebody who looks like you not have guys lined up for blocks?"

"For one thing, I attended all-girl schools."

Dana winced at the thought before a smile spread across her face. "Well, what do ya know?" she asked as she lifted a bottle of wine from one of the boxes.

Monty gave her a scolding look. "Dana, put that away."

"Maybe the priest included a mini-bar in the deal."

"That's sacramental wine," Monty informed her. "It's for Holy Communion only."

"I don't know about you, but I could use a little "holy" about now," Dana said as she read the label. "*Domus Santa Messa Vino Rosso Dolce Sacramentale.*"

"Dana, please," Monty scolded. "Don't be sacrilegious."

But Dana was already unscrewing the cap. Then, when she downed a swig right from the bottle, her face contorted and her eyes watered. "Whew—a little on the maple syrup side if you ask me, but it's got a good kick."

"That is so wrong," Monty admonished.

"Yeah, well I'll see you in hell, sister," she replied, holding the bottle out to her. When Monty ignored her, she shrugged and took another drink. "It gets better on the second pass, in case you change your mind."

Monty shook her head disapprovingly, which Dana ignored as she resumed her questions. "Okay, so there weren't a lot of men in your life," she ventured, "but there had to be some boyfriends."

The statement caused Monty to look up from the binoculars and explain. "Before Giancarlo there were really only two, one in high school and the other in college. I fell rather hard for the college guy, but broke up with him when he got drunk and made a pass at my roommate."

The remark caused Dana to lower the bottle from her mouth. "Wait a minute," Dana returned with confusion. "You're telling me some guy had YOU for a girlfriend and he still put the moves on somebody else?"

"She was very good-looking," countered Monty.

"How hot could she have been?!" Dana challenged. "You're practically a supermodel."

"That's nice of you to say, but evidently he didn't think so."

"What a putz," Dana assessed before taking another pull from the bottle while trying to imagine a woman more perfect than Monty. "That's it?" she resumed. "There had to be more romance than that."

Returning to her binocular search, Monty said, "I don't know if this qualifies, but I was pursued by one of my professors at Wellesley."

Dana sat upright. "Now you're talkin!" she remarked, intrigued. "What was his story?"

"Actually, it was a woman," Monty described with a tinge of discomfort. "Margaret Lassiter, my art appreciation instructor. She was quite a bit older than me and married. The whole thing was rather awkward."

"No kidding!" Dana screeched. "What happened?"

"Well," she started, "at first our conversations were harmless enough. We had so many wonderful philosophical exchanges about aesthetics. You know, what is beauty and what is art ...."

"Not really."

Monty got back to the point. "Over time, our meetings turned into coffee at Starbucks or a quick bite to eat off campus. We even visited an art museum once."

"That doesn't sound so bad."

"... and then one day she invited me to spend a weekend at her family's lake house," Monty finished.

"A weekend getaway—lemme guess. Without the family, right?"

"She failed to make that clear at first," Monty added. "I only learned at the last minute that she had other ideas about our relationship."

Dana whistled. "Pretty shady move."

"It gets worse," Monty continued. "She did not react well when I turned her down. I mean, she took it very, very personally. It wasn't long before she was emailing and texting me several times a day and calling at odd hours. The more I ignored her, the more aggressive she became. Once she even sent me a topless photo of herself."

"Holy crap, this's a Lifetime movie! What happened?"

"I shared the picture with my academic adviser and that afternoon Margaret went home. A day or so later her office was empty and no one in the department ever spoke of her again."

"That's some amazing shit, Monty."

"It was strange to be in the middle of it, that's for sure."

Dana thought about that and realized she was seeing her friend in a whole new light. "Sounds like college kinda sucked for you," she observed.

"Those two episodes certainly did," Monty confirmed. "But you know, I never gave up on the notion of love. I knew from my parents' marriage that good things in life were possible and that life partners really do exist."

Dana scoffed, "Yeah, and then numb-nuts comes along and screws all that up—nice."

Monty let the comment sink in. It was painful to hear that spoken aloud, certainly, but she also accepted that it was a necessary part of her recovery.

As their meeting drew to a close, Connelly stood and extended a hand to DeLuca. "Do we have an agreement about your investment?"

DeLuca nodded and accepted the handshake as Citrano unfolded a letter of understanding and set it on the coffee table with a $1,500.00 Montblanc *Meisterstück* pen.

When Connelly finished signing the document, he handed the pen to Citrano only to have DeLuca wave him off. "Keep it," he said.

Connelly was well-aware of the pen's value and nodded his appreciation. "Thank you very much," he remarked. "It will be a pleasure doing business with you."

Meanwhile, Lange had crossed to the door. "Gentlemen, speaking of pleasure, we have taken the liberty of arranging some entertainment to commemorate our new relationship."

The Italians reacted with raucous delight at the sight of four eye-catching call-girls entering from the hall.

"What about you, Dana?" Monty was inquiring as she continued to scan the hotel windows with the binoculars. "Were there other men before Alex?"

"You could say that," she answered before taking another sip of wine. "A bunch, actually. Not hundreds or anything, but you know, I could party with the best of 'em." She glanced at Monty to make sure that she did not think less of her because of her romantic past. "But those were sprints, and not marathons, if ya know what I mean," she clarified. "And most were kinda shallow."

Dana paused as a reminiscence unfolded in her mind. "The worst guy was a *Fifty Shades of Grey* wannabe," she recalled. "I mean, he was into all kinds of kinky stuff. I told him to go screw himself and believe me, if he could've figured out a way to do that, he would've."

The girls chuckled and the feeling of camaraderie between them felt good.

"Unlike you, I never thought I'd meet the right guy," Dana acknowledged. "Then Alex said all the stuff I wanted to hear, and I never knew what hit me."

As the women reflected on that, Monty saw something through the binoculars that made her tense up. Dana read her body language right away and set the bottle of wine aside. "Wuzzup?"

Monty became even more rigid. What she saw was the prostitutes cavorting with Connelly, Lange, and their new partners. As one of the women danced in her underwear, the others were giving nude lap dances to Lange and the Italians.

"I'm not sure ...." Monty answered in what was not a very convincing stalling maneuver.

"Either you found him, or you didn't," Dana came back.

"Um, well, it's hard to say ...." she said hoping to stall.

Dana impatiently stuck her hand out for the binoculars. "Come on Monty. Don't be a dick. Fork 'em over."

"Would you please be patient?" Monty asked in a last-ditch effort to prevent Dana from seeing the truth. A truth that now included an undressed woman removing Connelly's clothes in the bedroom.

"The priest won't let us stay here forever, ya know," Dana told her.

"I thought you bribed him," Monty said, continuing to stall.

"Even God's got an hourly rate," Dana stated. Holding out her hand once again, she demanded the binoculars.

Monty reluctantly handed them over.

As Dana took a look, she said, "Man, we can really see into these rooms! Which one's his?"

Monty slumped against the wall and answered so quietly her voice was barely audible. "Top floor, corner."

"Got it," Dana responded. But then her face sank. "Oh," was all she could say upon locating the suite.

"Are you alright?" Monty asked with dismay.

Dana lowered the binoculars with a thunk on the windowsill. "A hooker's doing the big nasty with my ex. What do you think?"

"I'm so sorry."

Dana turned away and flopped against the wall. Anguish was etched on her face.

"I didn't want you to see that," Monty confessed.

"You shoulda tried harder."

"Is there anything I can do?"

"Gotta high-powered rifle?" Dana asked before catching Monty's dismayed response. "Just kidding," she corrected.

Monty masked her worry as much as she could. "I knew that."

"No, you didn't."

"You're right. Sorry," Monty told her. "I'm sorry about all of this."

They fell into a long silence as Monty picked up the wine bottle and took a drink, both to give her time to sort out her feelings and because alcohol seemed like an excellent idea under the circumstances.

"It's funny," Dana mused. "No matter how many people have been put through this, no matter how many hearts have been trashed, it feels like I'm the only one it's ever happened to."

"I understand," said Monty as she handed her the bottle. "Listen to me. If the offer is still open, I'd love to help you get even with that ... that ... pelt piccolo."

Dana did not decode the reference right away. Then as the deduction came, she said, "... skin flute?"

"That's the one."

Dana was dumbfounded. "You're really up for this?"

"You were so right about getting even," Monty proclaimed. "Why should we tolerate this agony because of two men's callous pleasure?"

"Are you sure you just don't want to have Giancarlo killed?" Dana asked.

"I know you don't mean that."

"Okay, okay," she answered, waving her off. "Man, you really know how to take the laughs outta getting dumped by a guy, ya know that?"

The sense of dread that Monty had previously felt over how to deliver news of Giancarlo's probable death to the sisters at the orphanage was nothing compared to the emotions that overwhelmed her before phoning her parents that night. While the conversation started out well enough, as Grant and Rosemary's excited inquiries about the honeymoon helped to partially restore the energy that had drained from Monty, her mother soon detected the fragility of her daughter's brave front.

Monty had been able to keep other calls with them brief, but everything about this one was different. Rosemary knew that something was wrong, and her intuition could not, would not, be ignored. "Montell," she finally asked, "are you alright?"

Monty did not respond at first. She had done her best to match their cheerfulness with something other than despondency, in the hopes of easing them toward the disturbing truth about Giancarlo. But now she had fallen silent, which caused a knot to form in her father's stomach. "Honey, what's going on?" he asked.

"I don't know where to begin—" Monty told them through her tightening throat.

"Start anywhere you want," Grant gently encouraged her.

"Yes, take your time," added her mother, sensing the seriousness of what they were about to hear. As most parents would, they feared the worst, as irrational thoughts of cancer diagnoses, violent incidents, or the death of a loved one ricochet uncontrollably through their minds.

Monty forced herself to take a breath. "It was all a lie," she hesitantly disclosed. "Giancarlo isn't who I thought he was ... in fact, I don't know anything about him, except that he's a hustler and a thief ...." Her voice trailed as she fought back the feelings surging inside her.

"Oh, my God, are you alright?" her father asked with alarm.

"I'm fine, daddy," Monty answered. "But he's gone. He stole everything from me and then he disappeared."

"Disappeared?" Grant repeated incredulously. "I can't believe this!"

"When did this happen, Montell?" her mother asked.

"Last week in Saint Tropez," Monty admitted. "He had it all planned out. He even faked his own death in a car crash—" She wanted to tell them so much more, but her ability to speak was impeded by the grief that gushed forth.

Grant and Rosemary were devastated, their dismay over Monty's dilemma compounded by the utter helplessness that they felt. Their daughter was stranded across the Atlantic and hurting.

Thankfully, over the next thirty minutes the phone call yielded the information that they needed for the time being. And regardless of the outrageous details of Giancarlo's deceptions, their daughter was safe.

But the couple also learned that Monty was struggling with far more than a broken heart. They came to understand that she was also suffering from her decision to withhold from them the truth about the money she was obligated to spend on restaurant repairs, and more importantly, for failing to confide in them earlier.

Monty declined her father's insistence on catching the first flight to Rome. She explained that since this entire situation was due to her lack of judgment, she wanted to resolve it herself. What she omitted, of course, was her pact with Dana to somehow get even with both Giancarlo and Alex Connelly.

In the end, Grant and Rosemary were relieved to hear that she had reported Giancarlo's crimes to the Italian police and that she had enlisted the emotional support of a new American friend, Dana Zimmer.

At least their daughter was not alone.

Dana was nursing her third glass of tequila at the Inn at the Spanish Steps rooftop bar when Monty arrived, looking depleted. "So, how'd the call go?" Dana inquired.

"My parents just learned that their whole family was swindled by an Italian *gigolo*," Monty began. "How do you think it went?"

Dana reacted to her despondent tone. "I didn't mean to be insensitive," she responded, pointing to her glass. "I've already had a couple of these."

"No harm done," Monty replied before taking a sip of Dana's drink. "Is this the tequila that you like so much?"

"AsomBroso," Dana explained somewhat apologetically. "You said to order whatever I wanted."

"It's not bad."

Dana tried to force a smile. "After what we've been through, maybe you should order one and catch up."

But Monty's attention was lost somewhere in the far-off city lights.

Dana studied her carefully. "What else did your folks say?"

"I'd rather not relive that now, if you don't mind," she answered before taking another sip of Dana's tequila. "They're wiring me more money tomorrow."

"You don't seem all that happy about it."

"I have mixed emotions," Monty explained. "They think they're supporting my legal case against Giancarlo."

"So, you didn't tell them what we're up to, after all."

"I felt terrible about deceiving them again, Dana," she began, "but I didn't know how to tell them that I don't want a protracted legal battle to be my lasting memory of this."

Dana handed her the rest of her drink and motioned for a waiter to refresh and double the order. "Then drink up, sister, because from this moment on, you and I are letting go of all the bullshit. We've got some serious planning to do!"

Chapter Twenty-Two
We Have Come To Collect

Giancarlo was leaving his apartment that night when he found two surly tattoo-covered skinhead thugs leaning against his car. He understood all-too well what their conspicuous *SPQR* ink advertised: membership in the violent fascist gang named after the government of the ancient Roman Republic, the *Senate and People of Rome*.

Luigi Brancatto was known on the street as The Enforcer, while his sidekick was known only as Ice Pick. No one knew his given name because no one had the courage to ask.

Both men looked decidedly peeved at the moment and Giancarlo forced a light-hearted greeting as he approached them with an unconvincing synthetic smile. "Well, this is a nice surprise!" he squeaked through his anxiety-wrenched throat.

"Is it?" The Enforcer grumbled. "Your *Serie A* and *La Liga* bets went bad this week."

"Very bad," Ice Pick underscored with a pointed glower.

Giancarlo swallowed and hastily decided to keep his friendly demeanor going. He had no choice. "I know! Can you believe that? *Fiorentina, Sevilla,* and *Celta Vigo* are dead to me now."

"We believe it," added Ice Pick as The Enforcer nodded in agreement.

"I don't know what got into those teams," Giancarlo continued, determined to turn this into a conversation and not what he feared, which was a severe beating. "They did not play like themselves!"

The Enforcer lit a cigarette and flicked the match on the hood of Giancarlo's Peugeot. "That brings your losses to 41,260.50 euro."

"Are you sure?" Giancarlo asked as he tactfully retrieved the match from the car and dropped it in the gutter. "I made a payment two weeks ago."

"You did," Ice Pick recounted, "but your losses have climbed since then."

Giancarlo gulped as The Enforcer met his look. "You are over the 20,000 euro limit we approved."

"I don't know how that happened—" Giancarlo sputtered, never taking his eyes off The Enforcer as he tried to gauge his fate. "I mean, for all three clubs to fail me at once. What are the odds of that?!"

"The way you bet, typical," Ice Pick answered.

"Maybe you should stick to your lucrative art career and leave gambling to the professionals," The Enforcer added with a vicious laugh. He knew all about Giancarlo's fake profile as an artist, which made the joke seem especially ironic and funny.

Ice Pick laughed, as well, which forced Giancarlo to nervously join them.

Then the joviality ended. "We have come to collect," The Enforcer announced.

"21,260.50 will be an acceptable figure," added Ice Pick.

Giancarlo gasped as his mind raced in search of a way out of this mess. "Of course," he professed. "I know this will sound strange, but I had the money for you this morning ... there was a problem at my bank."

The Enforcer took a long draw from his cigarette and exhaled the smoke in Giancarlo's face. "We know you withdrew your savings. Where is it now?"

The comment caught Giancarlo off guard. "How—how did you know about that?"

"Unlike you, we're good at our jobs," The Enforcer established. "You were at the bank with a girl you were hustling."

"Yes! Yes, I was! Olivia Zironi, but she cheated me!"

The two skinheads roared with laughter. Then Ice Pick abruptly turned serious again. "How do we know you aren't trying to con us?"

"I ... I ... just need time to straighten everything out ... that's all!" Giancarlo stammered as he looked at them pleadingly. "Can't you give me a little more time?"

The Enforcer had no reaction. "We will get back to you," was all he said.

Giancarlo felt a sudden rush of relief. *He would not be murdered today!* "Thank you—thank you so much! An extension would really help me out."

Ice Pick glared at him for what felt like an eternity, as if he might be meticulously planning the details of Giancarlo's painful demise. "We aren't promising anything."

"I understand, but still, thank you for trying. You guys are the best," he said. "Please tell everyone that I will find a way to get the 20,000 euro."

"21,260.50, The Enforcer corrected.

"Certainly ... absolutely ...." Giancarlo stated, cursing himself for stupidly being imprecise with these known killers.

The Enforcer flicked what was left of his cigarette onto Giancarlo's loafers, causing him to jump aside. "We are not a charity, Giancarlo. Remember that."

Minutes after the Bank of Italy doors were unlocked in the morning, Giancarlo was extremely agitated as he spoke to a desk officer. The man's name plate identified him as Felicio Aiello. "Please, *Signor* Aiello, there must be a way to cancel that transfer!" he insisted.

"Unhappily, there is not," Aiello answered as he handed him a document. "These are the rules and regulations to which you agreed before the transaction."

Giancarlo's frustration was getting to him. "But it was made under false pretenses!"

"That would be a matter for law enforcement officials," Aiello replied dryly. "And as I review your banking history, they might very much want to speak with you, as well."

Giancarlo's breath came up short. "What ...?"

"Let me just say that your financial records make for entertaining reading," he stated. "Unexplained financial windfalls every few months ... opening and,closing accounts ... frequent changes of address and telephone numbers ...."

"I resent your implication, *Signor*," he said in a show of righteous indignation.

Aiello was not swayed, however. As a knowledgeable banking manager, he recognized Giancarlo's pattern of illicit activity. "I'm sure you do," he announced, turning his computer monitor off with a polite smile. "But as far as the Bank of Italy is concerned, you twice confirmed the transfer to a valid deposit account at another institution."

"But that account has been closed!" Giancarlo protested. "I called them this morning."

"It was closed upon receipt of your funds yesterday," he explained. "Unfortunately for you, *Banca Monte dei Paschi di Siena* has determined the account was opened using false identification."

"That is disgraceful!"

"The employee who made the error is being reprimanded for her carelessness."

"Reprimanded?" Giancarlo gasped.

"Our people receive better training."

Giancarlo was near tears. "That's it?! What about my money?!"

"There is nothing to be done by us," Aiello added. "The owner of the closed account cannot be traced."

Chapter Twenty-Three
Was All This Really Necessary?

Connelly and Lange arrived at the DeLuca Family Bakery in *L'Annunziatella* south of the city in the back of a dark sedan. Had they been fully aware of their location, they might not have found their proximity to the Appian Way particularly comforting—given that is where the famed gladiator Spartacus and his army of 6,000 slaves were crucified in 71 B.C.

DeLuca and Citrano were waiting at the entrance to the large commercial facility. DeLuca's sullen goon Beppe Caruso was at their side, as always.

"Welcome to my family business," DeLuca announced.

Connelly was not happy about having been held captive, in his view, for the forty-five-minute ride. "Was all this really necessary?"

"My associates are cautious people," DeLuca explained. "Take no offense."

"The meeting is a formality," Citrano claimed.

They entered the building, where dozens of tall metal rolling racks filled with fresh loaves of bread and rolls were being checked by workers wearing hair nets, disposable gloves, and face masks. As they moved past huge kneading troughs and mechanical mixers Connelly, Lange, DeLuca, and Citrano were besieged by the aroma of sweet and yeasty baking dough.

"Wow, it smells amazing in here!" admired Lange.

"It is something that I never grow tired of," DeLuca replied. "My family has produced bread for five generations. My grandfather expanded from a little shop with two ovens and my father built what you see here, a respected high-volume facility."

"Very impressive," Connelly observed, still trying to overcome his lingering irritation over having to be there at all.

"We bake one hundred varieties. When you leave be sure to take some with you," DeLuca offered.

Then upon entering a massive walk-in refrigerator filled with ingredients, a wall of shelves mysteriously swung open to disclose a secret door leading to a warehouse where a trio of stone-faced men were carefully watching packages of white powder being removed from bags of flour. It was heroin.

Connelly noticed that DeLuca carried himself differently as he entered the room, with his chin higher and shoulders back, as if to put everyone on notice that the boss had arrived.

"This is one of our distribution facilities," Citrano explained. "Drivers deliver special cargo to associates around the city, in addition to their regular bakery deliveries to cafes and stores."

Lange glanced over at men inserting heroin packets into carved out loaves of bread. "May I ask how many more of these facilities there are?"

Citrano seemed amused by the question and smiled at DeLuca before returning his look to Lange. "It would be better if you did not."

"Understood," Lange answered apologetically.

However, on second thought DeLuca felt that a limited answer was appropriate. "Let me just say that our structure is fine for Italy," he added. "But as you know we are eager to expand."

"I hope you still believe I'm your man for that," Connelly remarked.

"Let me introduce you to some people," he replied. "We will see what they have to say." They approached the three cohorts and DeLuca continued, "Alex Connelly and Greg Lange, I would like you to meet *Signori* Tonioli, Calvino, and Manara."

"G'day gentlemen, it is a pleasure," Connelly stated as he shook their hands.

Tonioli spoke for the group. "*Signor* DeLuca believes you to be trustworthy. Are you?"

"I am," he vouched.

"How do we know this to be true?" Tonioli followed up.

"I will leave that answer to *Signor* DeLuca, since he's the one who investigated me in the first place," Connelly answered. "I've had prostate exams that were less thorough."

The men laughed at his joke, but then Tonioli looked Connelly squarely in the eye. "Do you remember crossing the Tiber River during your drive here?"

"I do," Connelly answered, wondering where the exchange might be heading.

"Good," Tonioli replied. "The bridge you were on goes past *Riparazione Barche Magliana*, a boatyard that we own. It is a very private place, particularly in the darkness of night. And the river there is deep. Such a facility eliminates the need for retirement plans for associates who do not meet expectations." He paused to let his meaning sink in. "Do I make myself clear?"

Connelly nodded his understanding of the threat. "Personally, I never cared much for boating, *Signor* Tonioli."

"That is comforting to hear," the mobster responded grimly.

Chapter Twenty-Four
Well, I'll Be Damned

Monty felt ill at ease as she turned in a circle while Dana looked her over critically. "I feel ridiculous doing this," Monty balked.

"Just spin the goods, will ya?" Dana instructed from the couch in Monty's hotel living room.

Monty apprehensively continued to rotate in her t-shirt and shorts, but Dana seemed confused. "Okay, I gotta ask, has your skin ever seen sunlight?"

"What's wrong with my skin?" Monty asked as she stopped.

"You're pulling my chain, right?"

"I'm sorry, what?"

"You're practically albino," Dana ridiculed.

"My dermatologist says that I have a very healthy complexion," disputed Monty.

"I've seen vampires with more color," Dana came back. "I almost need sunglasses to look at you."

Monty rolled her eyes. "Ha, ha."

"I wasn't kidding," Dana clarified. "Now, take off your clothes."

"What ...?"

"You heard me. Off!"

"I'm not doing any such thing," Monty defiantly proclaimed.

Dana stared at her. "Do you want to stick it to this guy, or not?"

Monty deflated. Of course, she did. Then, as ordered, she removed her shorts, already beginning to regret agreeing to this partnership.

Thirty minutes later, an extremely self-conscious Monty stood naked in her large shower stall while Dana applied a can of Norvell spray-tan to her marshmallow white body. "Are you almost finished?" Monty peevishly asked.

"Oh, I was done ten minutes ago," Dana announced as she panned the spray across the back of Monty's legs. "I just couldn't get enough of your naked butt."

"Dana!"

"By the way, do you have a license for that ass?"

"You are disgusting," Monty informed her.

Dana ignored the remark and continued to spray.

"How is it that you happened to have spray-tan in your luggage, anyway?" Monty asked.

"Hey, ya never know when you're gonna have a tanning emergency."

Within an hour Dana was taking portrait photos of Monty wearing different outfits, while arranging her beautiful long hair in various ways: full, swept to the side, and up.

Then, posing before a green muslin backdrop and bathed in flattering softbox lighting, Monty was the girl-next-door in a pair of Dana's daisy dukes and a torn *Ciao* t-shirt in one angle and standing with her hands in the pockets of ripped acid wash jeans in another.

At one point, Dana paused to make an aperture adjustment to the new Nikon camera in her hands. "This rig's a whole lot better than the one I've got at home, Monty—nice!"

"I was happy to buy it for you," she replied. "It's fortuitous that you know so much about photography."

"Yeah, well I've been shooting a long time," Dana told her. "It's the only good thing I ever got from my old man growing up."

"You really know what you're doing!" Monty remarked, meaning it. "What's the purpose of this green screen, anyway?"

"That's so I can composite you over stock backgrounds to make you look like the real deal."

"Well, I'm impressed."

"Thanks," Dana answered. "I thought about doing this for a living once, and now that I'm outta work maybe I oughta give it a try."

"Are we almost done?" Monty asked.

"Hell no," came the answer. "We're just getting started on your portfolio—now we cut your hair."

Monty was stunned and defiant. "You are NOT cutting my hair!"

Dana pointed to her own head. She had been expecting this reaction. "Monty, I hate to tell ya, but this is the look Alex goes for."

"But I love my hair!" she whined.

"I know," Dana told her, "but if we're gonna do this, we gotta do it right. Besides, I know what I'm doing. My mom worked in a salon for a while."

Monty clutched the ends of her hair. "Isn't there a chance he could be attracted to me without having to go to these extremes?"

Dana sat on the couch and took a long pull from a bottle of *Castello Di Udine* beer. "Don't get me wrong, kid, you're a knockout … I just saw you buck naked," she explained. "But I know what turns the man on and you don't."

With Dana's help Monty's metamorphosis into an exotic French fashion model was unquestionably startling. In addition to giving her an identical pixie hairstyle to her own, she did a great job of creating sophisticated and sensual make-up variations. With the help of other outfits from Dana's suitcase, and items from a shopping trip that day, there were incendiary shots of Monty in red sheer mesh and lace baby-doll lingerie, and others in a deep V-neck halter mini club dress, assorted stretch suede over-the-knee boots, thigh-high fishnet suspender stockings, garters, slinky see-through blouses, and intricate lace-up bikini swimwear.

Soon Monty had a remarkable inventory of photo images. Yet while Dana managed to establish visual drama in many shots with a floor fan blowing Monty's clothing, it was more difficult getting the model herself to comply.

"For Chrissakes, Monty," Dana complained at one point. "Wear it like you mean it."

Monty groaned at the comment. "Not everyone can be the picture of fashion like you, I suppose." Her eyes locked on Dana's well-worn Los Angeles Dodgers *Bellinger* jersey.

"When you can hit like Cody Bellinger, we'll talk," Dana rejoined.

"I don't know what that means."

"You never know what anything means," Dana responded. "Super cute baseball star."

That was a losing argument, so Monty changed the subject. "Why must you take so many pictures of me in these revolting outfits?" she asked.

"Because revolting is what works with Alex Connelly," Dana came back. "How is it that somebody that looks like you never did any modeling?"

"There were offers when I was young, but my parents didn't want that life for me," Monty answered. "My mother was a Paris runway model in her teens and hated feeling like a living mannequin. She found the whole thing debasing and now I know why."

"Well, suck it up buttercup because you're a model in this scam."

"Some models have standards, you know," sulked Monty.

"Can't you color outside the lines just once?" Dana asked.

Monty could only roll her eyes. "Ugh!"

"What, you think it's easy being a slut?" Dana asked as she met her look. She was not joking. "You're still up for this, aren't you?"

"Of course, I am," Monty replied with diminished enthusiasm. "I want to give Alex and Giancarlo a taste of their own medicine."

"And I want to destroy them," Dana came back. "Ya gotta be the trophy Alex can't have, okay? That'll be irresistible to him."

When the photography session ended, Monty changed back into her normal clothes as Dana worked on a Facebook fan page for an international fashion model named *Montell*. The use of graphics and design with Photoshop software was extraordinary. Dana had composited Monty's pictures over frames downloaded from the internet so she could now be seen at the Grand Canyon, Great Wall of China, Taj Mahal, and other prominent locations.

Monty approached the laptop computer screen and reacted to one of the shots, "Oh, my gosh ... this is so professional!"

"Thanks," Dana replied. "Too bad I have such a dog for a subject."

"Very funny."

"Thanks for noticing."

"Where did you learn so much about computers?" Monty asked.

"One of my brothers is a geek and it rubbed off," Dana answered as she continued her work.

Monty could only shake her head in amazement. "I can barely use my iPhone," she said before a realization struck. "But wait, what if my friends or family find this page on the internet?"

Dana took another pull from her Italian beer. "No sweat. You'll be a diva model no matter what we call you," she decreed. "What's your middle name?"

"Cherie."

"Cool," she replied as she effortlessly changed the logotype over a suggestive photo of Monty wearing a lynx fur coat, long strings of pearls, and not much else. "I now pronounce you the French model known as *Cherie*."

"My goodness!" Monty remarked, astounded. "You did that so fast!"

"That was easy—so was scoring this toll-free number," Dana grinned. "The rest is gonna take a while to get right."

She clicked through a series of Monty's winsome photos, which were now cropped, and color corrected for aesthetic impact. She stopped at one art shot of Monty on a beach in Tahiti wearing a tiny pink bikini with matching pink hair. "Oh, man!" she thundered enthusiastically. "Alex will go ape for this one! You are a hundred twenty pounds of awesome here."

Monty stared at the image. "Actually, I'm one hundred five," she corrected, as if the correction actually mattered.

"In your bra, maybe," came Dana's sarcastic reply as she advanced to another photograph on the screen, this one a close-up of Monty licking a giant novelty lollipop with a naughty sparkle in her eye, "And check this one out—you are totally killing it here, sister!"

Monty could only roll her eyes in distaste.

Then Dana clicked to a decadent shot of Monty wearing nothing but a bath towel and stiletto heels. "You are freakin' hot in this one!" she exclaimed. "Get it off the grill, will ya?"

Once more, Monty rolled her eyes.

Dana clicked frames again to unveil Monty lying on the bed wearing a t-shirt and panties. "And this one. Gimme a break," she cheered. "You are an assassin!"

Dana stopped at the next photo, which featured Monty seated on an ottoman with her naked back to the camera. "Whoa! Hurt me, mamma!"

Monty glanced at her disdainfully. "Are you going to editorialize about every one of these?"

"Pretty much," she came back just as another shot appeared on the monitor. This one featured Monty posed in a black fishnet body stocking in the middle of a deserted Times Square. "Somebody get me an insulin shot," Dana crowed. "Cuz, I just found some eye candy!"

Monty erupted in horror. "Oh, God. My butt looks huge in that outfit, doesn't it? I knew it! Delete that one."

Dana reacted with incredulity, then cynically turned back to the screen. "Yeah, what was I thinking? What self-respecting guy'd want to hit that?"

"Are we done with this now?" Monty impatiently asked.

"Sure," came the answer. "I don't know how much more of your whining I can take."

"Good," Monty said as she stood. "Now let's see what I can do with you."

"Kinda hard to improve on perfection, don't ya think?" Dana joked.

Monty lifted a long blonde wig from a shopping bag. "But not impossible."

Dana's eyes grew wide at the sight of the hairpiece. "You don't expect me to wear that!"

"Certainly," Monty replied, approaching her.

"It's like a freakin' throw rug!"

Monty ignored the comment as she put the wig on Dana. The thick flowing hair completely changed her appearance. "There!" she announced. "What do you think?"

"Good God," Dana grimaced at her reflection in a mirror. "How could you stand having all this shit on your head?"

"Don't be so negative," Monty rebuked. "Giancarlo has a thing for long hair, and you look fabulous."

Dana moved to the dressing table and reconsidered her reflection more seriously. "You really think so?"

"You're joking again, right?" Monty questioned. She was not having much luck figuring out her friend's sense of humor.

"I'm serious."

"Dana, you are the most beautiful woman I've ever seen," Monty certified. "Giancarlo will think so, too."

"Thanks," Dana answered. The truth was, hearing a compliment like that from someone as refined as Monty meant a lot to her.

"You're welcome," Monty replied as she fluffed the wig. "But your appearance is only part of the challenge."

"What are you gonna do to me now?" came the suspicious reply.

Fifteen minutes later Monty watched as Dana walked across the living room in an expensive designer dress and heels. "No, no ... you can't move like that."

Dana stopped to face her. "What's wrong with it?"

"Everything."

"I've been walking like this forever," Dana contradicted.

"That won't get you into Giancarlo's life," answered Monty. "He must believe you have wealth, not an orthopedic problem."

Dana frowned and tried again, but the result was the same.

"Not so much hip," Monty drilled. "Let the fabric cascade over you."

"This's hard," Dana objected as she tried to tone down the mechanics of her walk.

Monty ignored the remark. "Toss your hair a little bit, too," she directed. "Take advantage of all that glorious new volume."

When an opportunity to extract herself from Monty's instruction availed itself, Dana seized the chance to show her how things are done in her world. She found the video for Shakira's dance hit *Hips Don't Lie* on YouTube and cranked it as loudly as she could through Monty's small portable desk speakers.

Monty looked on in shock as Dana perfectly replicated the mesmerizing hip thrusts and booty shakes from Shakira's repertoire. "Why am I being subjected to this?!" she yelled over the music.

"Because Alex likes to fly his freak flag and you don't even know what that means."

"I assume it's not a compliment."

"You're catching on," Dana confirmed as she danced around her, hips rolling. "His middle name is *party*."

Monty bristled at the remark. "I'm every bit as capable of having a good time as the next person," she claimed.

Dana sneered and folded her hands behind her head before moving towards her like an exotic dancer. It was a riveting sight.

Monty swallowed at the concentrated sexual content of Dana's choreography. "I don't know if I'm THAT capable."

Dana continued to dance. "Come on, Frenchie. Show me the money."

Monty timidly tried to mimic Dana's dancing but was failing miserably. *They sure never taught this at cotillion!* "I can't do this," she quarreled in defeat.

"Sure, ya can," Dana coached as she danced closer. She was unbelievably sensual. "Think of it as doing it with your clothes on see? Set your phasers to stun."

Monty's eyes grew wide at the raw eroticism of what she was seeing. "How in the world do you do that?" she gulped.

"That's what the guys usually ask."

"You are terrible!" Monty howled.

Dana grinned. "Not according to them."

Monty did what she could to imitate Dana's movements. Soon her inhibitions dissipated, and the girls danced even closer. Their bodies were almost touching now and as unlikely as it might have been, Monty liked it! "Oh, my God, this is fun!" she conceded.

"Yeah," Dana came back. "I checked the weather forecast and they predict cloudy skies with a good chance of whoop-ass."

Monty stopped dancing. "What?"

"Never mind," she replied. "Now, lay some leg on me. It's time to ink you up."

Monty's leg was arched on a chair as Dana put the finishing touches on a colorful stenciled long stem rose ankle tattoo. "There! Just like the real one Alex bought me," she observed, comparing it to hers. "The man likes a little ink on a woman."

From that point on, Monty and Dana did not resist what the other tried to teach as their seduction bootcamp continued throughout the day: While Monty educated Dana in the fine art of pouring wine, Dana showed her how to chug beer—and inevitably, while Monty demonstrated how to properly sit at the dinner table, Dana shocked her with such taunts as licking her fingertips and grabbing a man's buns with one firm squeeze.

That evening an emotional aria played on the computer as Monty created drawings in a sketch pad. Unlike the feisty woman from earlier, Dana was now quiet. "Can we kill that noise?" she asked, irritably tossing a pizza box aside. "I gotta monster headache."

Monty gave her a scolding look. "*La Traviata* is hardly noise."

"Coulda fooled me," Dana told her sourly.

"Dana," Monty began, "I won't belabor the point, but this is an important concept if you expect to deceive Giancarlo. This aria is *Di Provenza il mar, il suol* by Giuseppe Verdi. It means *The Sea and Soil of Provence.*

"Giancarlo knows that?"

"Every Italian citizen knows it. *La Traviata* is the classic tale of a tragic affair between a young man and a terminally ill prostitute."

"So, it's a comedy," Dana derided.

Monty ignored the joke. "The title *La Traviata* translates into English as *The Fallen Woman* and the heroine Violetta earns redemption through sacrifice."

"How the hell am I supposed to remember all that?"

"Giancarlo's entire persona is built around the arts. Fortunately, he's a fraud, so you only have to sound acceptable."

Dana turned the music off anyway. "Whatever," she grumbled.

"Come on. While you aren't one for academics, you must try."

"It's not the studying that bothers me. Or even that opera crap. It's all these books," she finally divulged with a gesture to the piles of reference books on various surfaces. "They remind me of Alex."

Monty looked at the research pile in a different light. "I'm terribly sorry."

"He was always talking about this stuff," Dana recalled. "One painter is famous for this ... another for that ... blah, blah, blah. I pretended I understood." She flipped a page in one of the art books and did a double take at a watercolor of two buxom female nude figures embracing in a pond. "Hey, I know this one. I could never get Alex to shut up about him. Vecchioni, right?"

"Yes," Monty confirmed. "Bernardo Vecchioni."

"He paints naked bimbos."

Monty smiled like a schoolteacher correcting a child. "Vecchioni is a modern master of the classic nude. His most recent work commanded two hundred fifty thousand dollars at auction."

"Where I come from, he's a perv," Dana replied, pointing to a rather graphic painting on the next page. "Check out the muff on this one."

Monty studied her skeptically. "I don't see you, of all people, taking offense at nudity," she observed as she closed the book.

"And I don't see you not being turned off by pictures of chicks doing each other," Dana countered.

Monty did not take the bait for an argument, however, and Dana realized it was time to talk frankly. For once she did not resist.

"It's the whole art thing. I only went along with it because it made me feel like I was something more to Alex than I really was. A willing piece of tail."

"You're worth a lot more than that," Monty disagreed.

"Sorry, kid, but the truth's out," Dana refuted. "You teamed up with a loser."

"Why, because you have feelings?"

"No, because I'm full of shit."

Monty looked at her supportively. "Would you like a laxative?"

Dana reacted, only to find her smiling. "Good one," she acknowledged, appreciating Monty's jest.

"Now maybe you'd care to explain why you're so down on yourself all of a sudden?"

"It's not all that new," said Dana. "I just didn't want you to know about it."

"But why? I bared my soul to you."

"Okay, okay," she replied, setting her usual defensiveness aside. "The thing is, at first I lied to myself that he was just a hot guy on the rebound from a bad marriage and the weekends in Laguna were all I was in it for." She took a long pull from a bottle of beer before continuing. "I thought nothing like this could happen to me, ya know? But he made me feel so special ... and that Aussie accent, forget about it. That was my kryptonite. That damn accent!"

"I felt the same about Giancarlo's," Monty concurred.

Dana paused before continuing. "For the first time in my life I really opened myself up to somebody. I'm such a dumbass."

Monty put a hand on her arm, consoling. "That isn't true."

"Sure, it is," she came back. "I was just a booty call to him, not a for-real."

"As I recently learned for myself, those distinctions are not always readily apparent," Monty confided. "Dana, I know this is hard, but you'll get through this. We will. Together."

Dana's jaw dropped. "Well, I'll be damned—who woulda thunk it? Here you are telling me to keep it together. Of all people. Thank you."

But instead of a characteristically gracious response, Monty's body language hardened. "Yeah, yeah," she growled, mimicking Dana in one of her less-than-tolerant moods. "So, ya wanna put on your big-girl pants and get back to work here, or what?!"

"If I was gay, I'd kiss you right now," Dana told her with a grin.

"And if I were gay, I'd let you," Monty returned with a grin of her own.

Chapter Twenty-Five
In Case You're Not Paying Attention

In the *Buona Fortuna* Casino outside the city limits, Giancarlo was frazzled as he frantically played one losing hand of *Punto Blanco / Baccarat* after another when the two skinhead thugs, The Enforcer and Ice Pick, unexpectedly appeared on either side of him.

He jumped out of his chair at the sight of them. "Please don't hurt me!" he squealed.

"We won't," stated Ice Pick. "At least, not here."

"Come with us," added The Enforcer.

Giancarlo shot a helpless look at the casino dealer, who knew to turn away without comment as the skinheads escorted their trembling prey from the table.

"Giancarlo, why are you wasting your money when you owe us 21,260.50 euro?" The Enforcer wondered as they walked.

"I'm trying to win what I owe you," Giancarlo stressed.

The Enforcer looked at him dubiously. "When was the last time you slept?"

"Two days ago," he answered sheepishly. "I haven't left the table."

"You need a more productive plan," The Enforcer threatened. "We came to tell you that you have one week to pay us—at twice the original amount."

"That's two times 21,260.50," Ice Pick added, "in case you're not paying attention."

Giancarlo gasped. "What?! But who could get that much money so fast?!"

"Then take another week," The Enforcer advised. "At four times the original amount."

"Four times 21,260.50," Ice Pick reminded him. "I hope you have a calculator app on your phone."

"Oh, my God!" was all Giancarlo could spit out as panic grabbed him like a vise around the chest.

The Enforcer stepped into his face, going nose to nose with him. His voice was low and menacing. "And if you fail to pay us then, the following week your debt will be eight times the original amount."

"Do you see the pattern?" Ice Pick asked with a grim smile. "The total doubles every week from now on."

"But that's an impossibility!" Giancarlo protested.

"How unfortunate for you," confirmed The Enforcer.

Giancarlo's eyes were filled with terror. He had no idea how he was going to dig himself out of this mess. None.

Chapter Twenty-Six
Ready As I'll Ever Be

Dana was completely transformed, as she sat alone in the café near Giancarlo's apartment. She was now impressively dressed and accessorized with an expensive diamond necklace and matching bracelet. And she wore the long blonde wig that made her look a lot like Monty.

She was practicing sipping cappuccino with an extended pinky finger when her phone rang. "Stud Magnets R Us," she answered sardonically.

"Very funny," Monty retorted from her hotel dressing room, where she was assiduously giving herself a glamorous Cherie makeover. "Are you ready?"

"Ready as I'll ever be, I guess."

But there was an uneasiness in Dana's voice. "I know you can do this," Monty assured her. "You know everything about art that you need to dupe him."

"Thanks," responded Dana. "Your crash course was pretty great. I shoulda sat next to you in school to copy your test answers."

Monty humored her. "You were a good student once you started listening to me."

"I know, I know," Dana affirmed, hoping to mask her insecurities. "By the way, I hafta tell you that the hotel you put me in is off the charts amazing!" she added. "Remind me to use you as my travel agent from now on."

"Let's hope it impresses Giancarlo."

"What's not to impress?" Dana came back. "I'm just glad I'm not paying for it."

"It's the least I could do ...." Monty said before trailing.

Dana heard the hesitation in her voice and could tell that something was being left unsaid. "What?"

After a long silence, Monty fretfully completed her thought. "I just wanted to remind you that he's an extremely crafty man."

Dana snorted, "Monty, this ain't my first rodeo. I'm not falling for his horse shit." But just then she saw Giancarlo approaching the café from his apartment building. "Okay—here he comes. Time to throw it down."

"Good luck," Monty offered.

"He's gonna need it!" Dana promised as she ended the call. Then, after checking her wig, she opened her sketch pad and unobtrusively watched Giancarlo speak to a waiter, obviously asking about the nice-looking woman sitting alone.

He could tell that she had money, which was of critical importance to him at the moment. He took a deep breath and headed in her direction. And as he approached, his anxious demeanor was replaced by a veneer of supreme self-assurance.

A moment later Dana looked up and drew in a short breath. The way Giancarlo carried himself radiated masculinity and his easy casual style was nothing less than magnetic. When he turned it on, people were inexorably drawn to him; a trait that he had honed to perfection over many years.

And he sure was turning it on now.

Her eyes scanned his custom tapered shirt and snug pants, which he filled out notably well. *The man was sexy. Really, really sexy.*

"*Buon giorno, Signora. La disturbo?*" he opened with a solicitous smile.

Dana blushed a little, as a schoolgirl might upon meeting a cute boy on the playground. But it did not require any particular acting skill on her part. Her face was turning a rainbow of colors all by itself. "Pardon me?" she said, mimicking Monty as much as possible. "Gosh, I'm sorry. I don't speak Italian."

"That is a surprise," he replied in English, pointing to her sketch pad. "From your style of drawing I thought you to be *Italiani*. You are influenced by Loprieno, yes?"

She tried to not react to his spellbinding dark eyes. The man had bigtime presence, no question about it. He filled the crowded room with charisma, yet persuasively made Dana feel that she was the only person there. And that she was the most fascinating woman he had ever met. "I ... don't believe I know him," she professed.

"Gianni Loprieno, a most talented man," he continued. "There is much similarity in your work. May I please sit?"

She fluttered her eyes and stroked her wig on one side the way Monty often did. "I'm not waiting for anybody."

He accepted the seat and turned her sketch pad to face him. "The statement of shadows and light, it is powerful."

"Hey, thanks," she reflexively replied before quickly adjusting her grammar. "Thank you."

Giancarlo resumed, "Technique very much speaks of the artist and this tells me that she is quite beautiful." He nailed her with his most heartfelt look. "Of course, I could see it also with my eyes."

"Thank you again, Mister—"

"Forgive me. My name is Giancarlo," he said with his patented predatory charm.

Good God, this man was something else! Someone as inexperienced as Monty didn't stand a chance with this guy, she thought. "Dana," she heard herself answer. She extended her hand to shake, but he kissed it instead.

"Sono incantato," he sighed. "That means *I am enchanted* in my language. "You are studying art at the institute in Rome?"

Once again, she allowed herself to blush just like Monty would. But with this guy that was not difficult. Her physical reaction to him was entirely visceral. "Goodness no, I'm on holiday," she demurred. "As for my drawing, you flatter me. That's just a hobby."

"One more time I am surprised," he proclaimed. "You have very much talent."

Dana hesitated shyly. "And once again I find myself saying thank you."

"If I may ask, how can such a gift not be your life's work?"

"My family believes that success in financial matters is everything, if you know what I mean," she complained. "A career in the arts would never be allowed."

Giancarlo frowned. "I do not believe that I like this family."

"You aren't the only one," she confided.

"Are they also in Rome? I will tell them how wrong they are."

Dana answered quietly, "No, I'm alone."

He looked at her hopefully. "That is good, *si?*"

"It seems to be working out," she said, nailing him with a flirtatious glint in her eyes.

Inside Giancarlo's apartment Dana struggled to project awe as she studied the artwork on his walls, even though it was the same mass-produced garbage that she and Monty saw on the factory assembly line. She showed special interest in a clone of the painting that was on display at the *Piazza Navona.*

"Giancarlo, this one is terrific!" she hailed. "You are so talented!"

He met her look. "I am pleased that you like it, Dana."

"Like it?!" she enthused. "I adore it. I must own this for my Malibu beach house! How much do you want for it?"

He turned away, affecting his best deep emotional reaction. "I could never part with *Orphan Boy,*" he explained. "You see, it is from my childhood."

It was all Dana could do not to laugh out loud, but she repressed it. *What a jerk-off!* "Oh, Giancarlo, you poor man! You were an orphan?" she asked as innocently as she could without vomiting.

He turned to face her again. Astoundingly, while her attention was fixed elsewhere, he had somehow managed to summon big crocodile tears! "Yes, I was," he replied softly. "Thanks to the nuns at the orphanage, this was not so bad. They treated me very well. And today my artworks they are my family."

She continued to fake admiration for the work. "Your use of texture and space is quite wonderful."

"*Grazie,*" he said. Just then, a tear traveled down his cheek. "The lines they symbolize my breaking heart as a young child."

Dana stifled the choice profanities that were rising in her throat. She did what she could to compose herself as she moved around the apartment. "Just look at these incredible paintings!" she beamed. "How could you have ever liked my dumb little drawings?"

He followed her to the grouping that she was talking about. "What is not to like?" he asked.

"They're so unsophisticated, compared to yours," she answered as she faced him again. "And my paintings, well, forget it."

A gleam appeared in Giancarlo's eyes as he inched closer. She was providing him with the ideal opening to win her trust and get closer to her money. "You did not say that you paint also."

She did her best impression of Monty's modesty. "Well, if you wanna—want to—call it that," she admitted with hesitation.

He inched closer and his magnetic pull was mesmerizing, as strong as any man Dana had ever met. "I am intrigued," he told her in a near-whisper. "What medium do you like?"

Dana was rattled by the question. *Medium? What the hell's that?* Her mind churned for a clue, but then she remembered what Monty taught her: *he was a fraud and probably knew less about art than she did.* "Oh, I pretty much like it all," she stated.

Giancarlo grinned in a way that was all his own. It was not so much a grin as a masculine assurance that he understood things about her he could not possibly know. Intimate and electrifying things. "A woman who is free," he said, sizing her up. "I find that exciting."

Their eyes locked and the sexual tension between them could be cut with a palette knife. Even by a man who did not know how to use one. His personal charm was undeniable, and his eyes were like bottomless wells. He inexplicably projected manliness, sincerity, and spiritual calm all at once.

"Why don't you meet me at my hotel later and I'll show them to you," she offered.

The *Parco dei Principi* Grand Hotel is regarded as one of the finest hotels in the world, and the Royal Suite that Monty booked for Dana was appropriately extravagant for the wealthy artist she was posing to be. The sophisticated draperies and expensive vintage furniture were accented by lush wood and Italian marble touches everywhere.

And it all smelled of money. Lots and lots of it.

While Dana adjusted her wig and make-up in a mirror, Monty was busy inserting mattes in the frames of four paintings to cover the artist signatures. The hotel gallery had not only proved to be convenient, but it had a nice selection of artwork for sale.

"What if he asks me how I made those?" Dana asked. "I already shot the wad with him on what I know about art."

Monty smiled patiently. "Tell him you prefer working in watercolor but recently tried your hand at oil paint," she told her. "That one is oil, and the rest are watercolors."

"Okay … oil … watercolors," Dana repeated. "Why's one better than the other?"

"It's not better. Watercolor is popular because it is versatile and inexpensive," Monty explained. "The paint trays are easy to work with and the vibrancy of liquid watercolors is an advantage."

"How the hell am I supposed to remember all that?!"

"Then just tell him you like it because it's cheap and portable."

Dana nodded hesitantly as Monty checked her watch. "He'll be here anytime, so I should leave," Monty announced, heading for the door.

"Do you really think I can pull this off?" Dana called out.

Monty stopped. "Dana, your beauty and wealth are more than enough to lure him in. Artistic talent is just icing on the cake."

When Giancarlo arrived, he methodically evaluated Dana's paintings, which had been placed on various surfaces. The fact that the work was light-years better than his bulk junk was a revelation. *Not only did this woman have money, but her paintings had value he could exploit!*

He was so excited that he never even noticed the panoramic views of Rome, *Villa Borghese* Park, or dome of St. Peter's that her accommodations had to offer.

"Promising," he mumbled as he pretended to assess Dana's talent. "Absolutely, most promising."

Dana had to repress her amusement. "Do you really think so?" she asked innocently. "I'm honored that an artist of your experience would say that."

"And you created all of these during your visit?" he wondered.

Dana smiled at the chance to fortify the story of her wealth. "The oil was. The watercolors are from Madrid and Amsterdam."

He was duly absorbed by the body of work. "You have had a most productive holiday!"

"Anything to be away from my parents."

Nodding thoughtfully, he tried to estimate how much of his gambling debts the paintings might cover.

"You have framed them excellently, as well."

"Oh, I was just getting them ready to ship home."

Then he stopped at the last canvas, an enchanting still life done in oil. He tried to hide his excitement.

"That's my newest," Dana told him as she moved to his side.

Giancarlo flashed a smile. "Let us enjoy it in the proper light, 'eh?" he said as he picked it up and carried it to the open terrace doors.

But Dana was jolted to see a gallery SOLD tag hanging from the back. "WAIT!"

"Not to worry," he told her. "I will treat your baby as my own."

Thinking fast, she grabbed the gilded frame and stuffed the tag in her sweater as she pretended to hold the painting in the air for him. "Art should be seen at the right height, don't you think?"

"Not when it hides the divine face of the artist," he said as he lowered the artwork and leaned in for a kiss. His lips graced hers with such tenderness that she was left breathless.

Dana leaned against the couch for stability. *Holy shit!*

"Forgive me, Dana," he whispered. "I could not help myself."

"No problem," she answered weakly as she tried to calculate how she was going to stay out of bed with him. The man clearly knew what he was doing when it came to women.

Chapter Twenty-Seven
Enchantée

Two miles south of the *Parco dei Principi* Alex Connelly and Greg Lange emerged from the lobby of the Raphael Hotel. "Where the hell's that driver?!" Connelly complained.

Lange glanced up the narrow street from the courtyard. "Maybe he got hung up in traffic."

Connelly knew that, of course, but his nerves over the pending deal with the crime syndicate were getting the best of him. Usually he was unruffled, but now he was swimming in unfamiliar waters, and he did not like the feeling. "These fucking Italians," was his perfunctory retort.

"It'll be fine, Alex," Lange suggested. "You were the one who told me to expect anything."

Connelly shot him a resentful look. "I don't know why he wants another meeting. I already signed an agreement."

"He's just being cautious," Lange explained. "I think you have to trust his judgment on how to handle his partners."

"I've already had two job interviews," Connelly warned. "This is the last time."

Just then a white Aston Martin Vanquish convertible zoomed past them and stopped outside the Raphael's walled patio on *Via di Tor Sanguigna*. But it was not the shining $300,000 car that caught Connelly's eye, it was the arresting woman driving it: Monty.

She was beyond gorgeous.

Connelly gaped, "My God, look at her!"

Then he saw them. Monty's legs. Miles and miles of them, smoothly swinging from the car. As she stood, she fired a look at him. It was knife-like and blunt. Heart-stopping. And with her clinging leather miniskirt, sheer blouse, tanned skin, hot European fashion model make-up, cute short haircut, and new ankle tattoo she was a most enticing package.

She tossed her keys to the valet and sauntered away from the Aston Martin, making sure to move her hips slowly back and forth exactly as Dana taught her. It was a hypnotic sight, as if she had just stepped directly off the cover of *Cosmopolitan* magazine.

Connelly did not stand a chance. "That's the most incredible sheila I've ever seen!" he uttered to Lange as she passed them.

Lange nodded his own stupefied concurrence.

As Monty arrived at the corner sidewalk *trattoria*, Alfredo, the owner of the establishment that Monty and Dana destroyed in the fight, was adjusting Monty's new Nikon DSLR on a tripod near the softbox lights. It certainly looked like a professional photography set-up.

Alfredo's wife Isabella, a hard-working woman who had been somewhat worn down by a life of almost continuous toil, sat Monty in a canvas director's chair and brushed her cheeks with make-up. To complete the charade, Alfredo made a big show of using the light meter hanging from a strap around his neck, though he had no idea how to use it.

Monty stole a glimpse of Connelly who was intently watching from the courtyard and took a deep breath. Retribution was an entirely foreign concept for her. Her upbringing had always mandated a poised "turn the other cheek" response to every slight. But now the possibility of retribution was at hand and it was exciting.

And so was the sight of Connelly scrutinizing her. He was far more dashing than she had anticipated. *No wonder Dana succumbed so easily to his advances,* she thought.

"Alfredo," she babbled excitedly, "I'll pay you an additional five hundred euro if this works."

Alfredo threw her a grateful look. "For that much money, Isabella and I will be magnificent, *Signora*," he swore as he touched her arm. Then he beckoned loudly and gestured wildly, "*Siamo pronti!* It is time to work."

"I have not finished my make-up," Monty announced dismissively in a thick French accent.

Alfredo theatrically raised his voice and the energy behind his arm gestures. "I cannot be bothered with your vanity when I am losing my light!"

In turn, Monty matched his volume just as their script prescribed. "It is not your photograph going on the magazine cover, either!"

"What photograph?! I have not taken one yet!" he snarled.

"And if you keep badgering me, you never will!" she threatened.

Alfredo threw his hands in the air in mock-antipathy and turned to Connelly, who had drifted closer to eavesdrop on the exchange. "When will I learn my lesson, eh? French models, they are all spoiled children!"

For the next half hour, Monty gave the fake photo session— and Connelly's attentive gaze—all that she had. The tutoring that Dana had provided proved remarkably effective as she preened for the camera, casting a smoldering look over her shoulder for one shot, twisting her body with her hands on her hips for another, and leaning pensively against a scarred stucco wall for another.

A large group of tourists and *trattoria* patrons gathered to watch. But no one soaked in every moment of the scene more than Connelly, who could not help conjuring an array of fantasies about the dazzling model, about kissing her, and looking deeply into her bedroom eyes as he made love to her.

Greg Lange intruded on the moment by tapping him on the shoulder. "Alex, the car is here."

However, Connelly was not about to turn away from this. "He can wait."

"DeLuca isn't going to like that," Lange pointed out, nervously casting a look at the intimidating Beppe Caruso waiting by the luxury sedan.

Connelly spun to face him. "Well, he can wait, too!"

At a pause in the photo session, Alfredo fussed with one of the lights while Monty rested under a *Campari* umbrella at one of the restaurant's outdoor tables. Connelly saw his chance and moved in for the kill. "Excuse me ...." he opened to Monty.

She eyed him playfully. "From what do you wish to be excused?"

"From intruding on your work to introduce myself," he explained. "I couldn't help admiring you."

Dana was right. His Australian accent was captivating, as was his muscular build. And Monty immediately recognized what she knew from life in Darien, Connecticut: the look of money. *This man had it all,* she thought.

Doing her best to push those observations from her mind, she forced herself back into character as she stood to face him and coyly eyed his wedding ring. "And your wife, she also admires me?"

Good Lord, she was stunning! Connelly worked hard to appear casual while privately cursing himself for forgetting to take the ring off earlier. "My wife passed away," he quietly explained. "I know I should stop wearing her ring, but I guess I'm sentimental."

"That is sweet," she commented.

"My name is Alex," he told her, offering his hand.

"Cherie," she answered as she accepted it, holding it a second or two longer than necessary.

"It's nice to meet you, Cherie."

"*Enchantée.*"

"Will you be in Rome long?" he hopefully inquired.

She scoffed with just the right amount of diva melodrama. "At the speed Alfredo works, perhaps forever," she griped.

Just then Alfredo called from his camera position twenty feet away. "We will finish the series now!"

"Do not treat me like a servant!" she yelled back.

As before, Alfredo threw his hands into the air in exasperation. "Work is always the same with you! A nightmare!" he roared loudly.

Monty turned to Connelly and shrugged, "*C'est la vie.* I must go now, Alex."

She turned to leave but he touched her arm, stopping her. "Are you free to join me for dinner?"

"Oh, I think not," she replied simply.

"But you were enjoying our conversation, weren't you?"

Monty smiled coquettishly and it nearly melted him right out of his Bolvaint loafers. "*Oui,* but I am thinking that conversation is not what you wish to enjoy with me."

Then as she turned once again to leave, she firmly grabbed his butt just like Dana taught her. *"Au revoir."*

Alfredo resumed snapping away with his camera. Monty did the best she could to continue imitating what models do; tossing her head, shoulders, and hips into poses just like an experienced cover girl.

A minute later Lange glided up behind Alfredo. "Can I have a word?"

"*Mi dispiace,* but I am working."

"So am I," Lange clarified while thrusting a wad of bills in his direction.

Alfredo eyed the money, and his face registered his pleasure. "You may have as many words as you would like, *Signor.*"

Meanwhile, it was Monty's turn to pretend to be put out by a delay in the photo session. "I thought you were in a hurry to finish the series, Alfredo!"

"Have Isabella do something about your cheeks first!" he roared back. "You look like a circus clown!"

Lange reacted to his comment with surprise. *Circus clown? He had never seen a more desirable woman in his life!*

Fifteen minutes later, while Connelly and Lange were riding in the back seat of DeLuca's car, Connelly examined Monty's eye-filling Cherie website on his iPad. She was more than convincing as an international fashion model. She was fully incandescent.

"Just take a gander at her, mate ... my God, she's a bewdy bottler!"

"According to the photographer, she's as driven as she is lovely," Lange reported. "To get her attention you'd have to do something really big for her career."

"No problem. I'll find a way," Connelly avowed.

"That's what Leonardo DiCaprio thought," added Lange. "She dumped him when he didn't come through for her in Hollywood."

Connelly considered the information, his curiosity piqued. This was a challenge worth the effort and one he was very much looking forward to. "Well, this time she's met her match," he vowed. He was not about to let some privileged Hollywood star's failure dissuade him. No way. *Besides, if she dated DiCaprio then older men were not off-limits!*

He flipped through several more of Cherie's photos and then stopped. As if increased motivation were necessary, the last one was a sensuous shot of Monty looking directly at him and begging him to go for it.

Chapter Twenty-Eight
It Keeps Me Out Of Prison

Beppe Caruso pulled into the circle driveway of a five-story mansion in the exclusive *Monte Gianicolo* area of Rome. A dour Tazio Citrano was there as Connelly and Lange exited the vehicle.

"You are late, *Signor* Connelly," Citrano complained.

"Your driver was delayed," explained Connelly.

"This will be the last time that you keep *Signor* DeLuca waiting."

Connelly had overstepped his role, and it was time to back off his usual assertive attitude. "Understood," he answered respectfully.

"He is waiting for you in the garden."

Connelly had seen some impressive homes in his life, including his own 9,000 square foot estate in the Rivas Canyon section of Pacific Palisades in Los Angeles, but the 30-million-euro palace that engulfed Greg Lange and him as they walked to the rear gardens was without question one of the finest. More than three times the size of his home and opulent in every regard, it said everything that anyone might want to know about Augusto DeLuca's power, influence, and wealth.

Lange reacted to their surroundings nervously as their footsteps echoed in the majestic marble hallway. "Citrano did not look very happy," he whispered to his boss.

"He'll get over it," Connelly advised.

"I hope so," Lange remarked.

They found DeLuca calmly sipping cappuccino in the shade of a large ivy-covered pergola.

"G'day, *Signor*. I apologize for keeping you waiting," Connelly began.

DeLuca cast a raised eyebrow behind the thick frame of his sunglasses. "I trust that the attractive model outside your hotel was worth offending me for."

"No offense was intended," Connelly replied. "For what it's worth, she's the most beautiful woman I've ever met." He opened his iPad and showed him Cherie's Facebook page.

DeLuca smiled. "Ah, yes. In my youth I prized such things very much," he remarked with a trace of wistfulness. "Those days are over for me, but you are still young. I wish you good luck with her."

"Thank you very much. As you can see, she's a worthy challenge."

DeLuca turned on a loud white noise generator that was sitting on the table and gestured for them to have a seat. "Forgive the unpleasant sound, but it seems that the *polizia* are always interested in hearing what I have to say."

Connelly nodded. "You are a wise man to be cautious."

"It keeps me out of prison," DeLuca replied. "I wanted to tell you that my associates have approved our arrangement, but they do have one question."

"What's that?" Connelly asked.

"They want to know what will happen to our investment if problems arise with customs officials and the jets you have leased with our money are seized."

"No worries there," Connelly promised with confidence. "That won't happen."

"How can you be so certain?"

"Because I've been in import-export a long time and I know how to treat government officials right when I have to."

Greg Lange added, "We have key people in place at every international airport and their police agencies."

"And they are well compensated," Connelly finished.

DeLuca nodded approvingly. "I will pass along what you have said to my associates."

Chapter Twenty-Nine
He Only Paints Nudes

In the upper chapel of the *Basilica dei Santi Cosma e Damiano*, which incorporates original buildings of the Roman Forum between *Monte Palatino* and *Monte Capitolino*, Giancarlo and Dana were viewing the many paintings that covered the walls and ceiling. Giancarlo seemed particularly enthralled by the face of an infant angel in a massive virtuosic fresco.

"She is so innocent, yes?" he pondered.

"Angels usually are," Dana answered as she stroked the long strands of her wig.

Then when he turned to look at her it was impossible to not look back. "I believed that innocence was for heaven only, but then I met you," he submitted softly.

Dana blushed. She wished she were pretending, but she was learning that such emotions came naturally when she was around this man. "I'm not as innocent as you think," she confessed.

"The truth is in your art," he vowed.

"No one has ever seen that in my work before."

"Then they are fools."

Once again, she was drawn to him despite what she knew to be the realities of the situation. "They are?" she asked.

He inched closer. "Leonardo da Vinci said, "Where the spirit does not work with the hand there is no art"," he described as he took her hands in his. "And if I may say it, your hands are lovely."

"You seem to know a lot about art," she answered, flicking her puppy eyes in his direction. "And me."

He held her gaze carefully, as if caressing her face. "I hope that you will forgive me for this declaration, Dana, but I had given up my hope of meeting a woman like you. Until now."

He was extremely close now, and Dana again found herself flushed. "Well ... I'm flattered, but you don't know anything about me."

"Some things a man knows without asking," he replied. "The others he will learn when she is ready," he assured her as he kissed her hand. "I think that time will be soon."

Dana swallowed hard. *Monty was way, way out of her league with this guy!* "Giancarlo," she faltered, "this's moving awfully fast."

"Much faster than I ever thought to be possible," he concurred.

With that, they kissed. This time it was not gentle, either. It was highly charged, and contrary to her best intentions, it was even better than Dana thought it would be.

That evening the lights were low as Monty and Dana were relaxing in Monty's living room with glasses of wine in hand. "Dana," Monty wondered, "what do you suppose it is that drives some men to be as deceitful as Giancarlo and Alex?"

"I bet a lotta chicks want the answer to that one!" replied Dana.

"I'm serious," Monty corrected. "On one hand, Alex is a successful married man who should not have a care in the world."

"And yet he wants more," Dana griped. "What can I say, the guy's a pig."

"That might be giving pigs a bad name," noted Monty.

Dana smiled in appreciation. "Then maybe there really are sex addicts in the world," she offered. "I used to think it was all New Age crap when some guy said he couldn't keep it in his pants."

"I doubt this has anything to do with sex," Monty countered. "For a man like Alex it's probably more about power and control."

"He does like to be in charge," Dana remarked as she finished her glass and poured more for both of them. "So, what's Giancarlo's deal?" she asked. "He's all about the money, right?"

"Sex has a lot to do with it, too," said Monty.

Dana flashed to the impact that Giancarlo's kiss had on her and tried not to imagine the details of Monty's romantic experiences with him.

When she saw Dana's reaction, Monty felt the need to clarify her point. "On that count our relationship was quite remarkable."

Fortunately, her cell phone rang to interrupt them, and Dana grinned at seeing it was the toll-free line. "Holy shit, Monty—it's Alex!"

Monty quickly adjusted positions on the couch to watch as Dana sat up straight, cleared her throat, and answered in a pinched Southern drawl. "This is Ashley Ebert," she announced, remembering to put the phone on speaker. She may have sounded more like a clichéd character on the *Southern Charm* television series than intended, but it was an effective vocal disguise.

At the other end of the call was Alex Connelly, who was alone in his hotel suite. His laptop was open to Cherie's Facebook page that said: *For information contact Ashley Ebert at Euro Models International 1-800-555-2424.*

"Ms. Ebert, this's Alex Connelly. From Connelly Industries in Los Angeles," he started. "I wanted to inquire about one of your models. Cherie."

Dana winked at Monty. "Our newest star. She is exceptional, isn't she?"

"She certainly is," he remarked. "I happen to be in Rome at the moment and had the chance to meet her during one of her photo shoots. I think she's perfect for a campaign I'm planning."

Dana sneered. "Oh, Cherie won't have openings for at least a year. But maybe we can talk about one of my other girls."

"No, she's the one I want," he stipulated.

"I understand, Mister Connelly, but unfortunately there's nothing—"

"Money's no object."

Dana stopped as his determination sunk in. "I see ..." she replied with a smile and a thumbs-up to Monty. "What did you have in mind?"

"Something she's always wanted to do but hasn't yet."

"Oh, believe me, there's nothing that Cherie hasn't done," she told him while pantomiming a playful pelvic movement for Monty's benefit.

Monty scowled and hit her in the arm with a decorative pillow.

"There must be something," Connelly continued. "Tell me what it is, and I'll make it happen."

"Hold on, please," Dana said, muting the phone.

Monty was on the edge of her seat. "Oh, my God, Dana. What are you going to tell him?"

"Working on it," Dana told her. Then, thinking fast, she picked up an art book from the coffee table and resumed the call. "Sorry to make you wait, Mister Connelly," she resumed as she flipped to a page featuring graphic paintings of nude women. And there was mischief in her eyes, which Monty read with alarm. "There is one thing that might get her attention—Cherie has always wanted to work with the great Vecchioni."

"That's an absolute ripper!" he said, his interest piqued. "I'll see what I can do."

"I'll be waiting," Dana said, hanging up as she collapsed against the couch. "I can't believe he didn't know it was me!"

Monty was beyond incredulous. "And I can't believe you did that!"

"Did what?"

"Vecchioni, "the perv"!" she protested. "He only paints nudes, in case you've forgotten."

"I had to tell him something," Dana came back. "Besides, ya primed the pump and now we take him to school. Gimme five."

She held her hand out and Monty looked at it blankly. "What?"

"Gimme five," Dana repeated. "You know, with your hand. You slap mine."

"I know what it is. The question is why would I do it?"

"Because we're crushing this, that's why. Gimme five!" Dana insisted.

But Monty was having none of it. "Well, "priming the pump", as you put it, wasn't very difficult, considering what you dressed me in today," she declared. "It's worth three at best."

Monty held out three fingers, but Dana was losing patience. "What are you doing? Nobody gives three," she growled.

"Then, what good is this tradition if everything has the same value?"

With that, Dana decided she was having none of it. "I'll tell you what ... why don't we just make it one and call it even?"

Dana prominently held up her middle finger on the way to the bathroom. Before Monty could respond to the insult, the room telephone jingled.

When Monty stepped off the hotel elevator a few minutes later, she quickly located Sergeant Fazio waiting in the small lobby. But unlike his previous neglected appearance, his uniform was now cleaned and pressed, and his hair and mustache were trimmed to uncover the nice-looking man that he really was.

"Sergeant Fazio, don't you look handsome this evening!" she observed.

He smiled sheepishly. "*Grazie.* As do you," he responded before quickly correcting himself. "No, that is wrong ... in America you do not say a woman is handsome, do you? I am so sorry. Sometimes my English is not as good as I would like."

"Please don't give it a second thought," Monty said while touching his arm. "What Italian word would you have used instead?"

Fazio looked at his feet bashfully. "I would have used two words. *Estremamente bella.* That means, extremely beautiful," he told her as his eyes met hers. "I like your new hairstyle very much."

It took Monty a second to remember that Fazio had not seen her since her make over. "You can thank Dana for this," she explained. "She talked me into it."

"Well, it is very becoming," he reiterated. "Miss Zimmer will not be joining us?" he asked.

"I'm sorry," she answered. "I misunderstood your message. Should I call her?"

"No, no," he told her. "Perhaps you will instead tell her the news that I have brought?"

"Of course," Monty replied.

Fazio gestured to a seat with his unlit cigarette and she sat, crossing her legs in such a way that the shapely tanned leg protruding from the long slit in her skirt was impossible to ignore. He sunk into a too-deep couch cushion that made simple stability a challenge. It was like sitting on a rubber raft in turbulent water. Then, regaining his balance with as much composure as he could muster, he smiled nervously. The fact is, there are not many heterosexual men who would have been anything *but* nervous in her presence.

He finally composed himself. "First, I promised *Capitaine* Chouinard in Saint-Tropez that I would give you his regards," he began. "He was happy to learn that you are doing well."

"How kind of him," she said with a smile. "Thank you for telling me, Sergeant."

"Of course," he replied. "And I must say how pleased I am to hear that you and Miss Zimmer are getting along so well."

Monty returned his smile, and she was luminous. "Surprising, isn't it? As it turns out, we have a lot in common, starting with our knack for picking the wrong men."

He was not sure how long he sat there trying to envision a circumstance where someone like Monty could not meet the right man, but eventually he asked, "Surely this is something that ladies such as yourselves can remedy, yes?"

"Picking the right man requires meeting him first," she replied. "I wouldn't even know where to begin."

Fazio gawked at her and nearly dropped his cigarette before summoning what was left of his professional demeanor. "*Signora*," he announced, "I have come to report that since your difficulties with the proprietor of *La Cucina di Isabella* have been satisfied, all charges against you have been dropped."

"That's wonderful, Sergeant!" she exclaimed with a kiss on his cheek. "Thank you so much for your help."

He could feel his face redden as he blushed. *God, she smelled good!* "It has been my pleasure," he told her as he handed her a manila envelope bearing the official seal of the National Police. "Your passports. I trust that you will contact me if I may be of further service?"

"Oh, definitely!" she enthused.

Fazio smiled hopefully in return.

Chapter Thirty
Ever's A Long Time

In a place where ancient ruins seem to exist on every street the remnants of the Roman Forum epitomize the city, highlighting the fact that the entire municipality is a gigantic archaeological treasure within a modern and unruly metropolis.

Across from the *Basilica dei Santi Cosma e Damiano,* where a day earlier Dana and Giancarlo shared a memorable kiss beneath the massive frescos, the crumbling pillars and headless statues of the House of the Vestal Virgins served as the backdrop for another one of Monty's fake photo shoots—a series of provocative swimsuit poses.

A large gallery of tourists watched from the avenue above the low-lying area as Alfredo once again pretended to be a photographer, and judging from the perpetual grin on his face, this assignment was more rewarding than the restaurant business ever was.

His wife sensed it, too, and smacked him upside the head.

"What was that for?!" he cried out.

"I have seen that look, Alfredo. A long time ago when it was meant for *me.*"

He immediately became rattled. "Isabella, my darling—"

"I'm sorry that I ever let you talk me into this!" she decreed. A defiant hand gesture drove the point home in case he was not paying attention. "Tomorrow the American tramp finds someone else to look at her perfect body."

Unseen by Monty, Alex Connelly arrived at a location thirty yards away accompanied by a strange-looking little man with a massive head that did not match his frail build. With his disquieting beady eyes and a few pointless strands of long hair greased onto a bald head, he resembled a cartoon character more than an actual person. He was the infamous painter of nude women, Bernardo Vecchioni.

"That's the girl, *Maestro*," Connelly said, respectfully using the Italian term for Master. "Her photos don't do her justice, do they."

Vecchioni expertly assessed her body with a narrow smirk and more than a little prurient interest. "Yes, I see. Supple breasts ... exquisite buttocks and thighs ... marvelous flat stomach ...." He continued the checklist privately as he muttered to himself. No wonder he dedicated his life to paintings of naked women making love to each other. There was something patently unsavory about this guy.

Meanwhile, Monty politely listened to Alfredo's marital grievances, which he aired after Isabella's earlier reprimand. "Isabella is jealous of any woman who talks to me," he complained. "Sometimes I do not understand what is wrong with her!"

"You poor man," she remarked with concern. "Should I speak with her?"

He shook his head. "Oh, no, no. That would not be wise," he confided. "You see, she believes you to be romantically interested in me."

The remark was upsetting for Monty to hear. "Oh, dear."

Alfredo nodded in appreciation of her compassion and then took his shot, hopefully. "You ... do not happen to be ... do you?"

Monty could not believe that anyone would think such a thing! "Don't be ridiculous," she reassured him. "We're friends."

He forced a polite smile to cover his disappointment. "Of course."

Just then Monty noticed Connelly approaching and adjusted her tiny bikini top. "Alex is back. How do I look?"

"Like the woman a man would leave his wife for, *Signora*," he hinted.

Like so many other things in Monty's life, the real meaning of what he was saying passed by her completely unnoticed.

Connelly arrived with Vecchioni a few minutes later. And the little man was not very subtle in his appreciation for Monty's attributes as he stared her up and down and back again. "G'day, Cherie," Connelly said. "Alex Connelly, do you remember?"

Monty smiled modestly. "The man who wants only to talk. I am sorry to not be dressed for it," she said with a sly wink.

Connelly felt oddly ill at ease in her presence but forced himself to recover. "I'd like you to meet a friend of mine," he announced proudly. "*Signor* Bernardo Vecchioni."

And now it was Monty's turn to almost die on the spot. "*THE* Vecchioni?" she asked almost forgetting to use a French accent. Her shock was genuine, as were her unnerved feelings, caused by the way that he was staring at her chest and licking his lips. Monty quickly realized that Vecchioni was the creep that Dana figured him to be from the beginning. "This ... is such an honor," she mumbled. "I have admired your work very much."

Vecchioni reached out to shake her hand, and his felt like damp 40-grit sandpaper. But what was even more disturbing was the fact that his eyes bore a strong resemblance to cold rat droppings. His gaze never moved from her cleavage.

Monty self-consciously folded her arms, but with a body like hers there was only so much to be hidden in a bikini that small.

"I own several of *Il Maestro's* works," Connelly remarked. "I purchased another today."

Monty forced herself to look at Connelly enthusiastically. "I am impressed," she managed to say.

"As am I," echoed Vecchioni. And as Monty turned to face him it was obvious that he was talking about her breasts.

Connelly continued, "*Il Maestro* has agreed to do a commissioned painting for me, if you will agree to pose for him."

Monty felt the earth disappear beneath her feet, but she refused to faint. "Well," she choked out, "it is the dream of every woman to pose ... *au naturel* ... for the great Vecchioni. *Oui?*"

La Cucina di Isabella was now partially restored, following the drunken fight that first brought Monty and Dana together. The tables and white linens had been replaced by industrial light walnut furniture with beveled edges and a dramatic reclaimed wood accent wall was under construction. Workers did their best to not let the presence of Monty and Dana sitting at the bar be distracting, but they were failing miserably.

Dana was not wearing the blonde wig, which would have been a liberating feeling under normal circumstances, but was now obliterated by Monty's update. "You're goin' naked for him?!" Dana screeched. "This's freakin' unbelievable!"

Monty shot her a disapproving look. "Keep your voice down. I'm not going naked for anyone."

"Right. A cheesy see-through nightie's so much better."

"It isn't naked," Monty insisted.

Dana sneered back. "It's pretty damn close."

"And it isn't for Alex," continued Monty. "It's for that deviant Bernardo Vecchioni. You were so right about him," she added as she shivered with repugnance.

"At least we agree on one thing."

Before the exchange could continue, Sergeant Fazio approached from where Alfredo had been showing him renovations. He quickly gave his breath a shot of peppermint breath spray en route. "*Signore,* the repairs look very nice, do they not?" he observed to Monty and Dana.

"Yes, they do, Sergeant," Monty agreed. "Alfredo is doing an excellent job."

"It is good to see this for myself," he confirmed while glancing around the room. But in fact, it was apparent that he felt extremely awkward around the women. Eventually he turned to them and tried to appear casual. "I am pleased to see that you are again welcome here, as well. *Signora* Lombardi, it was generous of you to lend Miss Zimmer the funds for her portion." He paused to gaze warmly at her. "It tells me that my feelings about you were not misplaced."

Monty cordially smiled. "Thank you, Sergeant. You're a dear."

When his eyes connected with Monty's, Fazio fumbled his unlit cigarette and accidentally dropped it in her wine glass.

Mortified, he shuffled off anxious to salvage what was left of his dignity. "Alfredo ..." he called across the room, "... such a marvelous fountain!"

Meanwhile, Monty fished for the cigarette with a fork and waited for Dana to resume her rant. But she got only brooding silence instead. "Enough icy stares, Dana. Vecchioni was your idea, not mine."

"Yeah, well, I didn't think Alex was really gonna show up with the guy."

"He's a very resourceful man."

"That's one way to put it," Dana groused.

Monty stopped. "What is that supposed to mean?"

"I've been there, okay?"

"I'm not sleeping with him, if that's what you're insinuating."

"Yet," Dana stated.

"Ever," Monty replied resolutely.

Dana paused. "Ever's a long time, kid."

And that was all Monty could take. "Alright, then," she stated firmly, "if it bothers you so much, let's call it off."

Dana was caught short.

"I mean it," Monty continued, reading her mystified reaction, "just say the word and our plan ends this instant."

"What?" she answered, still in disbelief.

"You heard me. Let's call this off right now."

"But you'd be giving up revenge on Giancarlo."

Monty did not care. She was determined to get things back on track with Dana. "Some things are more important to me. Like our friendship."

Dana was bewildered. "No shit ...?" she asked, not sure if she heard her correctly.

"Of course," Monty verified.

Dana took a while to digest that. She found herself being moved, which was an emotion she did not experience very often. "That's amazing," was all she could get out.

"Then, we're agreed?" Monty asked with an extended hand.

Staring at her friend, Dana had a sudden change of heart. "No way," she finally decided. "You were so absofuckinglutely right before, Monty." Then the intensity of her voice increased as she added enthusiastically, "Let's run the play. Let him see your tits!"

The construction workers abruptly stopped as the announcement resonated throughout the restaurant. Nobody in the establishment moved as the men leered at Monty—and Sergeant Fazio reacted with manifest discomfort.

Horrified, Monty smiled weakly at Alfredo's glowering wife behind the bar. "Check, please."

Chapter Thirty-One
No Guy Would

Monty stood in a lavish waterfall of glowing afternoon sunlight descending from the array of skylights in Bernardo Vecchioni's studio. The little man ogled her with peculiar, unnerving intensity, which felt almost as if he were actually touching her skin.

At first, she had to resist the urge to run from the chamber. But then, remembering how much Dana was counting on her, she summoned the courage to shed her robe. The negligee beneath it was exposed, along with much of the rest of her.

"You will lean against the table now," Vecchioni directed as he began to sketch her image. His gape grew impossibly wide as she arched her back. "Yes, yes ... just like that ... very nice ...." he uttered while savoring each stroke of his pencil and grunting under his breath.

Monty did what she could to ignore *Il Maestro's* exceedingly crude visual examination and concentrate instead on Alex Connelly, who was watching from the shadows across the room. She was pleasantly surprised to find that his attention was non-threatening, by comparison. He somehow used his eyes like arms holding her and, if anything, his intense gaze provided a calming influence. Much to her amazement, as the portrait session dragged on, she felt increasingly comfortable being scantily dressed in his presence.

Meanwhile, Dana was being wined and dined by Giancarlo at the intimate Michelin starred Aroma Restaurant. The spectacular rooftop views of the Roman Colosseum across the street from the *Palazzo Manfredi* venue took her breath away. The stone arches of the Colosseum glowed as the setting sun shined through them, and the sky was already beginning to shimmer with stars that would soon blanket the night.

Dana sipped her wine and drilled him with the bewitching sparkle in her eyes. "I'm having the most wonderful time, Giancarlo," she said. "Are you?"

"I am, as well," he replied. "I never want this evening to end."

"It's been perfect so far," she softly confirmed.

"More perfect than I have ever experienced," he said as he took her hands in his. "I do not want to ever feel anything other than what I feel with you right now," he continued.

"That's awfully nice to hear," she said. "Thank you."

"It is you who should be thanked," he replied. "You have restored my belief in love, Dana. I hope that you will not be shocked to know that I want to make you my wife."

That night in Monty's hotel bathroom she was removing her make-up as Dana looked on from the doorway with chilly silence.

"What's the matter with you?" asked Monty.

"What's the matter with YOU?" Dana returned.

Monty deliberately avoided making eye contact. "Why would you assume that anything was the matter with me?"

"For one thing, you forgot your eyelashes. Are you gonna sleep with those things on? They're the size of small animals."

Monty quickly grabbed her glue remover and a cotton swab. "Thank you for reminding me."

Dana continued to study her carefully. "So, how'd the painting go?"

"The painting? Oh, fine," Monty answered in a markedly non-committal tone.

"Meaning ...."

"Meaning that eventually I managed to forget where the little weasel Vecchioni's eyes were," Monty came back hesitantly. "He never blinks, did you know that?"

Dana waited for the rest of the story, but when nothing came, she continued, "What about Alex?"

Monty became preoccupied with searching for something in her make-up case. "Oh, I really didn't pay much attention," she remarked. "Modeling turns out to be surprisingly demanding ... I don't know how those women do it." She busied herself with her quest. "What in the world did I do with those tweezers?"

Dana saw that she was stalling, which she demonstrated by reaching into the box to easily retrieve the tweezers for Monty. "Come on, lady!" she challenged as she handed them over. "You're laying skid marks all over the floor. I know the guy, remember? What happened today?"

Monty set the tweezers aside and stopped to look at her friend in the mirror's reflection. "I'm not sure."

"Gimme a break, you're not sure."

"I mean it," Monty claimed, turning to face her. "We didn't even really speak that much. We just did an awful lot of ...."

Dana's shoulders slumped. "... looking at each other?" she said, finishing Monty's sentence.

"How did you know that?"

"Women's intuition," Dana curtly answered before leaving the room.

"Dana, you can put your mind at rest," Monty vowed as she followed her into the bedroom. "It was nothing more, I swear."

"It was enough."

But Monty could tell she was upset. "We didn't do anything," she attested. "Please believe me."

Dana plopped onto the bed in defeat. "I do," she told her.

"Then, what is your problem?"

Dana did not put her feelings into words right away. "It's weird that's all, knowing that look, remembering," she disclosed. "And let's face it, you're a freakin' smoke show."

"Dana—" Monty began.

But before she could complete her thought, Dana was heading for the door. "I should let you catch some Z's," she said over her shoulder.

Monty was not finished with the conversation, however. "You haven't told me about your date with Giancarlo," she reminded her.

"I'm fried," Dana said as she reached for the doorknob. "I'll fill you in tomorrow."

Unfortunately, Monty misinterpreted her evasion. "Oh, my God—did he force himself on you?!" she blurted.

"Don't get your thong in a wad," Dana replied as she turned to face her. "It wasn't like that."

"What, then?" demanded Monty. "Why are you avoiding telling me about this?"

Dana met her look and knew that there was no way to leave now. She slowly returned to the room. "Okay ... well ... the thing is, he asked me to marry him," she finally said.

"Dana!" Monty screeched.

"I didn't say yes."

"That's not what I mean—marriage!" Monty regurgitated as the reference triggered a flood of emotions within her. "At least he had the decency to wait a few weeks before proposing to me."

"Maybe he needs the bucks."

"Whatever for?" asked Monty. "He took thirty thousand and my wedding ring, not to mention what he stole from his former wives. Sergeant Fazio left a message that he has located six so far."

"Six wives?" Dana repeated, "Holy shit!" The information was intriguing as she returned to the bed. "For a sketchy guy running scams on so many women, his crib sure ain't much."

Monty sat beside her. "Then what could it be? Drugs?"

"His eyes are too clear for that," Dana came back. "Believe me, I know. One of my brothers did a stint in rehab." Then after thinking about it another idea came to her. "Gambling tabs?"

"Of course! He often spoke of his fondness for games of chance."

"There ya go, he's a casino hound."

Monty settled back against the pillows and they withdrew into their respective thoughts. Then she finally told Dana, "I must admit to being somewhat relieved."

"... that it's not really me he's after?" Dana finished.

Monty met her look. "You understand, don't you?"

"More than you know," Dana said.

Another silence passed, then Monty added what she knew Dana was waiting to hear. "You don't have anything to worry about with Alex and me, either."

"If you say so," was Dana's unconvincing comeback.

"So, what are you planning to do about Giancarlo?" Monty asked.

"I dunno," she answered. "If I let the engagement bit happen, he'll wanna jump start my battery."

"And if you say no, he'll leave."

"Alex won't wait long, either," Dana added. "Not after seeing you rocking that skank-wear today. No guy would."

Monty drifted into her thoughts. "He believes I'm his fantasy. I don't dare prove otherwise, or you'll never get your retribution."

The statement hung in the air.

Ultimately, Monty confessed, "You know, Dana, I'd be less than candid if I didn't say that I understand how you could become involved with Alex."

Dana flopped back against pillows of her own. "Yeah, well Giancarlo's pretty intense himself."

"So, here we are in their lives just as we planned ...."

"And they wanna go to pound town," complained Dana.

Monty reacted quizzically, "Where?"

"The bone-zone, Monty," Dana explained impatiently. "Schtoopville. Come on, work with me!"

Ugh! Message received.

"The question is, what're we gonna do about it?" Dana posed.

Monty thought about that, before asking, "Is there a pharmacy nearby?"

"What?"

"I've got an idea," she said. "Hand me my Italian phrase book, would you?"

At the small pharmacy around the corner from her hotel, Monty approached a female druggist. "Can you recommend a sleeping medication?" But when the woman reacted uncomprehendingly, Monty consulted a carefully prepared list of Italian phrases that she had in hand. *"Puo consigliare un farmaco per dormire?"* she asked haltingly.

"Ovviamente," the woman answered as she handed her a bottle from the shelf behind her. *"Eccone uno molto forte che é raccomandato."* But as Monty squinted at the Italian language label the woman added a word of caution in broken English, *"Solo uno* ... only one. Very strong."

Monty beamed happily. That was exactly what she was hoping to hear. *"Perfetto. Grazie mille!"*

Chapter Thirty-Two
A Different Kind Of Fun

Inside *Dolce Disco*, the unrelenting staccato throb of techno music and billows of colored theatrical smoke pouring from the disc jockey's sound desk ignited the writhing dance floor under layers of panning lights.

Located in the very heart of the revelry were Connelly and Monty, who were not so much dancing together as suggestively undulating for their mutual voyeuristic pleasure. Thanks to Dana's mentoring, Connelly was engrossed by the sinuous way Monty moved in her suggestive clubwear, while she found herself spellbound by his muscular torso and the fabric of his fitted shirt clinging to his glistening skin.

A half mile away, Dana and Giancarlo were holding hands in a private balcony box at the 19th-century *Teatro dell'Opera di Roma* Opera House. The production of Gioachino Rossini's masterpiece *Tancredi* progressing before Dana's eyes was something special.

She may have previously thought that she hated this genre of music, but she could not help being swept away by Rossini's lovely melodies and intertwined choruses, arias, and ensembles emanating from the stage below.

Dana was not alone in her reaction. Every person in the capacity audience of 1,600 was enthralled by the stirring *Ah! Se Giusto, O Ciel* as it unfolded at the end of act one.

Back at the disco, Connelly's and Monty's eyes were now locked in a shared understanding. His attraction to her was overwhelming. Unable to be this close any longer without touching her, he swept her into his arms and kissed her powerfully. Her reaction was seismic, as the sounds and motion of the room around them seemed to vanish.

It was the kind of kiss that people never want to end, and notwithstanding her valiant efforts to the contrary, Monty was no different.

As the opera drew to a close, Giancarlo kissed Dana so intently that she could hardly stay upright. Her body seemed to overheat, and her confidence abandoned her as it dawned on her that she did not completely control the situation she was in. And when it came to men, Dana Zimmer had *always* been in control. Yet, she felt increasingly powerless under Giancarlo's spell and it was an unnerving sensation, to say the least.

What had she gotten herself into?! It scared the hell out of her.

The stirring *Secondo Finale* at the end of the performance was a contributing factor. "Wow," she proclaimed as emotions induced by *Tancredi* stuck in her throat. "I should see opera more often."

"I am happy that you enjoyed it, Dana," he shared in a quiet voice with a warm hand on her leg.

She smiled politely while scrambling to recover her equilibrium and remember Monty. *Not only what she taught her, but Monty herself. Her friend, the one who was willing to abandon their revenge plot to spare Dana's feelings. The one who was counting on her to make this guy pay for what he did to her!*

"Yes, well, I have to say that I always thought my favorite was *La Traviata*," she recounted from memory, "but this production may have won me over to Rossini."

"Excellent!" he replied while moving his hand ever-so-slightly up her leg. "I enjoy Verdi very much, as well."

Every nerve ending in her body was screaming from his touch and she had to repress the urge to scream herself. "Who can ever get enough of *Di Provenza il mar, il suol?*" she cooed. "But don't get me wrong. This was ... a lot of fun."

He took her hand and kissed it. "And now let us have a different kind of fun," he said, grasping her arm and leading her from the box.

At *Dolce Disco* it no longer mattered that the tempo of the music was fast. Monty and Connelly were now slow dancing in a sensual tight embrace. Very tight. Eventually, she crawled from the emotional fog to think about Dana and how much she was counting on Monty for payback.

Connelly kissed the side of her neck and sent shock waves up and down her spine. The momentary jolt caused her to turn her head—just in time to see Giancarlo lead Dana onto the dance floor less than thirty feet away!

Monty gasped at the sight of them. And when her eyes met Dana's, both women nearly died. Quickly turning to Connelly, she mumbled, "Will you excuse me for a minute?"

At the same instant Dana turned to Giancarlo. "I'll be right back," she told him before rushing to the women's restroom near the bar.

Inside the spacious make-up area, a dozen young women in mini dresses were chattering as they smoked, gossiped, and touched up their makeup. When Dana burst through the door, Monty pinned her against the wall. "What are you doing here?!"

"Giancarlo said it was a surprise!" answered Dana.

"Well, he was right!"

"What are YOU doing here?" Dana disputed.

"Alex likes to dance, remember?" Monty reminded her. "Where did you expect him to take me?"

Dana thought about that and deflated. "Here. Shit, this place's raging."

"We should have anticipated something like this," said Monty. "I didn't even think to text you that we were here."

"It's my bad," Dana concurred. "I brain farted that this's Giancarlo's hang."

"So, what are we going to do? We can't let them see us together."

"No way," Dana agreed as her mind searched for an idea. "Okay, I'll go tell Giancarlo it ain't happening for me and we'll split."

"Good. I'll wait here until you're gone," Monty replied.

Nodding in agreement, Dana opened the door only to jump aside at catching a glimpse of Alex and Giancarlo standing near each other as they waited for their dates.

"Oh, God—" Dana yelped. "They're both there!"

"What?!" Monty squeaked as she took a peek and instantly stepped away. "What are we going to do now?!"

The girls were panic-stricken. *Trapped.*

"Let's go out a window," Dana suggested.

Monty looked around and frowned. "There are none!"

"Then you think of something," challenged Dana.

"You're the expert schemer. Remember?"

"You're right," Dana came back. "Shit! Okay … okay … then what we do is wait. And whichever one of them has to drain the snake first decides who walks out of here."

Monty's face went blank. "Drains what?"

"Have you never talked to a guy?!" Dana objected. "Takes a whiz. Pisses. Urinates."

"That is repulsive, even for you."

Dana just looked at her. "Then you come up with something."

As Monty wrestled with the directive, a thought came to her. "How much money do you have?" she asked excitedly.

"I dunno, why?"

"Believe it or not, I have an idea."

Dana grabbed some bills from her purse. Monty combined them with some of her own and then turned to a cute woman who was refreshing her lipstick. "Excuse me, do you speak English?"

The woman turned and answered, "A little."

Monty smiled and opened the door a crack. "Do you see that man standing by the bar?" she asked. "The one on the left?"

"Yes, what about him?"

Monty held out the money. "This is yours if you convince him to dance with you for a few minutes."

"May I ask why you want me to do this?" the woman asked.

Monty made a point of looking vulnerable. "Well, you see, he's my date and my friend and I were hoping for some time alone ... if you know what I mean." She completed the statement by unexpectedly kissing Dana on the mouth.

Dana's eyes grew wide with surprise, but she did not resist.

Unfortunately, the woman was not persuaded by the lustful display. "No thank you," she said as she left the room.

Monty and Dana exchanged worried looks until another voice cut in. A distinctly MALE British voice. "I'd be happy to help."

Looking up, they saw a strikingly attractive young man dressed as a woman.

"You would?" Dana asked.

The attractive not-a-woman peered out the door to see Alex Connelly waiting by the bar. "Mmmm ... the one on the left, you said? Strapping piece of work, your date," he observed with flair. "Gorgeous!"

"We really appreciate your help with this," Monty stressed, putting her arm around Dana's shoulder, and pulling her tight. "What's your name?"

"Ian," he answered as he stuffed the money in his purse. "But tonight, you can call me Jasmine."

"Monty and Dana," Dana told him.

"Well, it's my pleasure, luv," he remarked with a grin. "You ladies have fun." Then he adjusted his bra and momentarily paused before heading out. "And by the way," he said, pointing at Monty's feet, "I adore those shoes!"

Monty and Dana burst into laughter as soon as he was gone. "Well played," Dana affirmed.

"I learned from the best."

The girls took another glance out the door just in time to see Jasmine pull Connelly by the hand onto the dance floor. He had no choice but to go with her, as his polite attempts to resist were useless in the face of Jasmine's formidable resolve.

Closing the restroom door, Dana flopped against the wall. "Man-oh-man, I'd give anything to stay and see this!" she chortled. "Alex isn't exactly the most woke guy I ever met."

"Well, you can't stay," Monty warned. "You've got to get Giancarlo out of here."

"Okay. Good luck tonight."

"You, too," Monty told her before adding, "By the way, if you kiss Giancarlo the way you kissed me then he doesn't stand a chance."

Dana brightened. "You weren't so bad yourself."

Monty's upbeat mood was all-too brief, however. Her heart sank as she watched Dana approach Giancarlo and ambush him with a kiss. Seeing him like that with another woman still hurt, even though she knew the other woman and why she was with him.

It took Giancarlo a few moments to recover from Dana's surprise show of affection. "For what do I deserve that?" he asked.

Dana batted her eyes seductively, adjusting her position to prevent Connelly from seeing her. "For being the man I'm falling for," she purred.

Giancarlo took her hands in his. "*Molto bene*," he responded tenderly.

Shortly after Giancarlo and Dana left the disco, Monty emerged from hiding and turned her sights on Connelly and Jasmine dancing wildly. *If Connelly only knew!*

"*Excusez-moi*," Monty asked sweetly as she approached the couple, "may I cut in?"

Jasmine smiled conspiratorially. "And here I was, developing a taste for Aussie cuisine," he remarked with a wink before disappearing into the throng of dancing bodies.

Monty slid in close to Connelly. "*Mon amour*, did you make a new friend?"

"She was a little on the strange side, if you ask me," he stated, unaware that his former dance partner was not female.

"That is good to hear," she said, suppressing her amusement. "I was afraid that you might decide to leave with her instead of me."

"I'd have to be out of my mind to do that," he avowed. "With her or anyone else."

Monty met his look and moved in close. "But she wanted you very much, *oui?*"

Connelly took her face in his hands. "It's only what you want that matters to me."

She gently cupped his fingers in the smooth skin of her palms and kissed them. "I believe that you know what I want, Alex," she whispered back.

In Dana's suite at the *Parco dei Principi*, Giancarlo pinned her against a wall of the bedroom hallway, where he delicately nibbled her earlobe while unbuttoning her blouse. She was trying as hard as she could not to enjoy the experience.

Finally, she managed to nudge him away. Her heart was beating fast.

"Is there anything wrong, darling?" he asked.

Wrong? Hell yes, something was wrong! Being with him like this and feeling the things she was feeling—THAT was wrong! But Monty was counting on her, she continued to remind herself.

Dana looked at him with the most innocent expression that she could muster. "Giancarlo ..." she answered, still catching her breath, "I have to ... ask you something."

"Anything, my love," he answered as he leaned in to kiss her neck.

Once again, she pushed him away, if only less urgently this time. "I was wondering," she began, "how you'd feel if I wasn't ready to get married."

He gazed longingly into her eyes. "A moment in time with you is enough for me," he assured her as he pressed his body against hers in all the right places.

"Really?" she continued. "You aren't disappointed in me?"

Giancarlo reacted as innocently as only a professional conman could. "I have longed for a traditional woman like you, Dana," he replied. "You are a rare discovery, indeed."

Dana forced herself to break free. "Then let's drink to that!" she said as she scurried over to the bar. "Why don't you have a seat?"

As Giancarlo went to the living room couch, she poured their drinks. "I hope you like Dom Perignon 2008," she continued while being careful to block his view as she poured the contents of a medication capsule into his glass. While the pharmacy instructions were to take a single dose only, she and Monty had combined the powder from several capsules for this purpose.

"That sounds very nice," he remarked with a grin. He was well aware that the vintage sells for nearly 180 euro per bottle. *God, how he loved his life!*

"To that moment in time you mentioned," she added as she handed him his glass. "May it lead to something special."

Giancarlo gulped his champagne and set his glass aside, never taking his eyes off her. "Now I think it is time for something *molto speciale*," he teased as he unbuttoned his shirt.

Meanwhile, in Connelly's hotel suite, Monty opened a capsule of sleep medication and poured the powder into his glass of eighteen-year-old Talisker scotch, as Dana did with Giancarlo's champagne. *"Fais de beaux rêves,"* she murmured playfully.

Connelly grinned. "Whatever you said sounds good to me," he said snuggling behind her at the bar.

She turned and handed him his drink, repeating softly in English. "I said, "to the night of your dreams"."

Connelly raised his glass. "I like the way you think, Cherie. In both languages."

He quickly downed his scotch and moved in for a kiss. As his tongue explored her mouth, his hands glided across the front of her dress. Frankly, although she was trying hard, it was nearly impossible to retain her composure.

He was so good at this!

She could not ignore her feelings of arousal but remained determined to remember what getting revenge meant to Dana. Unfortunately, that was more difficult than she expected.

Remember: revenge ... REVENGE!

Then when she managed to break free from his embrace, she took his hand in hers and led him into the bedroom, kissing him and unbuttoning his shirt as they traveled down the hall.

A similar moment was unfolding at the *Parco dei Principi* three miles away, as Dana took her time unzipping Giancarlo's pants ... slowly ... slowly....

Just as Monty did for Connelly at the Raphael Hotel ....

And then Giancarlo began to feel woozy ....

As Connelly did too ....

Giancarlo fell back against the couch, unconscious ....

And Connelly hit his bedroom sheets, out cold as well ....

Monty breathed a big sigh of relief. So did Dana. They had come perilously close to crossing a line with the men that neither woman was prepared to cross.

The next morning Dana was pretending to sleep in a living room chair as Giancarlo awoke on the couch. She was still wearing the clothes that she had on at the opera, including the jewelry that Monty provided. He had a whopping headache and looked at her in confusion, struggling to remember the events of the previous night.

Conspicuously, his shirt and pants were off, so he assumed that things went well in that department.

When his eye caught Dana's framed artwork, he remembered what he was there for. He quickly dressed and took the cash from her purse, which he was frustrated to find was only 300 euro. He considered taking her jewelry but dared not risk awakening her.

Then he gathered up the four paintings without so much as a glance in her direction. And a minute later he was gone. *His financial problems would soon be over!*

As the door closed, Dana sat upright, wide-eyed and alert. She had witnessed the whole thing and shook her head with a smirk. *What an asshole!*

In the bedroom of Connelly's suite, Monty awakened to hear hushed angry male voices in the living room. She gingerly walked to the door and opened it a crack. Connelly was pacing as Greg Lange sat at the dining room table.

Connelly was not a happy man. He also looked like he was suffering from a terrible hangover. "What are you talking about?" he was saying in a hushed tone. "What trial run?!"

"They called it a demonstration," Lange whispered back. "DeLuca says his associates insist on it."

"Forget it," Connelly raged. "I'm not putting my neck on a chopping block without financing in place."

"Are you sure that's a good idea?"

"You're damn right I am," Connelly declared. "Three job interviews are enough."

"But Alex—"

"Fuck 'em, Greg. We have a deal."

But Lange was clearly worried. "This is the Mafia we're talking about."

Upon hearing the reference from the bedroom door, Monty nearly died. *Mafia! What had she and Dana gotten themselves into?!*

"I don't care who they are!" Connelly insisted. "I'm not delivering their goddamn drugs anywhere unless I've got money for the planes in my account."

"Are you sure?"

Monty slowly withdrew from the door and returned to the bed. Her hands were shaking as she processed the revelation: *Mafia ... Drugs ...!*

Chapter Thirty-Three
Thelma And Louise

Monty madly strutted past the expansive beauty of the Orange Garden in *Parco Savello* without noticing the lush canopy of trees, perfumed scent of oranges, or delightful *Colle Aventino* views of the city and Vatican. A prized green space in Rome, the park is usually an oasis of peace and tranquility.

But it was not that today, not for Monty or Dana.

"That's it," Monty protested. "It's over!"

Dana fought to calm her down. "It's a setback, that's all."

"Setback?!" Monty repeated in amazement. "We've stumbled into an organized crime operation!"

"We don't know that for sure," Dana argued.

Monty was completely mortified by what she was hearing. "You can't be serious," she reacted before correcting herself. "What am I saying? Of course, you can. Dana Zimmer has no boundaries!"

"Don't have a meltdown, okay?" Dana appealed, thinking fast as she paced back and forth.

"I don't know any other way to react," Monty responded. "Our simple little seduction plan that was going to be so rewarding is neither simple nor rewarding."

Dana plopped onto a park bench like a balloon that just lost its air. "This's a disaster, you're right. The fucking mob—shit."

Monty sat beside her. "Well, at least we know we tried."

"Yeah," Dana answered. "We sure did."

Neither one said anything more for a long time, each absorbed by her own swirling cloud of defeat and regret. For Monty, the revelation of mafia involvement had also caused an unsettling re-awakening of her devotion to her Catholic faith. Disturbingly, she now found herself feeling guilty for wanting to get even with the men.

"But wait," Dana offered at long last. "What if there's a way to finish this without putting our butts in a sling?"

"It's over, Dana. As much as it hurts to say."

"Come on, humor me," said Dana. "What if there's still a way to bring these skuzzballs to their knees?"

"And just how would we accomplish that?"

"I dunno ... but there's gotta be a way."

"We're not exactly *Thelma and Louise*, you know," Monty reminded her with a reference to the iconic film about women who pay a tragic price for their misguided feminist awakening.

But Dana was determined to salvage the plan. "We'll figure it out," she persisted. "We're on track so far. They're totally into us. Giancarlo's toast for sure, so all we really have to do is find a way to wreck that deal Alex's putting together."

Monty could only stare at her, since believing her ears was apparently no longer a possibility. "Is there a history of mental illness in your family?" she probed. "That would explain a lot."

"Come on, Monty—don't give up. This's either an obstacle or an opportunity."

"We're not taking on the mafia."

"Of course not," Dana told her. "But they only want Alex because he's a legit import-export guy," she began. "Maybe we can make him look like a risky bet or something. The rejection would be a gut punch for him."

Monty was hesitant, of course. Yet with Giancarlo well on his way to being put in his place, could she really deny Dana the same satisfaction with Alex? *They made a pact to help each other!*

"Do you promise that we will not put ourselves in harm's way?" Monty finally asked.

"Hell yeah," Dana came back. "We just have to put our minds to it."

Monty softened slightly. She was still morally conflicted about her participation, but there was no way to ignore the desperation and pain on Dana's face. "A push up bra and short skirt may not be enough this time, you know."

"I hear ya," Dana admitted with regret. "We gotta use our smarts."

Monty struggled to subvert her concerns, at least for the moment. "I can't believe I'm saying this, but I'm sorry I became hysterical," she said. "I know how much this means to you."

"Thanks," Dana answered. "And as long as we're being honest here, I'd be bullshitting you if I said I knew for sure that we could pull this off."

"I know that."

Dana reacted to the response. "And you're still in?"

"Let me put it this way ..." Monty started, "I don't mind being *Thelma and Louise* with you as long as we don't kill ourselves like they did."

Dana tried to smile but it was more effort than she had in her at the moment. "Would you mind if we just kinda sat here a while?" she asked. "My heart's pounding so fast it might come outta my chest."

"Mine, too," Monty added as she put her arm around her.

Chapter Thirty-Four
Bring Us Real Money

In the shadowy *Pino & Dino* Parking Garage on *Via Lucrezio Caro* Giancarlo was eagerly waiting at his Peugeot when the two skinheads, The Enforcer and Ice Pick, arrived on their Vespas. Giancarlo smiled assuredly as he adjusted the stolen paintings from Dana's hotel suite, neatly leaning them in a row against the car.

The Enforcer climbed from his scooter and gestured at the canvases. "What are those?"

"Extremely valuable paintings," Giancarlo proudly announced.

The Enforcer reacted blankly. "What are we supposed to do with them?"

"They'll more than cover my gambling debts," Giancarlo explained. "I guarantee it."

The Enforcer looked at Ice Pick. "Does that look like money to you?"

"No way," Ice Pick replied.

The Enforcer grabbed Giancarlo by the shirt, lifting him to the balls of his feet. "Let me ask you a question," he pressed.

"Yes ... of course ...!" he stuttered.

"How did you think we were going to carry that shit on our motor scooters?"

Giancarlo stammered, terrified. "I ... I ... didn't ... think about that ...."

"Obviously not," Ice Pick remarked.

The Enforcer let go of Giancarlo. Roughly. "So, here is what you are going to do now. You are going to bring us real money. All of it."

"Not the minimum you were supposed to have for us," Ice Pick stated. "The full amount. 41,260.50 euro."

"In cash, plus interest," explained The Enforcer. "Let's make it an even 60,000."

Giancarlo began to shake in his loafers, prompting Ice Pick to pull a 9.2-inch *Tezzorio* stainless steel ice pick with a wooden handle from his boot. It was his favorite implement of persuasion. Waving the tool in Giancarlo's face, he smiled grimly. "For all the grief you put us through."

An hour later a terrified Giancarlo was outside his apartment building jamming belongings into his car. But he was in such a hurry that when he pulled from the curb, he nearly drove under the wheels of a passing truck! The truck blared its horn, and Giancarlo slammed on the brakes, stopping in the nick of time.

He sat in the car in a daze at having almost lost his life.

Then, remembering his dire circumstances, he shook it off and carefully pulled into traffic, disappearing into the congestion.

Chapter Thirty-Five
What Happens Next?

Nascondiglio Nastrini is a dimly lit restaurant on *Via dei Giubbonari*, a narrow canyon of shops and apartment buildings in the *Regoli* district. With its intimate private booths for two, red checkered tablecloths, and candles in old wine bottles, *Nastrini* has long been the ideal refuge for a romantic rendezvous.

Greg Lange seemed jumpy as he entered wearing a blazer and his best tie. He had no idea why Cherie, the French model that his boss was aggressively pursuing, would ask to meet him, but his mind was alive with amatory possibilities. Being alone with a woman like her exceeded any fantasy that he ever had.

After all, Lange knew he was unspectacular looking. *Was it possible that Cherie perceived his executive position as being more than it really was? Did she think he was a man of influence? The power behind the throne at Connelly's company, perhaps?* He could only hope.

When his eyes adjusted to the darkness, he located the justification for his nerves: bathed in warm candlelight, Monty was waiting alone in a secluded corner booth. He bit his lip at the sight of her in a sheer black off the shoulder blouse and snug white jeans that looked like they were painted on her. *Damn, she was spectacular!*

Smiling broadly as he approached, she momentarily set aside her growing moral quandary over the retaliation plot and let him have it with both barrels of her sexiest French-accented voice, "Gregory, I am so happy that you could meet with me privately."

He slid into the seat across from her but was unsure where to look. While her eyes were magnets that demanded his attention, the silky smoothness of her tanned shoulders and graceful neck were quite a distraction. "How could I say no?" he answered as he forced his eyes back to her face.

Getting his mind out of the fantasy gutter would be another matter.

"But I have to tell you," he opened, "I was a little surprised to get your message."

Monty blinked and pouted her lower lip. "*Mais pourquoi?* I saw the way you looked at me that first day at the shoot. Did you not see me looking back?"

"I thought you had something going with Alex," he told her, shocked that she even noticed him.

"He is nothing to me," she vented defiantly. "Forget about him."

Lange was thoroughly perplexed. *If she's not with Connelly anymore, then why did she invite him to meet her here?* "Easier said than done," he explained. "Since he's my employer. He went to a lot of trouble meeting you."

"Such as arranging the sitting with *Monsieur* Vecchioni?"

"Exactly," he confirmed.

"Really?" she appraised, unhurriedly fingering a slender bread stick that was protruding from a basket on the table. "Who was the one who spoke to my photographer about me?"

"Well, I did," he acknowledged, returning the smile that appeared on her face.

"Then it is evident who made the real effort," Monty decreed. Then she added pointedly, "I like a man to be in control."

She fixed her eyes on him and slid the bread stick into her mouth.

He swallowed. *Did somebody just turn up the heat in here?* The most unbelievably perfect woman on the planet was focused exclusively on him! And the messages she was sending were high voltage transmissions. "Guilty as charged," he said as his voice cracked.

"*C'est bien.* I wish that you were with me when I posed for my session with *Il Maestro*," she coyly offered. "You make me feel ... frisky."

Lange was so aroused now he could practically hear the capillaries popping in his neck. "Should we order some wine?" he hurriedly inquired.

"But of course," she responded with a promising gleam in her eyes.

Lange tried to get a waiter's attention. After all, getting as much alcohol into her as possible was the most important thing in the world. *What if she changed her mind?!*

Much to his chagrin, his effort was to no avail. Nobody noticed him. Damn it!

"So," he asked as casually as he could, "does Alex know it's over with you?"

Monty picked up a menu and pretended to examine it. "Who can tell? He talks only of business, and those problems with your government," she stated dismissively. "Why do these Italians use red sauce on everything?!"

However, he could not get past her previous comment. "I didn't know Alex had government problems."

She continued to pretend to read the menu. "Government, FBI … they are all the same to me," she announced with disinterest. "Do you think I should have the fish?"

But Lange was intrigued. "Wait a minute," he asked, lifting the menu from her hands. "Alex is talking to the FBI?! Are you sure about that?"

"That is what the man said on the telephone."

His ears perked. "Cherie, this could be important. Exactly what did the man say?"

"Well, he was calling from Washington," she recounted, "and his name was Braxton. It is such an unpleasant name, Braxton."

Lange continued to probe. "Do you know what they talked about?"

"Something about tax problems."

"Really," he commented. "Are you sure he wasn't from the IRS?"

"No, it was the FBI. Like in the movies."

Lange's mind was churning. "But that doesn't make any sense. Why would the FBI be talking to Alex about tax matters?"

Monty shrugged. "They are going to make everything better if Alex helps them with something," she added as she took the menu back. "Perhaps I should have salad and soup."

Lange was fully engaged now. "Cherie, did they talk about someone named DeLuca?"

She looked up from the menu with a smile of recognition. "*Oui, oui, c'est ca.* DeLuca"

Lange's eyes were practically glowing as he mumbled, "I'll bury him with this!"

Monty pretended to be confused. "I have said something wrong?"

"Hardly," he told her. "You're more helpful than you know,"

"But bury means dead," she corrected. "Gregory, I would not want what I have said to hurt anyone."

Concealing his excitement about what she divulged to him, he underplayed that as much as he could. "It won't," he promised.

She took his hands in hers. "Do you mean that, *mon amour?*"

His pulse quickened. "Whatever you say," he followed. "No problem." Of course, he would have said anything to keep the conversation going in this direction.

Monty squeezed his hand and gave him a straightforward look. "Good. I would not want anything to get in the way of us growing closer."

"All I want to do is improve my standing in a deal we have going. Believe me," he vowed. *But enough about Connelly. He was alone with the most astounding woman he had ever seen.* "So, what happens next? With you and me."

"I must return to Paris soon," she informed him before adding, "Perhaps you would like to be with me there?"

Alone in Paris with a dazzling model? Hell YES!

However, in his enthusiasm he forgot to articulate his answer. Monty pretended to be concerned about that and leaned forward. "Gregory, if you come with me, I promise that you will not be disappointed."

And with that concept and its enticing romantic possibilities detonating in his mind, Lange's pulse was pounding so hard he thought he might have a heart attack. But this time he remembered to answer. "Cherie, just tell me when and where."

Monty smiled. *"Merveilleux!"*

That afternoon, Dana and Monty watched from the shadows as two men unloaded housekeeping and kitchen uniforms from a delivery truck in a service courtyard behind the Raphael Hotel.

Monty felt nervous and out of place, as she was still wearing the sexy sheer blouse from her rendezvous with Greg Lange. "I cannot believe you are actually going to do this," she whispered.

"Yeah, well like the song says, *Here Comes Revenge,*" Dana answered while taking an L.A. Dodgers baseball cap from her purse.

"What song is that?" Monty asked.

"Metallica, of course," she answered as she adjusted the visor to cover her eyes.

Monty ignored the reference, which of course was unknown to her. In truth, at this point she was used to it from Dana. "Just promise that you'll leave the instant anything goes wrong."

"Nothing's gonna go wrong," Dana reassured her. But it was a thin statement, since this part of the plan scared the hell out of her. They could only hope that Connelly's recent Vecchioni purchase would be in his suite because its disappearance would not only save them the trouble of buying more art to entrap Giancarlo, but the famous artist would also provide a fresh twist to their unfolding scheme. "Trust me," Dana offered with fabricated confidence. "One of my brothers used to knock over houses when the neighbors were away."

"And he got away with it?"

"Until they caught him, sure," Dana answered. "He's always been an idiot."

Monty shook her head with incredulity and hugged her. "Good luck."

Dana nodded appreciatively. "Just make sure you call me if the cops show up. I'm pretty sure that Sergeant Fazio will never sign off on this."

Then, noting the position of a wall-mounted security camera near the entrance, Dana positioned her back to the camera and slipped through the entrance behind the delivery men while Monty waited outside.

Inside the utility corridor, the workers departed after depositing their neatly folded bundles on a large table. Dana grabbed one of the uniforms from the pile and stepped into a storage room. Before long she emerged looking like any other female housekeeping employee, allowing her to follow the conduit from the courtyard camera unnoticed.

She passed various laundry carts, cleaning supplies, and other service essentials as she moved along the curved concrete passageway. Pausing at the sight of maintenance tools in an alcove, she took a crowbar and wire cutters before continuing on. It did not take long to locate the conduit's destination in another alcove: a control box labeled *Sicurezza Video Dell'hotel*, which she remembered from notes that Monty gave her meant Hotel Video Security.

Glancing over her shoulder, Dana used the crowbar to pop the lid and wire cutters to sever the coaxial cables inside. She could not help smiling in the knowledge that the disruption of the video feed would give her time to get what she came for.

Concealed in the second-floor service hallway, Dana peeked at an unattended housekeeping cart stacked with folded towels, bedding, and toiletries. While the maid was busily working in an open guest room, Dana swooped in unnoticed and lifted the key card that was dangling on a lanyard before returning to concealment.

Then on the fourth floor, the most severe rage that she had ever felt surged through her. She watched from the service hall as Connelly exited his suite, and her sense of hatred was surprisingly strong. It was all she could do to contain herself as he passed within inches of her position on his way to the elevator.

It seemed like an eternity before the car arrived and the door closed behind him, but when it finally did, she advanced towards his room.

Once inside the suite, however, she hesitated. This was as close as she had been to Connelly since he so callously rejected her. The sight of the briefcase that she gave him for his birthday triggered a pounding level of angst that she had not expected.

Dana continued into the living room where a few more of his belongings came into view. Among them was a half-empty bottle of Talisker, his favorite Isle of Skye single malt scotch whisky. As she approached the bar and reached out to touch it, she forced herself to resist the urge to pour it down the drain. Her impulse to write insulting things in lipstick on the mirrored wall behind the bar was even more difficult to withstand. But she summoned the strength to keep moving. She was on a mission and deviating from that was not an option. For this new aspect of the plan to work, Connelly could never suspect she was in his room.

Dana fortified her willpower accordingly and soon found what she was looking for: an 18 x 24-inch unframed painting of six nude women in a graphic lesbian love fantasy that could only have originated in the aberrant mind of one man. She cringed as her eyes settled on the signature: *Vecchioni.*

She recoiled at the disgusting image, which was saying something since it took a lot to offend her. The scene depicting a gaggle of contorted amorous women was starkly graphic and raunchy. *Bernardo Vecchioni was a bigger pervert than she thought—and so was Connelly for spending good money on this.*

After locating the protective sleeve, she inserted the painting and was heading for the door when she stopped—*there was something that she absolutely had to do.* Returning to the bar, she poured salt into the bottle of Talisker. *So much for the peaty and dark smoky finish that Connelly loved so much!* The image of him finding his scotch ruined gave her almost as much pleasure as the thought of him discovering the theft of his latest art acquisition.

When her phone rang Monty was standing outside the Church of *Santa Maria a Trevi,* where upon arriving in Rome, she had spoken with Father Demetrio Vitale about the mysterious Sisters *di Sant'Angelo.*

On the other end of the call was Dana in the hall outside Giancarlo's apartment. She was just a few feet from his open door, and she could see that while his furniture was there, his personal possessions were gone. "Where are you right now?" Dana asked her.

Monty hesitated a beat before answering. "I'm running an errand. Why?"

"Because you owe me twenty bucks," Dana announced. "Giancarlo split, just like I said he would."

"No, you said you'd find him," contradicted Monty. "Not finding him means you failed and therefore you owe me."

"Are you always this annoying?"

"A bet is a bet, Dana."

"Just worry about your lip gloss, sweet cheeks," Dana groused. "I'm all over this."

Then, upon hearing the toilet flush in the apartment, she grabbed a nearby broom like a baseball bat. "Gotta go. My twenty bucks might be here after all."

Monty was going to wish her luck when the line went dead.

Meanwhile, Dana pocketed her phone and advanced into the main room. The floor creaked beneath her feet as she inched towards the closed bathroom door.

Suddenly a feeble old man in maintenance clothes emerged! *"Santa Madre di Dio!"* the man yelled.

"I'm sorry!" she shrieked back. "I thought you were somebody else!"

The old man looked at her, puzzled. "In Giancarlo's apartment?"

"I was hoping to find him," she said.

"With a stick?"

Dana thought about how much information to give him and then quickly came up with a plan. "Well, yes ... the door was open, and it looked like he was robbed."

"No, he has moved."

"Where did he go?" she asked. "We had plans today."

"I do not know. It was some sort of emergency."

"Emergency," she repeated.

"He was very upset," he confided. "I am worried about him."

Sitting on the bed, Dana forced a tear. "I am, too," she explained. "Is there any chance you'll hear from him?"

"He said only that he will call about his mail," he told her, pulling up a chair. "*Signora*," he queried, "if I may—you seem upset, as well."

Dana averted her eyes to convey her helplessness. "You are a perceptive man, *Signor*," she observed. "Giancarlo and I were together at my hotel, but after he left, someone broke into my room and stole my paintings."

"I am so sorry to hear this."

"That's why I acted the way I did," she described. "I was afraid the thieves came here and robbed him, too."

"Giancarlo will be most concerned to learn of this, I know."

She let out a long, exaggerated sigh. "Thankfully, the burglars missed my most valuable possession," she informed him, letting the remark hang in the air for emphasis. "My own artwork can't be worth much, but the original Bernardo Vecchioni that I had in my closet was very expensive."

"Good!" the old man said, shaking her hand. "My name is Umberto LaPaglia. If I speak with Giancarlo, I will tell him what has happened."

Chapter Thirty-Six
I Don't Want To Let Her Down

Monty did not tell Dana that her errand was an appointment with Father Vitale, who was her sole Catholic touchstone in the city. He had been exceedingly kind in trying to help her once, and she grudgingly conceded that she needed his counsel again. The questionable morality of what she and Dana were doing, retaliating against Connelly and Giancarlo, was weighing heavily on her mind. Especially now, given the shocking revelation of Connelly's mafia dealings.

She no longer knew if she could go through with her pact with Dana.

Seated alone in the front row of the Church of *Santa Maria a Trevi*, Monty was quietly asking the Lord for spiritual guidance when Father Vitale emerged from the vestry. He smiled at the sight of her and approached with a well-worn Bible in hand. "*Signora* Lombardi, it is so nice to see you again. I hope that you have positive news to share about your husband."

"Thank you, Father," she opened. "Unfortunately, my situation when I saw you was worse than I thought." She unconsciously clutched the cross on a gold chain around her neck. "Everything about my husband turned out to be a lie. His identity and faith, our marriage, his death ... it was all a cruel deception."

The priest's soulful eyes filled with sadness. "I am sorry to hear this," he replied. "It must be a terrible burden for you."

"It has been difficult, I'll confess," she told him before pausing. "Not only did Giancarlo break my heart, but he stole from me," she explained.

Father Vitale grasped his Bible tightly, a reflex that often-accompanied learning of a distressing parishioner crisis. "What can I do to help?"

"Well," she began slowly, selecting her words carefully. "I was wondering what the church would think about someone like me seeking retribution."

Father Vitale thoughtfully considered the question. "The desire for retribution is understandable, *Signora*. However, Christian moral law does not allow such actions."

"What about justice?" she refuted. "Isn't that a form of revenge?"

"Of course," he explained. "But if the outcome that you seek is born of anger, then that would be one of the Seven Deadly Sins."

Monty slumped against the pew. He had just confirmed the doubt that had been gnawing at her for days. "That's what I was afraid of," she admitted. "I feel so guilty over what I've been planning."

"Guilt is God's way of speaking to us. Of reminding us about the beliefs we hold dear."

Monty nodded. "What's complicating this is that a friend of mine was also hurt by someone, and we're supposed to help each other get even."

"An eye for an eye to avenge your sorrow?" he asked. "From the Old Testament."

"Yes, exactly!" she reinforced. "Dana has already been through so much. I don't want to let her down."

"Your commitment to her is an admirable quality," he pointed out. "She is fortunate to have a friend like you."

"Thank you, Father," she answered. "As you can see, my dilemma isn't only about me. It's about her, too."

"I can see that now," he replied. "And I can see that while your heart may be broken, because of your friend it is also full." Then, sensing the extent of her predicament he continued, "May I ask the nature of what you have been contemplating for this reprisal?"

"Well, Dana is arranging for my husband to be arrested for theft, while my job is to ruin a business deal that her ex-boyfriend is putting together with criminals."

"I see," he answered as the details registered. "So, in addition to revenge you would be interfering with a criminal enterprise?"

"That wasn't the original idea, but as it turns out, yes."

The priest took a moment before asking one more question. "*Signora*, if you were to do this thing, would there be violence of any kind?"

"Violence?" she answered. "Oh, no. Absolutely none."

Her answer made Father Vitale smile. "Then in my view, what you are planning does not go against the Church," he told her. "Jesus taught that while love is preferable to eye for an eye-punishments, delivering evil men to justice is not the same as bringing vengeance upon them yourselves."

"It isn't?" she responded hopefully.

"The Principle of Subsidiarity says that matters should be handled by the smallest or lowest competent authority," he explained. "From what you have described, that sounds like you and your friend."

Chapter Thirty-Seven
Some Stuff You Need To Know

Dana was waiting in her suite hoping that Umberto LaPaglia, the old man at Giancarlo's apartment, successfully delivered her message. As she pulled her blonde wig into a casual-looking ponytail, she wondered about Monty's assurances that Giancarlo's greed would be an irresistible lure. If that proved wrong, then Monty would have to take her chances with the notoriously unpredictable Italian legal system.

The regional version of something called *Ex On The Beach* was on television and there were plenty of hunky men and sexy women frolicking together. As far as Dana was concerned, it was useless trash. *What she would give for a WWE wrestling match right now!*

She turned off the audio track and took in the excessive surroundings that Monty had provided, wondering what it would be like to grow up wanting for nothing. Of course, wealth was not the only aspect of her new friend's life that she envied. Her close family bonds were even more appealing. Dana reflected on her own upbringing, on the mother who did not stand-up to her father's drunken temper and the brothers who protected her when they could. As dysfunctional as her childhood may have been, she realized, it seemed to prepare her for this—the opportunity to exact revenge on her ex and to help Monty punish a career slime ball like Giancarlo.

Just then, there was a vigorous knock on her door.

Opening it, she saw Giancarlo waiting in the hall. He was a disheveled wreck, looking like someone who had not slept in days.

"Giancarlo ...!" she sobbed as she hugged him. "I was so worried about you!"

"Darling, thank God you are here," he cried.

She gave him a puzzled look. "Where else would I be?"

"I dare not to even say," he sniffled in what she was sure was the run-up to an Academy Award-winning dramatic performance. "After what has happened to me, I had only nightmares for thoughts."

He entered the suite, deeply immersed in his elaborate charade. She followed him with manufactured confusion and concern. "What are you talking about? What happened?"

Giancarlo turned to face her, choked with emotion. "When I awakened yesterday to see your exquisite face, I wanted to surprise you with a beautiful flower," he claimed. "But outside the hotel two men struck me on the head. For many hours I was not able to even say my own name."

She pulled him into another emotional embrace. "You poor dear!"

He continued, milking it as he pretended to put the details together. "I then could remember a little ... at first my name and my home," he said faltering. "I was frightened because the men they might return. I moved from my apartment ... and then finally I remembered you, my love. But I saw that the terrible men had also stolen my key to your hotel room."

"Well, they used it," Dana bemoaned as she flopped into a chair. "Giancarlo, something terrible has happened. I was robbed."

Glancing around, his face registered the horror of what he pretended to be seeing for the first time. "No—not your paintings!"

Dana nodded and fought back her tears. "Yes, but they missed a wonderful piece that I recently purchased."

She savored his curiosity as she crossed to the couch and uncovered the Vecchioni lesbian orgy scene.

Giancarlo's eyes flared as he stood to review the canvas. He may have been a fraud as an artist, but time had taught him to recognize value when he saw it. And this original Bernardo Vecchioni looked like the payday that he so desperately needed. "Vecchioni!" he said, practically sobbing with elation. "But my darling, if I had stopped the thieves you would have the others, as well."

Dana moved to his side. "The important thing is that we're both okay."

"It is because of me that you suffer," he claimed, ardently stroking her face. "How may I help?"

She turned away, as if unable to handle the words she was about to speak. "Giancarlo, I'm broke," she sniffled. "I spent everything I had on this painting and when they heard about the robbery, my family was furious and cut me off. Without their financial support, I can't afford this hotel or even a flight back to America. What ever will I do?!"

He paced the room, seemingly working hard to find an idea. "Let me think … there must be something …."

Dana clutched her bosom and hoped she would not ruin the moment by laughing.

He gradually made his way back to the Vecchioni. "Perhaps I could sell the painting for you."

Tears of gratitude cascaded down her cheeks. "Gosh, do you think you could?"

"Absolutely. Vecchioni is very famous."

"Oh, my darling, thank you … thank you!" She threw her arms around him and hugged him hard. "I wouldn't even begin to know where to find a buyer!"

As a rule, an emotional encounter like this in Giancarlo's life would lead to lovemaking, but there was one thing that he liked even more than sex—money. And considering his issues with the skinhead gang, he was more than a little obsessed about his finances at the moment.

He could not escape with the Vecchioni painting fast enough and did not even bother to wrap it for safekeeping before he left.

As a tour guide in his teens, Giancarlo learned early to connect with women, especially rich Americans on holiday. *They were such eager lovers and, oh, how they ate up his starving artist persona and heart-wrenching fiction about his pitiable orphan childhood!* He emerged from Dana's hotel with the Vecchioni painting under his arm, grinning ear to ear over this unforeseen bonus from his latest victim.

He was so proud of how proficient he had become at his con game. His father, uncles, and brothers could only dream of being this good, he knew, though they had certainly tried. *Perhaps he should write a book about it, he thought. He could make millions if he did.* But then the recognition came that writing a book would require doing actual work, and he had zero inclination for any such thing.

Besides, why would he share his trade secrets with the world when there were still so many unsuspecting rich women in need? So many gullible flowers to be plucked.

He had a triumphant spring in his step as he approached the end of the hotel's hunter green awning that covered the tiled front entrance. He had only to convert the Vecchioni into cash to have a clean slate with the skinheads. And there would be plenty of money left to live the good life for quite a while. *Dana had given him a way out of his troubles! It was too bad that he never got the chance to sleep with her.*

He paused at the sight of a serious looking policeman ascending the steps from the street with his side arm unholstered. It was Sergeant Fazio.

"*Attenzione!*" Fazio ordered. "Put the painting down carefully and raise your hands."

"Certainly!" Giancarlo answered as he complied with the instructions. "What seems to be the problem, officer?"

Fazio glowered at him. "You are under arrest for theft."

Giancarlo recoiled. "Theft?! You must be mistaken."

"An original Vecchioni is valued at over two hundred thousand euro." Fazio pronounced.

A smile of relief appeared on Giancarlo's face as his confusion cleared. "Oh, this ... it belongs to my girlfriend. She asked me to sell it for her."

"I think not," Fazio informed him. "You are going to prison for a long time, *Signor* Nunziato." As he held Giancarlo's attention, he relished the moment. After all, this was something he had eagerly anticipated since first learning how ruthlessly Monty was fleeced by this man. *An Italian man, at that!* That was an insult Fazio could not stomach. As a result, he delighted in letting Giancarlo stew in his own befuddled juices before dropping the hammer on him.

And drop it he did. Another police officer stepped out from behind a decorative lion statue, on cue, and brusquely slapped handcuffs on Giancarlo's wrists as Fazio cautiously set the painting aside.

Giancarlo was getting really nervous now, but then brightened at the sight of Dana emerging from the hotel. "Dana! he called out with torqued urgency. "You cannot believe what this officer is accusing me of!"

She took her time on her approach, glancing from Giancarlo to the policemen and back, playing her earnestness to the hilt. "May I ask what's going on here?" she inquired.

Fazio turned to her with his most official comportment, "You are acquainted with this man, *Signora*?"

Dana considered Giancarlo a second before dropping a gigantic hammer of her own. "Why no, I've never seen him before."

"WHAT?!" Giancarlo screamed in a sniveling panic. "But my darling—"

"Silence!" Fazio demanded, which promptly shut him up. Turning the canvas around to face Dana, he explained, "He claims to have your permission to be in possession of this artwork."

"Really?" she asked, savoring the theatricality of it all. "Oh, he must be talking about my friend!"

Fazio and Giancarlo followed her look to discover Monty as she materialized from the hotel lobby. "Darling, how funny meeting you here!" she jauntily called out. "I didn't know you were in Rome!"

Beads of sweat formed on Giancarlo's brow and he gasped what could only be described as something resembling a dying man's death rattle. "But officer ... I ... I ... I am innocent!" he squeaked before his throat went dry.

Fazio gave him a grim stare. "That is not what the other women have told me."

And if a color more colorless than white exists in the universe, then that is what Giancarlo's face became. He looked absolutely lifeless. "... other women?" he gagged.

"Yep!" Dana gloated as she pointed to the bottom of the stairs where six glaring women ranging from twenty to fifty years-old disembarked from a Municipal Police van.

Amazingly, Giancarlo's face became even whiter than before.

"And the gentleman from Barcelona," Fazio added with a censorious frown. "*Señor* Contreras."

Giancarlo groaned at the spectacle of a sobbing man in his seventies joining the women on the sidewalk.

"It took a while for me to locate them," Fazio added proudly. "But it was worth the effort."

Dana snickered at Giancarlo, "Dude, you are so toasted!"

Meanwhile, Giancarlo, who was exceedingly distressed by this point, turned to Fazio and pleaded, "Officer, I beg you—help me."

But Fazio remained stoic and he was loving every second. He did not often have the chance to deliver justice personally, nor so dramatically. This opportunity was more than he could have hoped for. Not only was he helping Monty, but in that instant, he felt like Kevin Costner standing up to Al Capone in *The Untouchables*, the popular film that inspired him to become a policeman in the first place. "Confess to all charges or remain here with your wives and husband," he tersely offered. "I will let them pass judgment on you. It is your decision."

Giancarlo practically jumped out of his skin in horror. "NO— for the love of God! Take me with you. PLEASE!"

Dana looked away from the spectacle of Giancarlo's meltdown in time to notice that Monty was now heading in their direction. Her attention jerked back to the weepy *Señor* Contreras and her pulse quickened—*there would be no graceful way to break the news about his relationship with Giancarlo to Monty.*

Dana hurriedly moved to intercept her. "Monty, listen. This might be a good time for you to tap out," she advised. "There's some stuff that you need to know."

However, Monty's reaction was astonishingly unemotional. "Thank you, Dana, but if it's about that poor man from Barcelona, Sergeant Fazio already told me."

That caught Dana off guard. "Hold on—" she faltered. "You know about him?!"

"Sergeant Fazio didn't want me to be blindsided by the revelation," she explained. "*Señor* Contreras and Giancarlo were married two years ago."

But Dana still could not believe it. "Wait, you know Giancarlo plays for both teams and you're not totally unhinged?"

Monty was uncharacteristically nonplussed. "Not in the least."

Dana tried to digest that but could not. And in that moment, she was every bit as confused as Giancarlo. "Okay, then who the hell are you and what have you done with Monty?" she demanded.

Monty chuckled in response. "All I did was channel my inner Dana Zimmer and ask myself what you would do if you were in my shoes."

"Which was?"

"This ...." Monty announced before strolling over to Giancarlo and grabbing him in the crotch. With both hands. Roughly. His eyes bulged as he yelped in extreme pain.

And she did not let go. In fact, she squeezed even harder, which made him squeal as if he were being murdered. It was wonderful to watch.

Dana was duly transfixed by the display. "Good talk."

Meanwhile, Sergeant Fazio captured the moment with his cell phone and grinned at Monty. "*Capitaine* Chouinard will enjoy this video very much."

Chapter Thirty-Eight
Wonders Never Cease

Greg Lange was working on his laptop when Alex Connelly answered the phone in his hotel suite. "Hello?" A huge smile appeared on his face as he listened to the caller. "Excellent!" Connelly excitedly said. "I'll be right over."

"Good news, I take it?" Lange asked.

"You know it, mate," he answered enthusiastically. "The coppers found my painting!"

Lange was impressed. "That sure was fast."

"If I sign the paperwork today, they said I'll have it for the flight home," Connelly told him as he put on his jacket.

"What about DeLuca?" wondered Lange.

"He can get his own jets," Connelly stated.

Lange was surprised by his change of attitude. It was not like his boss to walk away from a lucrative deal, even one with shifting terms. "Do you really think that's a wise move?"

But Connelly was resolute. "I'm through with those fucking wogs!" he announced using the Australian slang for people of Mediterranean ancestry.

At the *trattoria* where Monty met Connelly at her fake photo shoot, she and Dana sat outside wearing hats and sunglasses to be discreet. They slouched behind their menus upon seeing Connelly step into the Raphael Hotel courtyard to retrieve his car from a valet.

"Well, that didn't take long," Dana observed as he drove off.

But even though Father Vitale had given her his blessing, Monty was still struggling with ethical misgivings. "Are you sure this is going to work? Alex is a formidable man, as you know."

"Maybe so," answered Dana. "But when the mob gets wind of Uncle Sam breathing down his neck, no way are they gonna do a deal with him."

"I hope you're right."

"Trust me, Monty. He's gonna be majorly depressed when this falls apart and that cues him up for Cherie to pick up the pieces."

"When that happens, just make sure you get the photos quickly," Monty replied. "I don't know how long I can pretend to be his willing sex kitten without throwing up."

Dana kept her attention on the hotel. "You better go without me. If I run into Greg Lange, I might strangle him with my bare hands."

Monty grinned. "Well, wonders never cease—Dana Zimmer showing personal restraint!"

"Just deliver the message and get out, will ya?"

Monty entered the lobby, where she slid a slip of paper across the desk to the clerk. She did her best not to stare at his thick black eyebrows and iridescent yellow hair that does not exist in nature. "For *Signor* Connelly," she instructed.

"*Benissimo*," he replied with a courteous partial bow.

As Monty turned to leave, the desk clerk entered a number into his phone, waited a few seconds and said, "A message for *Signor* Connelly: "Mister Braxton in Washington will call at ten o'clock"."

Upstairs in Connelly's suite, Greg Lange wrote the message down word for word. "Thank you," he said grimly. *This confirmed what Cherie told him; Alex was talking to the government!* He immediately recognized this as the kind of information that Citrano and DeLuca might appreciate having brought to their attention.

Then he smiled. Maybe they would show their gratitude by letting him take the lead on the deal now that Connelly wanted out. Considering that he knew as much about the arrangements as his boss, he hoped to find himself generously rewarded for his loyalty.

Chapter Thirty-Nine
I Didn't Mean For This To Happen

That evening, the city of Rome was uncommonly quiet as it was wrapped in a gelatinous blanket of fog that shrouded the tops of buildings and made driving even more hazardous than usual. All seven of the famous hills on which the city was constructed, and their many ancient structures, were obliterated from view.

As Alex Connelly emerged from the Metropolitan Police Station, he was a supremely happy man. Having completed the necessary paperwork to retrieve his valuable painting, it would be delivered to his hotel by police officers in time for his flight home in the morning.

Connelly stood on the sidewalk and took a minute to locate his car in the thick smoke-like air, which had worsened since he arrived. But as he prepared to step from the curb, a dark limousine mysteriously appeared from the murk and stopped.

It was an alarming sight, one that was punctuated by a handgun being pointed at him through an open window. "Get in, *Signor* Connelly," DeLuca's goon Beppe Caruso tersely told him.

Connelly froze. Running was not an option, since the dark barrel of a Defiant Force Plus 9mm semi-automatic handgun was plainly evident. So was Caruso's scowl. And while the limo's other occupants were seated in shadow, Connelly suspected their identities. But he frantically hoped he was wrong. "Yes ... yes ... of course," he stuttered.

As Connelly climbed into the backseat with Caruso, his worst fears were realized when he saw Citrano, DeLuca, and Greg Lange watching him from the rear-facing seat. *What the hell was Lange doing with them?! Something was wrong. Really, really, wrong.*

The limo pulled away from the curb. "What's this about?" Connelly asked as calmly as he could.

Citrano was stone-faced. "We understand that you have decided to part company with us, *Signor* Connelly," he intoned. "We agree."

Connelly stared at the gun that Caruso was still pointing at his ribs. "I don't understand," he answered. "What's with the gun?"

Citrano reacted darkly. "We know about Braxton."

"Who?!" Connelly questioned. He had no idea who they were talking about, of course, because Monty and Dana had made the name up.

"The American government official you have been conspiring with," Citrano clarified.

His emphasis of the word *conspiring* was particularly troublesome. Suddenly, the dire implications of the situation came crashing down on both Connelly and Lange. *To crime figures such as these, feds plus conspiring equals death!*

"Wait a minute, I never said anything about conspiring," Lange protested. "I'm sure they're just fishing for information."

But Citrano ignored the remark and directed his attention exclusively at Connelly. "He left a message for you at your hotel," he revealed.

Connelly glared at him. "If I was working with somebody in the government why didn't he just call my cell?"

"Why does that matter?" Citrano asked.

"You can check my phone," Connelly asserted. "There are no messages from anybody in Washington!"

Citrano smiled cynically. "And no trace of your betrayal. Very smart. It would be like the FBI to arrange that."

"I told you, I'm not working with anyone!"

"It was just a phone message," Lange nervously added, hoping to repair some of the damage that he had caused.

But now it was time for DeLuca to speak. He lowered his sunglasses to look Connelly in the eye. "Were you not leaving police headquarters just now?"

Connelly did a doubletake. "I was filling out paperwork from a robbery. Greg knows that."

"So, you are working with the National Police," DeLuca remarked.

Lange was really starting to get worried now. "What? No—"

"They recovered something that was stolen from my hotel room!" Connelly insisted.

"Of course," Citrano stated with smug satisfaction. "The intriguing thieves who took only one painting, leaving your other valuables untouched."

"But that's what happened!" Connelly argued. "It's worth a fortune."

DeLuca's eyes were dead. "It is also a convenient cover story for you to help the police with their efforts against me, yes?"

The full weight of what DeLuca thought was happening landed on Connelly, and his life passed before his eyes. "*Signor* DeLuca, you have to believe me!"

"From now on, young Lange will handle our business," DeLuca added with a sense of finality.

Connelly glowered at Lange. "You double-dealing prick!"

Lange tried to speak, but his emotions rendered the effort indecipherable. He was in over his head and felt as if he were drowning.

Then the limo pulled to an abrupt stop. Citrano turned to Lange and decreed, "You will leave us now."

"But Alex—"

Citrano completed the sentence for him. "—is coming with us."

Lange's eyes grew wide as he digested the statement. "But you said nothing would happen to him!"

DeLuca's eyes were burning like two festering sores. "I changed my mind," he said as he put his sunglasses back on. "Thank you for your assistance."

Caruso waved the gun in his direction. "Good night."

Lange did not need to be told twice. The weapon being pointed at him said it all. Scrambling from the limo as fast as humanly possible, he stumbled onto the sidewalk as if he had been thrown there.

Moments later the limo was gone. As it disappeared into the folds of haze, Lange stood alone in the unsettling darkness, where he disintegrated into a full melt-down. "Oh, God. OH, GOD!!!!" he screeched.

He was about to wet his pants when a burgundy Citroën C3 appeared from nowhere with a taxi close behind. Dana called out through the open passenger window. "Where's Alex, Lange?"

"The mafia's going to kill him!" Lange cried. Just saying the words intensified his fear to an unbearable degree.

"Kill him?!" she repeated. "What are you talking about?!"

"Kill him, as in a hit!" he explained. "They took him away just before you showed up!"

"SHIT!" she cursed as she leapt from the car and motioned urgently at the taxi.

Seconds later, Monty approached wearing one of her sexy Cherie outfits. "What is it?" she asked without using a French accent.

"The mob has Alex!" screamed Dana.

Monty could hardly believe her ears. "What?!"

"Ask Lange," she responded, getting back in the car. "Let's go!"

Monty immediately opened the passenger door and turned to Lange as she climbed in. "You heard her, Greg!"

He did not move right away, however. He was still confused by Cherie's presence. "What happened to your accent?"

"I'll fill you in later—come on!" she replied.

Lange had not fully complied when Dana stomped on the gas. His open door slammed loudly, and he was thrown against the back seat as the car burned rubber.

Somehow Dana had to find that limousine! With no clue about what to do if she did, she clung to the idea that Connelly's survival hinged on it. "Which way'd they go?" she demanded.

"Turn right at the corner," he answered, still processing the perplexity of seeing Connelly's two mistresses together. "Cherie, what are you doing with her?" he finally questioned.

"Chick's got taste," Dana declared as she adjusted the bill of her baseball cap and fishtailed around the corner onto *Viale Aventino*. "Okay Lange, now what?" she thundered.

"How am I supposed to know?" he asked.

"For goodness sake, slow down!" Monty interjected as she held on for dear life. "You'll run someone over!"

"Not the way I drive," she came back. "One of my brothers is a Nascar champion." She turned her baseball cap backwards on her head, as if that had something to do with efficient driving.

Monty threw her another look. "Is there anything people in your family can't do?"

"I don't see them!" Dana barked as she strained to see in the condensing soup.

"Oh, God—he doesn't have a chance," bleated Lange. "I didn't mean for this to happen!"

Dana fired him a glance in the rear-view mirror. "Neither did we!"

"Actually, I told you it was a bad idea," Monty returned.

But Dana was in no frame of mind to deal with semantics. "Can we talk about that later, Monty?"

Monty folded her arms defiantly. "I just want to set the record straight, that's all."

"Unfuckingbelievable," Dana fumed.

Meanwhile, Lange was sluggish to react to something that he just heard. "Wait—Monty? I thought your name was Cherie."

"It's a long story," Monty answered.

The next forty minutes were harrowing. Under the best of circumstances, navigating the streets of Rome in fog would be a strange adventure, but on this night, the chase after the limousine was downright scary. Since many locals wisely decided to stay off the streets that night, things were unusually still.

Monty shrieked repeatedly as Dana powered through the streets like a pro, evading obstructions and potential victims with skill. It was like being in a demolition derby blindfolded, however, and that made keeping track of the limo nearly impossible. Unfortunately, with so few taillights to help guide Dana through the poor visibility, the handful of cars and pedestrians that were out made driving extremely treacherous, as they seemed to pop out of nowhere.

Swerving around a truck that unexpectedly appeared in the chunky morass, Monty and Lange screamed. But seconds later, the limo could be seen a half block ahead as it turned onto *Via Ostiense.*

"There they are!" Lange hollered excitedly.

"I'm on it," Dana replied as she weaved through traffic. But despite her best efforts, the fog seemed to be gelling, and that made keeping the limo in sight an impossible challenge.

Monty strained to see. "Don't let them get too far ahead."

"You wanna drive?" Dana slammed back.

"I'm just trying to help," Monty returned sheepishly.

Just then, as they were turning onto *Lungotevere Paolo,* their Citroën engine sputtered pathetically a few times before the car slowed. "Fuck a duck—" Dana cursed.

"What's wrong?!" asked Monty.

And then the engine stopped completely. Dana tapped the dashboard angrily. "We're outta gas!"

Monty was bewildered. "We're what?!"

"I forgot to fill up, okay?"

"How could you overlook something like that?!"

"I had other stuff on my mind—like taking care of Giancarlo for you!"

"Fair enough," Monty admitted. "What are we going to do now?"

Then Monty saw that Dana's attention was concentrated elsewhere. She realized that she was looking at an Iveco delivery truck filled with open side panels of wine. Cases and cases of it. The truck was double-parked with its emergency flashers on as a delivery man hoisted one of the containers to his shoulder and walked into a restaurant.

"We hafta punt," Dana disclosed as she exited the car and ran to the truck. "Follow me."

Moments later Monty and Lange rushed up behind her. "You are not seriously thinking of stealing this truck," Monty challenged.

"Get in or say goodbye to Alex," Dana warned. "Your choice."

Monty and Lange reluctantly climbed in beside her as she dropped the manual transmission into first gear. Monty was in the middle of the bench seat. "Please tell me we're not doing this!" she implored.

"Okay, I won't."

As the delivery truck lurched from the curb, several unsecured cases of wine crashed to the pavement. But that was not the only time it happened. As Dana careened through foggy intersections, she triggered several fender-bender accidents, narrowly avoided others, and sideswiped more than a few parked vehicles, grinding the truck's gears, and leaving an avalanche of exploding wine bottles in her wake.

Before long, they were driving along the Tiber River, and the swampy conditions worsened near the water. When they turned onto *Viadotto della Magliana,* they found themselves in a less populated area filled with darkened factories and warehouses. And whether the fog was denser there or not, it sure seemed to be. The truck headlights were unable to make a dent in the solidifying cloud.

Dana downshifted and decelerated, struggling to see more than a few feet ahead. "Where are they, Monty?!"

"They were here a minute ago."

"What have I done?!" Lange moaned.

Dana yelled over Monty. "Shut up, Lange." Then she turned her attention back to the chase. "Keep looking, Monty,"

"I am," she confirmed. "But they've vanished into thin air!"

"They gotta be here someplace," insisted Dana as she aimed the truck down one of the darkened alleys. It was solid fog.

"Please be careful, Dana!" Monty begged.

"I'm doing the best I can, okay?"

"But what if you find them?" bawled Lange. "Then what? THEY'LL KILL ALL OF US!"

And that was about all that Dana could take. "Lange, if you don't put a sock in it, I'm gonna climb over there and do it for ya!"

"This's all my fault—" he wailed, holding his head. "It's a nightmare!"

Suddenly, Dana thought of something. She grabbed her phone from her purse and shoved it at Monty. "Call Sergeant Fazio."

"Of course!" Monty said. "What's the number?"

Dana reached into her bra and handed her a slip of paper. "Here."

Monty reacted blankly. "You keep his number in your bra?"

"Will you just freaking call him?!"

Monty punched in the number and spoke into the phone, "I'd like to speak to Sergeant Fazio immediately. It's an emergency." Then Monty's optimism dimmed, and she turned to Dana with agitation. "Italian, Dana. They speak *Italian!*"

"Damn foreigners," Dana carped.

"I don't believe this!" protested Lange.

"Don't you ever shut up?!" Monty challenged.

"Just look for the limo," Dana commanded in an effort to get them focused again.

Monty yelled into the phone, "Wait—*momento*—" And she turned to Dana as an idea came. "My phrase book!" she explained.

"Good thinking!" Dana cheered.

Monty dug a booklet from her purse and flipped the pages, though what came out of her mouth only vaguely resembled the Italian language, as she butchered phrases when she hurriedly found them. "I would like to speak to ... *Vorrei parlare con ...."*

Just then the truck hit a pothole, flipping the pages of the phrase book as she went on, *"Vorrei fare l'amore con il Sergente Fazio."* Unfortunately, what Monty actually told the police receptionist was, "I would like to make love to Sergeant Fazio."

She turned to Dana resentfully. "She's laughing at me!"

"Let's see ... you have a poor attitude ...." she continued into the phone as the truck hit another bump in the road. Finding what she thought were the right words, she said, *"Hai un culo grande!"*

Click! The cell went dead.

"She hung up on me," reported a deeply offended Monty. What she did not realize was that she had once again badly mangled an Italian phrase. What she actually told the receptionist was, "You have a big ass!"

Lange flopped against the passenger window and whimpered. "Alex is a dead man."

Dana continued to drive. "Okay, Monty where would you take somebody you were planning to whack?"

"How would I know?" Monty yelled with rising alarm. "Don't you have a brother who's a professional assassin? They do everything else."

"Wait—assassin. That's it!" Lange recalled. "The mafia has a boatyard where they get rid of people!"

"A boatyard? Dana asked. "How do you know that?!"

"They told us about it when we drove by here ... as a warning."

"Where is it?" Dana demanded.

"I don't know."

Dana yowled, "You hafta know!"

"I don't remember, okay?!" he screamed. "It's on the Tiber somewhere!"

"Monty, check the map," Dana ordered.

Monty pulled out her iPhone and stared. "I don't know how to use that feature yet."

The admission stunned Dana. "What?!"

"It's a new phone," Monty reminded her. "Giancarlo took the other one, remember?"

"Then try a real map," Dana challenged.

"Oh," Monty answered. She dug through papers on the dash and in the glove box. "Not everyone has your computer savvy."

"Yeah, I get that."

Pulling a soiled pair of men's underwear from the glove box, Monty contorted. "This vehicle is disgusting! I don't even want to know what its carbon footprint might be."

In the meantime, Lange continued to work his memory. "I remember the bridge we were on. Mangle. It was Mangle something ... Mangle ... Maggot ... Magnolia ... *Magliana!* That's it!" he screamed victoriously. "The MAGLIANA BRIDGE!"

Monty found a weathered and greasy map and opened it as if she might catch a disease touching it. And she might not have been wrong about that. "The print is microscopic," she reported before reading aloud. *"Ponte del Risorgimento ... Fabricio ... Mazzini ... Magliana!* That's it—turn right!"

Dana yanked the truck into a sudden turn, spilling most of the remaining wine cases on the pavement.

They had only traveled four miles from the Municipal Police station where Sergeant Fazio worked, but they might as well have been on another planet. This place was certainly not cosmopolitan Rome, particularly the way it looked in the opaque air that enshrouded everything. It was dark and remote. Knowing it was also a mafia facility used for making people disappear was the capper on an already extremely frightening concept.

As they crossed the Magliana Bridge, the streetlamps were grossly inadequate in the impenetrable visibility. Dana downshifted again and slowed the truck, but the limo was nowhere to be found. "This bites," she snapped. "Come on, Lange. Help me out here."

He referred to Monty's filthy map and looked out his window. "Wait ...!" he faltered. "I think he pointed down there when he mentioned the shipyard."

He excitedly thrust the map at Dana. "And here it is— *Riparazione Barche Magliana!*"

Dana pulled to a stop and shook her head at the foggy void. "Well, at least it's not creepy or anything," she sarcastically griped. "Good place to off somebody, though."

Monty, all the while, was becoming more upset. "Will you watch your language?" she beseeched. "What are we going to do?"

Dana thought about that a beat and then grumbled, "Fuck it— hang on, kids." She pulled the truck into a sharp U-turn and headed back across the bridge. "There's gotta be an access road around here someplace," she told them.

"You aren't really going to drive down there," Monty said.

"You got a better idea?"

By now, Lange was beginning to shiver uncontrollably as visions of what he was sure was going to be his execution played in his head. "Oh, God ... oh, God ...." he muttered.

Then, locating an old wooden sign identifying the shipyard, Dana killed their headlights and entered the turn-off. The entire truck was swallowed by the dense fog, which only became heavier the further they descended the single lane dirt access road.

Even without zero visibility conditions, this would have been a place to avoid at night, Dana thought as she inched the truck past the solid wall of trees and tall overgrown bushes on both sides. They were fully committed now, she realized. There would be no backing up if something went wrong.

"I don't like this, Dana," Monty objected as she imagined mafia gunmen behind the foliage preparing their weapons for the slaughter.

"Yeah, well I'm not that crazy about it myself," she complained as she stuck her head out the window hoping to see better. The air was cold and clammy on her face.

"We're going to die ..." Lange whimpered. "I know it!"

"Oh, grow a pair, will ya?!" Dana snarled.

They continued down the sloping road for several minutes, though it seemed like a lifetime. Dana brought the truck to a crawl as several speedboats and piles of mechanical parts came into view. It was unearthly and more than a little horrifying as the fog seemed to attach itself to objects like sticky grey cotton candy, and the sounds around them became disturbingly muffled and sluggish.

When they entered the boatyard compound of rusting structures with corrugated metal roofs a single pair of taillights became visible through the mist. In time they could make out the image of the limo parked at the riverbank.

Then they could see a man standing beside the limo as someone large draped him in heavy chains. *It was DeLuca and Citrano's goon Caruso preparing to kill Alex Connelly!*

The girls traded worried looks and Lange was beside himself. "Oh, God, they're going to drown him and then we're next! OH, SHIT!" he wept in a desperate whisper before jumping from the truck and running up the road into the night, completely terrified.

The girls watched in dismay as Connelly was blindfolded by Citrano and DeLuca checked his gun. "Okay, these guys are the worst," Dana confirmed.

Monty shot her a look. "Thank you for that assessment."

"At least they're not going to drown him," Dana observed.

"Really?" asked Monty. "How can you tell?"

"Because they're gonna put a bullet in his ear first."

Monty was beside herself. "Dana, we have to do something!"

"You don't think I know that?" she growled. It did not take long for her to answer her own question. "Aw, what the hell—" she said as she dropped the transmission into first gear, punched the accelerator to the floor, and leaned on the horn.

The truck churned dirt and gravel as it practically flew down the hill toward the mobsters. DeLuca and Citrano reacted with shock and disbelief as Caruso fired his gun over and over, shattering the windshield. The girls screamed and ducked, even as Dana managed to shift into second and third gear. Then DeLuca pulled his own pistol from his shoulder holster and fired wildly, before leaping into the limo with Citrano as Caruso scrambled for the driver's door.

Meanwhile, Connelly tried to make a run for it, but his blindfold and chains made for slow going.

Dana aimed the truck for the limo and rammed it from behind with a deafening crunch of twisting metal. The ear-splitting explosion was like being in the middle of a fireworks display, followed by a waterfall of windshield glass that covered the girls as the limo was shoved from a narrow wooden pier into the murky river below.

Then the world around them plunged back into eerie silence.

"I cannot believe you did that!" Monty shouted.

Dana could not believe it herself. "Copy that," was all she could say. She was having enough trouble breathing, never mind talking.

But as soon as the words left Dana's lips, Monty saw the image of Alex Connelly in the fog, standing in stark relief against the refracted glow of a work lamp hanging from one of the buildings. He was stumbling, blindfolded, panicked—and heading straight for the water's edge. A twenty-foot drop.

Monty yelled at the top of her lungs, "Alex, STOP!!!!!"

And he did, confused beyond description. "Cherie—" he called out, "is that you?"

"*Oui*, my darling!" she returned in her French accent. "I have been looking for you! Do not move!" But then Monty turned to Dana in a panic. "What do we do now?"

"Do you know how to drive a stick?" Dana asked.

"It's been a while, but I used to."

"Then you take him back in the truck," continued Dana. "I'll call Fazio for a ride."

"But Alex will have a lot of questions," Monty worried.

Dana thought fast. "You got any more of those sleeping pills?"

Monty wracked her brain until the memory finally came. "In my purse!"

"Then maybe he needs a drink to calm down," Dana added as she grabbed one of the surviving wine jugs from the truck.

Meanwhile, Connelly called from the water's edge, still blindfolded, confused, and scared, "Cherie? Where are you?!"

"I will be right there, my darling!" Monty proclaimed in her French accent. "Do not worry! You are no longer in danger!"

Meanwhile, Dana unscrewed the top of the jug as she and Monty poured the contents of the remaining capsules inside. "This oughta take care of him for a while," said Dana.

"Wish me luck," Monty told her before approaching Connelly. "I am coming for you, Alex!"

As Monty removed his blindfold, Dana stepped out of sight.

"Alex, I am so relieved that you are safe!" Monty professed.

Connelly was still terrified and bewildered. "What are you doing here, Cherie? What the hell happened tonight?!"

Monty thought fast. "Gregory told me what the criminals were going to do, so I asked a friend to follow the limousine." She handed him the wine. "Drink this, my darling."

He gratefully gulped the wine before looking across the darkened boatyard. "I ought to thank your friend. Where is he?"

"He ran away, *mon amour*," she explained. "He was afraid."

Connelly met her look, still trying to process what took place. "He's not the only one," he admitted before taking another drink.

Monty put her arms around him and kissed him. "May I give you a ride to your hotel?"

"That's a bonzer idea if I ever heard one," Connelly grinned.

Ten minutes later he was passed out in the passenger seat of the truck as Monty drove back into the city.

Chapter Forty
Your Fantasy Is Waiting

Twelve hours later, Monty was feeling extremely fulfilled. Not only was the harrowing rescue of Alex Connelly successful, but Sergeant Fazio called to report that two more of Giancarlo's jilted spouses had been found. *What glorious news that was to hear!*

She leaned closer to the dressing room mirror and touched up her makeup in preparation for Cherie's final appearance in his life.

When he awakened on the living room couch, he was groggy and drugged. Then, taking a sip of his beloved Talisker scotch, he winced. *Why did it taste so awful?!* His body ached as he shuffled over to the bar in search of an unopened bottle.

That is when Monty appeared in the dressing room doorway. She was wearing a sheer black negligee and the sight of her made him forget all about finding more scotch. She was radiant looking.

"Cherie ...." he gasped.

"I hope that you are feeling better now," she murmured as only Cherie could.

He ogled her in the negligee through bleary eyes. "I'm still pretty knackered. How long was I out?"

"Twelve hours."

"Wow," he exclaimed. "You know, I feel like a drongo having a sheila rescue me like that."

"What does that mean, the word *drongo*?" she asked.

"That's Aussie for fool," he explained.

"I would not say that you are a fool," Monty whispered as she sauntered in his direction. "But I am happy to be called Sheila if that is what you would like."

Watching her body move in the negligee was downright tantalizing. "I still can't figure out why Lange told you about the mob's plan," he told her as he tried to piece the memory together.

"He would not be the first man to try to impress me with his connections," she replied with a shrug.

"I don't doubt that," Connelly affirmed as his imagination crackled. "So, what happens now?"

She kissed him softly and leisurely began to unfasten his pants. "I am going to make you forget all about what happened at the river last night," she promised as she kissed him again.

"River? What river?" he said with a smirk as his pants hit the floor.

Taking him by the hand, she smiled. "Come with me."

"*Oui, oui!*" Connelly answered, laughing with delight.

In the bedroom, she tore his shirt off him before shoving him hard onto the bed. "I want to do things to you, Alex. Special things."

Connelly watched her looming over him. "No argument here."

"Mmmmm. I like how that sounds," Monty returned as she held up a pair of handcuffs from an overnight bag on the chair. "What do you think of these?"

His eyes were ablaze with expectation. "You are a devil!"

"I am that and much, much more," she assured him as she locked his wrists to the bedposts. "Are you comfortable, my darling?"

He could hardly speak he was so excited. "I can't move," he replied as his voice tightened.

She bent over him, providing him with a remarkable view of her cleavage that nearly drove him out of his mind. "And this is agreeable for you?" she asked.

Agreeable? Hell yeah, he thought. "You have no idea," he said with a slight yelp.

She giggled playfully as she ran her fingers through his hair with one hand while reaching into her overnight bag with the other. Soon she lifted a sexy strapless stick-on brassiere into view.

His eyes grew wide. "What's that for?"

"To make my fantasy complete," she teased as the bra dangled in his face.

Another look at her body and Connelly was ready for anything that she might have in mind, no matter how kinky or strange. "Whatever turns you on, doll!"

Again, Monty smiled. "This will make me feel very good," she explained as she carefully positioned the brassiere across his chest.

She paused to savor the image.

"Well?" he asked. "Your fantasy is waiting."

Monty nodded. *"Une chose de plus,"* she purred, reaching into the bag one last time. She produced a curly yellow Little Miss Muffet wig, complete with exceedingly long ringlets. *"Voila!"*

"Come on, really?" he chattered. "That's ridiculous."

"Au contraire, it is perfect," she concluded as she plopped it on his head and adjusted the ringlets to frame his face just-so.

Then untied her negligee. "And now my surprise for you …."

Every cell in Connelly's body was energized as she removed her negligee jacket. He stared, speechless. She was an absolute vision of all things exotic and erotic.

Suddenly, the door to the bedroom flew open and a pregnant woman walked in—it was Heather Connelly!

She glared at the incriminating scene. "Alex?!"

Connelly could only lay there, disoriented and wearing the bizarre outfit. "Heather … I … I …."

"You what?" she challenged.

"I … what are you doing here?" he finally got out.

"Surprising my cheating bastard husband!" she announced, her voice dripping with contempt. "And it certainly looks like I have."

Just then Monty stepped forward as if nothing untoward was happening. "Darling, are you not going to introduce us?" She extended her hand to Heather, *"Bonsoir,* I am Cherie. His lover."

Connelly panicked at the words. "No—I can explain!"

But before he could try, he turned white at the sight of someone else at the door: Dana in a hotel uniform.

"Signora, your bags have arrived," she announced.

"Never mind," Heather responded. "I won't be staying."

"Heather, wait!" Connelly screamed as he stared at Dana. "I KNOW THAT GIRL!"

Heather's reply was to aim her iPhone at him. "Smile for the judge."

And as the shutter clicked, Monty leaned into the frame at the last second, photobombing him with an alluring fashion model pose.

"I'll see you in court," Heather snarled before leaving.

Dana was right behind her, but stopped just long enough to add, "Dude, you are so busted!"

Heather leaned against a wall outside Connelly's suite, composing herself as Dana emerged from the room. "I can't tell you how satisfying that was!" she blurted. "Thank you for calling me."

"It's amazing you got here so fast," Dana told her hesitantly.

"A company jet does come in handy," Heather replied as she caught her breath. "But I can't wait to meet Monty. Not many women would go to such trouble to shut down a philanderer."

Dana nodded her agreement, though she was subdued. "She's something else, alright."

Reveling in the memory, Heather laughed grimly. "God, the look on his face ...!"

Dana fought the guilt rising inside her, but that was a losing proposition. She was unable to even look Heather in the eye. "Heather, about that," she began slowly. "There's something you need to know."

It did not take long for Heather to pick up on what was coming next. "Monty isn't the only one Alex has interest in, is she."

Dana stared at her feet. "It's worse than that," she began. "I was interested back. The truth is, I thought I was in love with him."

Heather stood up-right and her complexion reddened. "So, you're the one—" she began. "I knew he was seeing someone."

"I feel like such a jerk—" Dana started.

But Heather was not really listening. Her emotions were already fully charged, and a million repressed details flooded forth. "The signs were all there. I saw them ... but I just couldn't prove anything."

"I didn't know he was still married," protested Dana before correcting herself. "No, that's not true. I mean, I knew he was married, but he said it was over a long time ago."

Heather did not respond as she stood there in shock, studying her. Dana was practically shaking. "Please don't hate me—I already hate myself enough for both of us."

Heather flopped against the wall for support, but still did not say anything.

"If you wanna punch me in the face or something, I'd understand," Dana added. "I totally deserve it."

Heather's mind raced as she imagined what it would be like to take Dana up on her offer. But, ultimately, she could not do such a thing. At long last, she caught her breath and softened. "No," she answered. "This isn't about you, Dana."

Dana was incredulous. *How could it not be about her? She was sleeping with this woman's husband!* "It isn't?" she finally asked.

"He cheated before," Heather clarified. "I don't know how many times. When he agreed to counseling this last time, I foolishly thought there might be a chance to save our marriage."

Dana flopped against the wall beside her, relieved that Heather seemed willing to forgive her. She was also thunderstruck to hear that she was not Connelly's first affair.

"I should have left him long ago, but as you know, the man can be very convincing," Heather reflected. She gently touched her stomach. "Like when he said he wanted to start a family. I thought that he had finally turned the corner."

Dana's head was spinning now. Her guilt, dismay, anger, and embarrassment were off the charts. "But still—" she confessed, "I shoulda known better than to believe him."

Heather nodded sadly and touched Dana's arm. "Maybe we both should have."

Back in the bedroom a shattered and numb Alex Connelly was still handcuffed to the bed as Monty put on her negligee jacket. "Cherie, where are you going?" he nervously asked.

She cast her eyes on him and batted her lashes. "You could not want me now," she suggested, "after that unpleasantness with your wife."

"But I do!" he claimed. "She means nothing to me! Please stay."

She looked at him quizzically. "The mood for lovemaking is gone, is it not?"

He shook his head vehemently. "No! I'm still into it ... the handcuffs ... everything!" he claimed before adding what he hoped would seal the deal. "You can do anything you want to me."

She let the offer hang in the air, pretending to give it consideration. "Anything?"

"Whatever you want!" he announced in equal measures of hopefulness and desperation.

Monty let a smile slowly return to her lips, as if this were the most engrossing opportunity that she had ever received. "Well, since you have offered ...." she said.

Connelly relaxed in eager anticipation of what he thought was about to happen. Monty lifted a bottle of champagne from an ice bucket and set it aside with a spicy smile, before lifting the waistband of his boxers and pouring the freezing contents of the bucket down the front. He screamed bloody murder as the ice covered his genitals, and Monty walked to the door.

Then she turned to address him without her French accent. "God only knows why Dana fell for a reprobate like you," she charged. "But what is inconceivable is that you let her get away."

Before he could respond she left the room. As the door closed, his voice could be heard echoing throughout the suite, "Wait! Cherie, you can't leave me handcuffed like this! Wait! PLEASE!"

Monty was greeted in the hallway by Heather and Dana, who helped her into a negligee-covering trench coat that Dana had at the ready. "Thanks, Dana," she said as Connelly continued to bellow for help from inside.

Heather motioned her head in the direction of his pleading. "You know, I think I could stand here listening to that all night!"

Dana's time with Heather Connelly that afternoon was less awkward than she feared it would be. Having heard the extent of her husband's contemptible manipulations, Heather invited Dana and

Monty to continue the conversation at a nearby café. Monty was careful to listen, but not intrude. Fortunately, it became apparent rather quickly that Heather and Dana's mutual source of pain was Alex.

Monty admired Heather for the gracious way she handled the exchange of individual and collective heartaches, and Dana for her willingness to show remorse.

Then, after devoting two hours to sorting out the lies that Alex told them, it was evident that Heather had actually grown to like the young woman who was her husband's mistress.

She stood to leave and gave Dana a hug. "Dana," she offered, "When we're both feeling a little better about all this, would you let me take you to lunch?"

The invitation came as a shock, to say the least. "No shit? I mean ... really?"

"We have too much in common to have hard feelings over what happened to us," Heather answered. "We're both victims here. Let's not let that son of a bitch win."

Chapter Forty-One
That Would Be Entertaining

Back at her hotel, Monty wrapped herself in a thick terry cloth bathrobe and tried to decompress. She would be meeting Dana and Sergeant Fazio later for a victory dinner, but this quiet time was something to be treasured. With Fazio's assistance, she and Dana had accomplished the impossible: they got revenge. And now that it was over, she was realizing just how audacious the whole thing really was.

As she stepped onto her terrace, a full moon was already visible in the cloudless blue sky, and the warmth of the late afternoon sun enveloped her. She reveled in the splendid feeling on her skin and drifted off to another time and place, when the world in which she lived was innocent, and Italy held only romantic and cultural associations for her.

A favorite Percy Shelley verse that recalled those days came to mind:

> How beautiful is sunset, when the glow
> Of Heaven descends upon a land like thee,
> Thou Paradise of exiles, Italy!

As it turned out, Italy was not much of a paradise for Monty. Nor did it turn out to be for her new acquaintance, Dana.

The thought of Dana caused Monty to pause and consider their highly unconventional bond. While it would take a long time for her anguish to fade, their successful campaign against Giancarlo and Connelly was proving to be remarkably restorative. Theirs was an odd-couple relationship to be sure, but it was one for which she was most appreciative. She wondered if any of her college classmates would have been as effective as Dana in this crisis—or if they even would have been minimally capable.

Dana, she had come to realize, was a truly exceptional person.

Monty also understood that while Dana was adept at hiding behind her tough façade, she was every bit as vulnerable to heartbreak as anyone else. Monty admired her most for her tenacity, however, and wished that she could be more like her. She hoped that Dana might visit her family summer home on Lake Hayward in Connecticut one day soon. The only thing better than enjoying a peaceful morning coffee on the deck and listening to the chirping birds would be sharing it with her partner in crime.

The extraordinary feeling of living in an aviary was not the only thing about the lake that she wanted Dana to experience. The peaceful bioluminescence of fireflies blinking as the tree crickets sang at night was another.

And then there was the crystal-clear natural spring water that often made it impossible to tell where the lake ended, and the sky began. The feeling of stepping into a living landscape painting had always been special to Monty, and she was sure that Dana would enjoy it.

The image of her parents' reaction to meeting her unusual quirky friend brought a smile to her face. *That would be entertaining, indeed!*

Meanwhile at the *Parco dei Principi*, Dana was savoring a glass of tequila along with a long bath. While she had never been one for meditation, if this soak in a hot tub was anything like it then she considered finding a class when she got home.

But what would home look like now? she wondered. To start with, she was newly unemployed and single. She was hemorrhaging emotions, though she did what she could to convince herself that what she was feeling was more embarrassment than hurt. Nobody had forced her to put her street smarts on hold and fall in love with a married man, she reproved herself. *That was so unbelievably stupid! She should have known better than to get involved with him in the first place. She should have sensed that he never meant the loving things he said.*

On the other hand, with Monty's help she had gotten more than the payback she had hoped for: Heather Connelly had helped to resolve the guilt that she felt over becoming Alex's mistress. In fact, her gracious nature reminded Dana a lot of Monty and she wished that she possessed a few of the many fine qualities the two women shared.

That realization prompted her to think about how much her opinion of Monty had changed since their crazed fight, and she wondered if any of Monty had rubbed off on her. Monty's generosity was admirable, but Dana envied her most for being so optimistic. For her unbending, glass-is-half-full vision of the world. That point of view had been foreign to Dana before they teamed up, and it was inspiring to be around it. Her own glass-is-almost-empty approach to things was a hell of a way to go through life, and she privately swore to do better.

She wondered if the reason for Monty's outlook might be her faith in God. If so, she thought that could be something worth looking into.

Dana was determined to remember these lessons as she launched a new beginning. Whatever that might turn out to be.

Chapter Forty-Two
Call Me Anything You Want

By nine o'clock that night at the *La Cucina di Isabella*, Monty and Dana looked rested and content as they basked in the glow of their triumphs over Giancarlo and Connelly. Every table in the restaurant was occupied, and Alfredo gleamed with pride over the fully restored and upgraded space. Thanks to Monty's restitution funds, the new wooden accent wall was stunning, and it included framed natural slate water features which were hung like works of art. And the bar's liquor display had been expanded and redesigned with floating acrylic LED bar shelves.

It was outstanding.

Meanwhile, the pianist in the white dinner jacket was back at work in the corner, and Monty was glad to see that he still had a job. She hated the idea of anyone's livelihood being interrupted because of her.

As Alfredo arrived at Monty and Dana's table with a bottle in hand, a burly bear of a man sitting near them was inhaling massive bites of tortellini with *Bolognese* sauce. Nothing about his eating resembled anything close to dining, and the women traded silent amused looks with Alfredo.

He shrugged and whispered to them, "It seems that he enjoys my wife's cooking very much!"

Dana shook her head, "You're more patient than me, Alfredo."

He nodded and opened the bottle, which was champagne. "I believe everyone to be more patient than you, *Signora*."

"True-dat!" she agreed with a laugh as she raised her glass.

Monty joined her, then paused. "Alfredo, I just realized that we never asked for champagne."

"This is complimentary, to congratulate you both on what you did about those horrible men who hurt you," he informed them.

Dana and Monty were overjoyed. "Wow, really?" Dana said.

"Sergeant Fazio told me everything," he commented. "Well done!"

"That is so nice ... thank you!" Monty replied.

Dana shook her head in wonder. "It was a little hairy there for a while, Alfredo, but it all worked out."

"I was delighted that I could play a small part in your quest for justice," Alfredo proclaimed.

Monty smiled at him as she lifted her glass in a toast. "To justice!"

"And to your family not disowning you," Dana added, "or we'd both still be stuck in the slammer."

"I will certainly drink to both of those!" Monty happily remarked.

Alfredo felt like a proud papa as the girls downed their drinks and then re-poured. "Please permit me ...."

"You are such a dear, Alfredo!" Monty gushed.

He smiled at her, though cautiously. *"Grazie tanto,"* he responded. "But there will be no fights this evening, yes?"

"Of course not!" Dana confirmed with a chuckle.

Monty concurred. "Those days are over for us, trust me."

Alfredo's smile widened. "Excellent! My wife she will be very happy to know this."

"I'll second that—take five!" said Monty, holding her hand out to mimic Dana.

Alfredo and Dana stared at her.

"Monty, what are you doing?" Dana asked.

"Commemorating our moment," she came back, again extending her hand towards Dana. "Take five!"

Alfredo was still in the dark and Dana could only shake her head. "It's gimme five, not take," Dana corrected.

"Take five, give five, it's still five, isn't it?" Monty challenged.

Dana halfheartedly slapped her hand. She had learned the hard way that some things were not worth an argument with Monty.

Meanwhile, Alfredo had no clue about what just happened. "Let me bring you *antipasti* while you wait for Sergeant Fazio," he said as he placed the champagne bottle in a bucket and exited.

Dana checked the time on her phone. "When's Fazio supposed to get here, anyway?"

"Any time now," Monty said. "It was sweet of him to offer to meet us for a celebration, wasn't it?"

Again, Dana could only stare. "Sweet? Monty, the guy's got a thing for you."

"Oh, don't be ridiculous."

"He got your jewelry and paintings back, didn't he?"

"Of course, he did," Monty stated. "He's a law enforcement professional, which is why he was able to convince Giancarlo to tell him where they were."

Dana reached for her champagne glass with obvious skepticism. "Yeah, right," she scoffed. "Professional."

"Well, he is," Monty added.

"I suppose he invites all of his crime victims to a dinner out."

"That doesn't mean anything," Monty insisted.

Dana chortled, "Sure, it does."

"You are such a cynic," accused Monty. "To you everyone has an agenda."

"Look, I'm just telling ya," Dana argued, "the guy's got it bad for you."

"Hopeless and ridiculous," Monty said, correcting her previous assessment.

"Suit yourself," chuckled Dana as she returned to her drink. But then she saw something in the distance. "Check it out ...."

Monty followed her look to the entrance, where Sergeant Fazio could be seen looking boyishly handsome in his best white silk suit. He had a bouquet of colorful flowers in hand. "Your boyfriend cleans up real nice," Dana observed.

"For the last time, he's not my boyfriend."

"Hundred bucks says you're wrong."

Monty shot her a reprimanding look. "You don't have one hundred dollars."

"I'll borrow it from you."

"You are incorrigible!" Monty observed. Then, as Fazio approached, she smiled at the large bouquet he was holding. "Sergeant Fazio, what lovely flowers!"

Fazio reacted bashfully. "They are, indeed, *Signora*." But then he shocked the girls by offering them—to Dana. "For you, Miss Zimmer."

And for once in her life Dana was completely caught off guard and baffled. "Me?!"

Fazio's already shaky confidence quickly evaporated. "You do not like them?" he asked with growing concern.

"Yeah, Dana, don't you like them?" Monty asked gleefully.

Dana struggled to recover. This was not expected. Not at all. "No ... I love them," she stammered. "Thank you ... Sergeant."

He exhaled as a look of relief appeared on his face. "Please, I would be honored if you would call me Cesare," he offered.

"No problem ... Cesare ...." she answered modestly.

Fazio beamed. "And may I call you Dana?"

"Well, sure, of course," she faltered. "Call me anything you want."

"Thank you," he returned. "I will put these in water for you."

As he headed to the kitchen, Monty rejoiced. "Call me anything you want!" she said, mimicking her with mocking exaggeration.

Dana flopped back in her chair. "How the hell did I not see that coming?!"

"Who cares?" Monty returned. "He's adorable."

A huge grin appeared on Dana's face. "I know, right?"

"I'll add the hundred to what you already owe me," Monty promised as Alfredo returned with a platter of *antipasti*. "And speaking of adorable, Alfredo, we could never have done this without you. Come here, you darling man ...."

Monty stood and planted a big kiss on his cheek. As luck would have it, at that very instant his wife emerged from the kitchen with a tray of food. Her jaw hardened at the sight of the gorgeous American woman kissing her husband, and he immediately went pale, which made the prominent lipstick mark on his face stand out even more.

"Isabella!" he pronounced with more apprehension than he intended to reveal, "we were just talking about you—"

"That did not look like talking to me!" she snarled.

"My love, it is not what you think—"

"I know what I saw, Alfredo!"

"What, this?!" he said pointing to his cheek chuckling nervously.

But she cut him off sharply, as if resuming a previous argument, which in fact she was. "I should have listened to my mother and married Lorenzo Di Vita!" she announced in a fury.

His face instantaneously turned red. "But ... Isabella ... my soul-mate ...."

"I was a fool to trust you!"

"No—"

"Sexy men like you always cheat on their women!" she asserted.

"But my precious darling ...." he begged.

"I am finished with you!" she yelled as she hurled the platter in her hands. It smashed near one of the diners, spraying pasta, and sauce in all directions.

Regrettably, the victim of the flying food was the big man who was inhaling tortellini at the next table, the one that had amused Monty, Dana, and Alfredo a few minutes earlier. But he was also someone that most people would go to great lengths to avoid. He jumped to his feet, furious. "What was that?!" he barked as he advanced on Isabella. "I am celebrating my anniversary tonight and now you ruined it!"

Recognizing that the situation was escalating fast, Dana stepped in. She was not intimidated by him in the least. "Hey Guido, put your ego in your pants and back off."

Even though *Guido* is a well-known slur in the United States and not Rome, the burly man deduced the insulting nature of it and shoved Dana aside. "Out of my way, bitch!"

But Alfredo was not about to let that stand. "You will not speak to my guest that way!" he ordered while approaching the big man. "You will leave my restaurant immediately!"

The big man did not even blink before slugging Alfredo and knocking him out cold, prompting Isabella to rush to her husband's side. "Alfredo, no!" she cried as she kissed him.

Just then Monty appeared beside the big man and broke the champagne bottle over his head. "Dickhead," she stated.

Unfortunately, the unconscious man did more than go down. On the way, he crashed into a nearby table, causing everyone there to leap to their feet. They were all covered in food and enraged. A flurry of Italian language profanities filled the air.

Monty turned to Dana sheepishly. "I think I might have over-reacted."

"Are you kidding?!" Dana countered. "You had me at *dickhead*."

Suddenly, one of the big man's companions threw a full carafe of red wine at Monty—who ducked at the precise moment that Sergeant Fazio was returning from the kitchen with a flower vase. Chianti splattered across his white suit and his startled face as a group of customers closed in on Monty and Dana.

The girls picked up wine bottles and trays as weapons and backed up slowly.

"I suppose you won't be paying me back now because you'll need bail money," Monty observed as she braced for the assault.

"Nah, it's all good," Dana replied with a wink. "My boyfriend's a cop, remember?"

The girls shared a roguish snicker and the incensed patrons lunged.

<u>THE END</u>

Epilogue
Where Are They Now?

After the fracas at the newly restored *La Cucina di Isabella*, the incensed big man who delivered the knockout punch to Alfredo Barone was persuaded by Sergeant Fazio's threat of criminal charges to pay for damages—and then some. That made Isabella Barone quite happy, which in turn made Alfredo extremely relieved.

Meanwhile, when Dana and Monty returned for Giancarlo's trial, Dana and Fazio finally had the opportunity to spend time together. A long-distance dating relationship followed, and she visited him twice that summer before deciding to stay. Fortunately, his distress about his mother's potential reaction was easily assuaged. Magda Fazio could not have been happier to learn that Dana's grandmother was born in Palermo!

Dana and Fazio were married fifteen months later. The ceremony at the Church of *Santa Maria a Trevi* was conducted by Monty's spiritual advisor and new friend in Rome, Father Demetrio Vitale.

Monty served as maid of honor, of course. Alfredo and Isabella were also in attendance, as was Saint-Tropez *Capitaine* Chouinard, who had become friends with Fazio during the investigation. Chouinard and Monty were surprised by how much they enjoyed seeing each other, and that initiated six months of transatlantic phone conversations. Realizing that they were falling in love, she moved to France, and they became engaged at the celebration of his promotion to Police Commandant.

Dana and Sergeant Fazio served as maid of honor and best man at the wedding in New York, and His Eminence Cardinal Timothy Dolan once again officiated.

As for Alex Connelly, his fears about potential mafia vengeance over what happened in the shipyard prompted him to sign everything over to his wife Heather and disappear. He now manages a small surf shop in Costa Rica, while she has full custody of their baby daughter.

The threat of mob retribution did not end there, however. Augusto DeLuca was blamed by his colleagues for botching the Connelly deal, and a series of mysterious explosions destroyed his bakery.

The ordeal in Rome sent Greg Lange into intensive therapy. He abandoned his business career aspirations to become an adjunct lecturer at his alma mater, Loyola Marymount University. He teaches classes in business ethics and continues to have vivid nightmares about the truck chase in the fog and Connelly's near execution.

Not surprisingly, Olivia Zironi—whose real name is Chiara Antonelli—was not a university student. After conspiring with Leandro Rossetti to fleece Giancarlo of his ill-gotten gains, they were married in the resort town of Positano, where they opened *La Galleria* tavern. One of Giancarlo's fake paintings hangs behind the bar.

And finally, since he did not contest the evidence against him, Giancarlo was sentenced to thirty years, three for each of his fraudulent marriages and larcenies. Upon arrival at Rome's infamous *Regina Coeli* prison, he became the object of intense interest to a group of *SPQR* fascist skinheads, who had not forgotten his outstanding gambling debts with them. He is now said to be the personal property of his cellmate, Bruno Abruzzese, a brutal ax murderer who is the gang's leader.

OTHER BOOKS BY TOM BLOMQUIST

SILENT PARTNERS
Lindstrom Legacy Publishing

EYE OF THE STORM
Directing for Film, Television & Emerging Media
Written by Maria Viera, Ph.D. & Tom Blomquist
Kendall Hunt Publishers

Made in the USA
Monee, IL
11 March 2021

62535178R00144